THE DEMANDS OF MRS. WEST, DECEASED

The Case Of The Dead Widow
By Reginald Clark

Bruce L. Willis

Amazon Books

ISBN-13: 9798372192003
ISBN-10: 1477123456

Cover design by: Art Painter
Library of Congress Control Number: 2018675309
Printed in the United States of America

This book is for my parents, who loved and guided me, and my wife and daughters, who always encouraged me to write. It was writing Blood is Blue, Stories of Growing Up in the Fifties and Sixties, that I decided to try something new; The Demands of Mrs. West, Deceased, the Case of the Dead Widow by Reginald Clark, and the Toronto that was but only in my imagination. I enjoyed writing the story and hope you will enjoy it.

INTRODUCTION

If you are looking for a book where a wisecracking reporter becomes involved with a ghost with unfinished business, read *The Demands of Mrs. West, Deceased, the Case of the Dead Widow by Reginald Clark.* This is my seventh book. I had finished six Klondike Detective books, five published and the sixth soon to be out when I published *Blood is Blue, Memories of Growing up in the Fifties and Sixties.* Then eureka, Reggie Clark, an inquisitive reporter, and his connected spirit, Mrs. West, wanting to find out who murdered her. Those two were meant for each other.

There was only one problem, Reggie was not the hero type. When you think of famous detectives, Sherlock Holmes, Philip Marlow, Sam Spade and Nick Charles, they sneered at danger and laughed at risk. Not Reggie; he would stay under his bed until the danger was over if he had his way. He did not follow the pattern of a brace detective since he is a bit of a chicken. Oxymorons like loyal opposition, jumbo shrimp and old news have a new one, cowardly detective. If you had asked Reggie, he would freely admit this and say he never wanted the job. It was not his fault that Mrs. West cajoled, scolded and nagged Reggie to carry out her task.

The setting is Toronto in 1957, a prosperous, growing city with immigrants from Europe. It took me back since I lived there as a boy for three years in the fifties and returned in the seventies to article, pass my bar admission course and work as a trial lawyer. I loved Toronto and think you will, too, since I will take you back to a wonderful period as Reggie tracks down the murderer.

Nonfiction

Officers Life in Halifax 1749 to 1970, Halifax, Department of National Defence, 1970.

The History of the Shawinigan Engineering Company, Montreal, The Shawinigan Engineering Company, 1974.

The Effects of Disproportionate Infantry Recruitment in Quebec and Canada in the First World War, Acadia University, 1970, Thesis.

The Environmental Effects of the Yukon Gold Rush 1896-1906: Alterations to Land, Destruction of Wildlife, and Disease, University of Western Ontario, 1997, Thesis.

"Environmental Controls Affecting Exploration and Development of Mineral Resources in the Yukon" (co-author), Vol. 3, Canadian Journal of Administrative Law and Practice

"Bradish v. Warren: Further Juridical Observations on the Constitutional Status of the Northern Territories", Volume 4, Canadian Journal of Administrative Law and Practice

"Yukon Environmental Spills" contained in Environmental Spills: Emergency Reporting, Clean-Up and Liability, Carswell, 1993

"Lender, Receiver & Trustee Liability for Environmental Obligations", Volume 8, Canadian Journal of Administrative Law and Practice

Fiction

The Klondike Detective: Murder on King Solomon's Dome, 2017, Amazon Books.

The Klondike Detective 2: The San Francisco Scheme, 2018, Amazon Books.

The Klondike Detective 3: The Murder Conspiracy, 2020, Amazon Books.

The Klondike Detective 4: The Disappearance, 2020, Amazon Books.

The Klondike Detective 5: The Stolen Documents, 2021, Amazon Books

Blood is Blue; Stories of Growing Up in the Fifties and Sixties, 2022, Amazon BooksThe Demands of Mrs. West, Deceased

CHAPTER 1

Finger Nails on a Blackboard

Hell settled in Toronto on Friday, June 21, 1957, without the devil; since rumour has it, Las Vegas was his new home. Scorching and sultry, the dog days of summer had arrived. Waves of heat settled on roads, sidewalks and buildings and touching a car in the sun gave you third-degree burns. The hot wind felt like it was from the Sahara Desert, bringing exhaust fumes that stank worse than an annoyed skunk. The sewers were so dry they reeked worse than a two-day-old-blocked toilet, and I had to work.

A long lineup for the graveyard shift. Windows stayed open, and fans at maximum made no difference. Smokers remained inside, smoke filled the air, and ashtrays overflowed with butts. Typewriters, hard-backed chairs, and battered desks were our domain as phones rang, typewriters clacked, and people shouted for copyboys. We typed as we received and made calls, always wanting a scoop.

Crumpled papers and cigarettes that floated in used coffee cups filled our desks as we churned out the paper, constantly wiping brows with handkerchiefs or takeout napkins. I hated the night shift, who ate toast and jam at three in the morning and left sticky keys on my typewriter, which required cleaning. The cleaners could not disturb our work, which meant the office was a pigsty, and the few times someone commented, we pelted them with empty coffee cups. I blame that on the heat. We ignored those who asked about the weather and shunned those idiots who commented, "at least it isn't raining."

After a while, I became so tired of my fellow reporters saying, "boy, it's hotter than hell," I would ask, "did you enjoy it there?" An innocent joke, but maybe I struck a nerve, and the insults I received were exceptional in their coarseness. Again, I accuse the humid temperature, which created a Jekyll and Hyde scenario where mild-mannered reporters transformed into cantankerous curmudgeons.

Reporters delight in and savour words; occasionally, they resort to imaginative ones, and I was the recipient. They focused on certain parts of my anatomy or had me do the impossible toilet humour at its worst. It was a trade-off, and my six-foot two-height and one-hundred-eighty-five-pound weight meant no one invited me outside for fisticuffs. I took it like the tolerant fellow I was, but I may have remarked that some of my fellow hacks had their heads up their asses.

Anyway, brawling in the street in this heat was impossible, so we did the next best thing. We wrote insulting limericks to each other and posted them. I was the master of mirth, knowing anyone who read them would roll around the floor laughing and demand more. It was my genius at work with my knee-slapping hilarity. Or I would like to think so. However, two of my fellow reporters did not appreciate my work since they wanted ribald limericks. I had difficulty deciding what to call them, the smut seekers, the dirt diggers, the filth fans, or the crude crowd; it didn't matter; they took smut seriously. Those two cheated in their limericks since who calls a reporter a Ducker, a Duckface, a Brasswsipe or a Brasshole? And what rhymed with those names was coarseness at its finest for scribblers who demanded lewdness and vulgarity.

Besides jokes, newspaper offices are filled with insults, sarcasm and dark humour, and ours was one of the worst. We drank too much, smoked too much and swore too much; digging up dirt had consequences. A few nights ago, someone put up a sign, "Abandon Hope All Ye Who Enter Here," and no one took it down.

Outside pavements cracked, trees looked for shade, and people packed air-conditioned movie theatres. Police protected ice cream trucks and weathermen, and crowds filled the beaches. People slept in basements, and water from a lawn sprinkler was so hot no kid would run through it. Nobody was foolish enough to fry an egg on a road; if they tried, they would cook faster than the egg, and their head might explode.

I left my building at six-thirty, jacket over a shoulder, fedora dripping with sweat, with a pounding headache, after a long, hot, tiring day. I arrived at Champs Bar on Queen Street West at seven, and the first hint of a breeze from the windows gave me relief from a horrible day. It was the summer solstice, the year's longest day, but I didn't care. Beer was what I needed; beer was what I craved; beer was what I had to have, cold and frothy after a hot, hung-over day. If you are a drinker, you know the symptoms: hating loud noises, nasty headaches, sweats and coffee that burn your stomach. I sat alone in this bar to avoid my friends since I wanted to remain sober tonight and not send my liver into overdrive.

The beer was at my mouth when I noticed the sound. Fingernails scratched on a blackboard, a sound I detested. It was horrible and reminded me of my collegiate class of 1950, surprise tests, dodgeball and idiots scratching fingernails on blackboards. I put my beer on the table and looked around, but no blackboard. That glass had been in the refrigerator, nice and cold, and it bothered me not to taste it. It happened again, and I looked around the bar. A few customers sat at tables, and the fellow behind the bar read a paper, but no one looked up. The small television was muted, and I could see the news, but I did not know what the announcer said.

The sound began again, and I looked at the customers and then the bartender, but no one said anything. Perhaps I was in a secret meeting of deaf people, or I didn't like this thought; only I heard it. I stood up and asked where the bathroom was. The bartender pointed to the back of the opposite wall. His hearing was okay, which I found aggravating then I heard other conversations. I sighed, thinking nothing good would come from this, and strolled to the toilets.

I did my usual thing in the urinal, then looked in the mirror and intoned, "you are not crazy." A lot of good would do since I was the only one tuned into that dreadful sound. How did the *Oxford English Dictionary* define delusional? Believing things that weren't true, I heard fingernails scratching on a blackboard three times. The problem was only I heard them. Maybe if I had stayed here, I wouldn't hear the noise. As I washed my hands, I contemplated whether this was a bad dream, but apart from the sound, everything appeared normal. I could ask the bartender whether he had noticed anything, but what was the point? Tabloids published stories about persons with a third eye or understanding cats, and I hated to think they were now my people.

Back at my table, I downed the liquor control board regulation glass with the line near the top and picked up my fedora. I left a quarter and a dime as a tip and walked out onto Queen Street West. The streetcar had just left, so I went to my guest house to calm down. The sun was still overhead as I walked. Maybe I worked too much, or last night's bender had unsettled me. Perhaps it was just my imagination, but that noise seemed real when I was in the bar.

Those ads at the back of the comic books showed a bully kicking sand at a ninety-eight-pound weakling. After a few months of magic pills, they transformed the weakling into a two-hundred-pound muscle man. That was unbelievable, and no one in their right mind would accept it, and yet that is what I experienced in the bar with the sound. I shook my head and smiled. It was a momentary thing, and I couldn't explain it, but I was over whatever it was. I was sure everybody had one of those episodes and then stopped. What was I thinking, nails on a blackboard and only I heard it? I took a deep breath and sighed.

I thought back to last night. Mrs. Brown had spoken with me at breakfast about my behaviour. All I could do was apologize to her since I did not know how I got home. I found myself on the floor in my room in my guest house when I woke up this morning. I must have set my alarm clock, but I had no recollection of doing it. At least I could sleep in tomorrow since I was not on shift for the weekend. I worked as a crime reporter for the *Toronto Mirror,* and I might enjoy an extra hour, but if I slept too late, I would miss breakfast. Saturdays were when Mrs. Brown served bacon and eggs with pancakes.

Mrs. Brown promised to leave me dinner in the oven, and I stopped at a grocery store to buy her flowers and breath mints. I munched the mints and was at the guest house by seven-thirty. I found Mrs. Brown cleaning the dining room table. Once I gave her the flowers, she said I shouldn't have, but I could see she was pleased. She told me to wash up and that she would have my dinner at the table. This was real, and the world was unfolding as it should.

I walked up to my room on the top floor to take off my jacket and hat, and once I closed the door, fingernails on a blackboard again, but I had no blackboard. I sat on my bed and closed my eyes, trying not to break into hysterical laughter. Anyone who knows me can assure you I am a level-headed guy. I don't believe in ghosts or supernatural beings and found reading Edgar Allan Poe boring. But this was not right, then the noise stopped.

"Did that get your attention?" a voice asked.

"Holy shit," I said. "Big Fish, you almost gave me a heart attack, and it's not funny," I said. I searched for hidden wires, dropped to my knees to look under my bed and checked my closet. No wires.

"Where are you," I said. "I'm going to call you Ira," I said to Big Fish since he hated his name.

"Are you finished, Mr. Reginald Clark?" the voice asked. It was an older woman with a deep and distinguished voice.

"How to you know my name?" I asked.

"Frightened, are you?" the voice asked. "Your lips twitched."

"You can see me too? I asked. My reality collided with an otherworldly spirit, and I did not know why this happened to me, a hung-over reporter. A grand finale to a really crappy day.

"Why did you make that sound in the bar?" I asked.

"To make you leave, you drink too much," the voice said. "You need a haircut, and you are mischievous," the voice said as I smiled. I enjoyed being mischievous, along with being known as a wisecracker.

"That is not something to smile about," the voice said. "It is deplorable. I need you to be serious and end your attempts to be funny. You are a crime reporter for a disreputable paper; you are twenty-five and drink too much and sometimes use gutter language. They put you in the crime section because you helped convict murderers. You wear your socks two days a row and eat fast, put too much peanut butter on your toast and burp because of bolting your food. You go out with women you think are easy, but they never are, and that frustrates you, but it shouldn't. Looking for a cheap embrace is beneath you, and you must, at all times, be a gentleman. You should write to your parents and are trying to write a novel, but you have no talent or life experience. You are not bad looking but give away that check suit."

That did it; I was angry and no longer scared. You this and you that, listing my faults. I enjoyed being a wisecracker. And how else could I eat where we used forks as weapons over a choice piece of meat? It was the survival of the fastest, not the fittest, and my arms were in good shape after taking on members of the guest house at the table. I was a hardworking and hard-partying young reporter and no different from my fellow hacks. Chasing women was what we did, and who cared what this afterlife thought of me? She was a prude and a busybody. Maybe a busybody was the wrong word since there was no body. Buttinsky was better. Perhaps there was an entity on the roof not paying attention, so what was talking to me had a little walkabout.

The spirit might have mentioned my good qualities, a noted reporter who knew how to sidle out of situations. When required, I could slink away with no one noticing me, and some called me the phantom. I was also adventuresome and took risks to get the story. I won't mention other observations since no one is perfect, which the afterlife spirit had made clear to me with a list. It tempted me to ask for an example of my gutter language, but even I could not do that. When I used gutter language, I moved from profanities to expletives to obscenities in the blink of an eye. For that, I blame my two summers with regular army sergeants.

"You watched me?" I asked.

"I don't go into your bathroom down the hall, which needs cleaning, and I close my eyes when you change."

"If you have never been there, how do you know the bathroom needs cleaning?" I asked.

"I should have said I assume your bathroom needs cleaning. You live with four other men, and I doubt none of them bother to clean the tub after they use it. I can imagine a black ring on the side of the tub."

"Fair enough. It is a little disgusting," I said. "You sound like my mother, but older."

"I am older," the voice said. "Or I was, and I need you to be healthy and alert."

"For what?" I asked.

"To help me," the voice said. "I had to be satisfied you could do the job," the voice said.

"What job?" I asked.

"All in good time, since I have to be satisfied you are the one for my righteous cause," the voice said.

"World War Two is over, and I don't like religious crusades," I said.

"There is no need to be sardonic," the voice said.

"Until you arrived, with your objections to my behaviour, I enjoyed my life."

"What life," Mrs. West said. "Hungover, living in a boarding house and writing a dreadful book. It is time for you to change.

"It's a guest house, and how long have you been watching me?" I asked.

"Long enough," the voice said.

"Since you have such a low opinion of me, why are you asking for my help?" I asked and realized I was talking to thin air. Did I have a nervous breakdown or the "vapours?" No, that was what they called it for women in the nineteenth century. I waited, hoping that I would not hear another sound. After a minute, I smiled and sighed; it was a passing delusion.

"You are not imagining this," the voice said. "You have bad habits that a marriage may fix, with luck, but you are a talented reporter, which is what I need," the voice said

"Shit," I said. "You're still here."

"Language," the voice said.

"Why?" I asked.

"Isn't a reporter to do who, what, where and how?" the voice asked.

"Never mind that; why do you want my help?" I asked.

"I want you to discover who murdered me?" the voice said.

CHAPTER 2

Finding out about my Client

"Can this wait?" I asked. "My dinner is getting cold."

"Really," the voice said. "A typical man. You have the greatest story; all you can think of is food."

"I will eat slowly," I said.

"While you are gone, I will check your underwear to see if it is dirty."

"Wait a minute," I said.

"I am joking. I can't move anything."

"What was your name," I asked.

"It is Mrs. Alicia West. "I am here, so do not refer to me in the past tense," Mrs. West said. "Finally, a question, and since I can't write, you will have to make notes when you come back. Don't drink too much. I require you to be sober since I hate repeating myself. My father never took a drop of alcohol."

"Good for him," I said. "Is he still alive?"

"He went to his maker a while ago."

"When was that?" I asked.

"April 21, 1931."

"I bet he was glad to end it since he didn't drink," I muttered.

"I heard that, and my father was a wonderful man."

"What was his name?" I asked since he would be part of

my inquiries if I decided to take this on. My other choice was to check myself into 999 Queen Street West, the Ontario Hospital for Lunatics, otherwise known as the funny farm.

"Mr. Justice Horace Kingsmill."

"How old was he when he died?"

"Seventy-seven?"

"How old were you when you died?"

"You shouldn't ask a woman, her age, it is impolite, but I am seventy, born January 14, 1887."

"Pretty old" I said.

"Not at all" Mrs. West said.

"According to Stephen Leacock about the only good thing you can say about old age is, it's better than being dead" I said. My effort to be amusing was probably not appreciated.

"Did it ever occur to you that your last statement was cruel" Mrs. West said.

"I am sorry" I said.

"Try to be serious, if you can" Mrs. West said. "I remember the death of Queen Victoria and the coronations of Edward, the two Georges, and the other Edward. He was a scoundrel with that woman Wallis Simpson and recently, our Queen. I was in a relationship when I was twenty but broke it off. I went to Montreal for a year, and I began a relationship with Mr. West when I returned. We were married when I was twenty-four, in 1911, the year George the Fifth became king, so I was old when I married."

"You died younger than your father," I said.

"Yes, but he died of natural causes, and I was murdered."

"So, you say," I said. "When did you die?"

"I'm not sure but my funeral was on April 23, 1957, almost two months ago. Now go, eat and be back soon." I left my room, closed my door and went to have dinner. As I sliced the pork roast and ate a bite, my first question was, did I have a screw loose? Or as my Uncle Henry would say, the wheels are turning but the hamster died. I mean hearing a ghost, that no one else had heard was inexplicable. Looking at the bright side, apart from this teeny, tiny hitch in my mental process, I was fine. I was aware of today's date, my age, my hat size, where I worked and where I lived. My mother lived in Regina, Saskatchewan, was fifty-six and worked as a teacher. My father was fifty-nine and worked as an accountant. My parents were level-headed persons, and apart from Uncle Bert, who was a little strange, there was no insanity in the family. Uncle Henry had another saying, nuttier than a porta potty at a peanut festival but enough of Uncle Henry's wit, which I hoped didn't apply to me.

I took a deep breath, stabbed the mashed potatoes, put some on my fork, and ate. This whole thing was unbelievable, but I was interested. The voice, or should I call it Mrs. West, had searched for me because she thought I was a good reporter, something my editor Bill Wise had never said. Mind you, he never said anything to any of his reporters unless he had been drinking, and after that he was rude.

Upstairs I closed the door, and the room was silent. I sat and a chair and thought this was better; I had imagined the whole thing.

"No, you haven't," Mrs. West said.

"I didn't speak," I said.

"It doesn't matter, I can understand your thoughts."

"Oh, shit," I thought.

"Mr. Clark, I detest vulgarity and profanity. I was about to let her have it but stopped.

"How can you be here if you are dead?" I asked.

"I have no idea," Mrs. West said.

"That makes two of us," I said. "Did you get any parting words before you were sent here?"

"No," Mrs. West said.

"Not helpful?" I said. "I thought once we die, that is it," I said.

"I always believed that, but here I am," Mrs. West said. "We are connected."

"Couldn't you pick someone else? I asked.

"Even if you don't want our connection, you have no

choice," Mrs. West said.

"Go back and say I wasn't interested," I said.

"I am not sure where that is," Mrs. West said. "I assume it is heaven. There are more things in heaven and earth, Horatio, than are dreamt of in your philosophy."

"I don't want Shakespeare; I want to be free," I said.

"You are," Mrs. West said.

"Free from you," I said.

"I am rather charming when you get to know me," Mrs. West said.

"I am stuck with you until I find out who murdered you?" I asked.

"Yes, and you make it sound like an imposition," Mrs. West said. "Think of it as an adventure with a cultured otherworldly spirit."

"Holy Doodle, now that you put it that way, I can hardly wait," I said.

"Mr. Clark, really," Mrs. West said. "You must understand what I expect from you."

"What?" I asked.

"Let us begin by proper behaviour, Mr. Clark," Mrs. West said. She was good with admonishments, but I decided to try her patience. "If you have a question, you will ask, Mrs. West, I have a question. I require your intelligence, good manners and, above all, no sarcasm. Is that clear?"

"Rough around the edges, am I?" I asked.

"If you think annoying me will make me disappear, it won't," Mrs. West said; then I heard fingernails on a blackboard.

"Fine, Mrs. West, I surrender," I said. "Would you like a white handkerchief?"

"Did you forget what I said about sarcasm?" Mrs. West asked.

"No, Mrs. West," I said.

"Good," she said. "You are like a disobedient dog."

"Wait a minute," I said.

"Got you, didn't I?" Mrs. West asked.

"You have a sense of humour?" I asked.

"Don't tell anyone," Mrs. West said.

"Very funny," I said. "Why nails on a blackboard?"

"That was rather clever since every student detests it. It was that or a dental drill. Organ sounds are ridiculous, and if you read the Christmas Carol, using chains for Marley's ghost is too much. If I wanted to be dramatic, I could use a death gurgle when your throat is cut, but unless you had been around someone whose throat has been cut, you might not understand. I don't think of myself as a ghost; besides, it worked."

"Can you make the sound of an outboard engine?" I asked.

"Mr. Clark, I don't appreciate your humour, and I don't think you understand the seriousness of the situation," Mrs. West said.

"If you aren't a ghost, what are you?" I asked. There was a long pause, and I thought Mrs. West had disappeared before she spoke.

"Think of me as an afterlife detective."

This began my connection to Mrs. West which changed my life. She became fond of me, and I of her. She had a wicked sense of humour. I quickly discovered my attempts to be funny did not impress her since I was a wisecracker, like Groucho Marx, but without the fake moustache and cigar. I know it sounds ridiculous to have an affection for a spirit, but I did, and Mrs. West was quite the character. Over time her behaviour resulted in my developing patience, which was a great gift. Later her requests for me to play opera on my record player resulted in my growing to love the composers. That was a change from my previous affection for country and western music.

Mrs. West was a spirit who wanted my help, and the phrase rest in peace did not apply to her. The fact she was here and connected to me was an enigma. It went against everything I was taught and made me realize I was dealing with a presence from the great divide.

CHAPTER 3

Curiouser and Curiouser

I wrote for my university newspaper. They drummed this into us; the who, the what, the where and the how, so it was time to begin. The window was open, and I had turned on the fan since my room was on the third floor and hot, and I could hear street noises below.

"How are you going to pay me?" I asked. "I will spend many hours on this, and I may have to pay someone to help." Her laugh was high, long and infectious.

"Young man, this will be an adventure, and I can hang around and listen to your witnesses, or I suppose you call them your sources," Mrs. West said. I looked but of course, what was the point? I had no idea where this afterlife detective was standing, sitting or floating.

"Mr. Clark, you are gullible, which is not good. Not good at all."

"What do you mean I'm gullible," I said.

"I can't understand anyone's thoughts."

"But you did," I said.

"Guesswork Mr. Clark. I have brothers and sons, and I know how they think. I should find someone else for

"I am a good crime reporter. You can call me Reggie."

"I'd rather not, Mr. Clark. Fine, I will use you. You can write your book with something real, unlike your story about working as a spy in Paris during the war. I doubt you have ever been there, and from what I gather, your French is rather poor. Why else do you have a dictionary and a map of Paris if you have been there? No, this is the story you will tell as long as I am portrayed as a woman deserving of justice."

"Your righteous cause," I said.

"Precisely," Mrs. West said. "I am glad you listened."

"How did you die?" A simple question, shot, stabbed, poisoned, thrown over a cliff or hanged?

"I don't recall. I have no idea, so that will be where you start; find the medical report and obtain that if there was a coroner's inquest."

"Maybe it was old age since people die when they get old," I said. There was a long pause before she spoke, and I could tell she was unhappy.

"I was not old. I walked and ate well, and my doctor told me I was like a young person. You don't die of old age, young man. You die when your heart stops, and mine was fine, thank you very much" I decided to change the topic.

"When did you come alive as an afterlife detective?"

"Recently, although I wouldn't describe it as alive. I am more of a festering spirit that needs resolution."

"How long have you been in this state?" I asked.

"I have no idea, so you need to move if you want my help."

"I still don't have proof you were murdered," I said. "You haven't told me how you died. Why do you think you were murdered since you were....?"

"Not old, Mr. Clark. I had told you before I was healthy and had lived a long time, but I was not old, just mature."

"Ok, you were healthy, so why do you think you were murdered?" I asked.

"Motive, Mr. Clark. Motive: I am or was a wealthy woman, and my family was selfish. On September 15, 1956, I met with my solicitor. It was Saturday, the day of Our Lady of Sorrows when I changed my will and unfortunately told my family about it. I realize I should not have mentioned that, but that is what I did. I was upset, and you know how things happen when you are annoyed. I raised selfish children who made certain assumptions without checking with me." There was a knock on my door. I opened it to see a concerned Mrs. Brown.

"Is someone with you in your room?" she asked. "That is not permitted." I opened the door and told her to look inside.

"I am practicing my lines for a play, but I will try to keep my voice down," I said. She looked around, sniffed and left my room, and I heard her walking down the stairs. I closed the door.

"She is rather pathetic checking up on her boarders," Mrs. West said.

"I am not a boarder," I said.

"What are you?" Mrs. West asked.

"I am a resident of a guest house," I said.

"A place where no guests are allowed, so how can you stay here as a guest?" Mrs. West asked.

"I am a guest who is not allowed guests," I said.

"But you pay so you are not a guest, which makes you a boarder in a commercial arrangement," Mrs. West said. Her logic drove me nuts, so I did what I always did and ignored her argument.

"Mrs. Brown is all right and not a bad cook if you like everything fried or overdone."

"You mean burnt," Mrs. West said.

"Not exactly," I said. "Extremely well done is more accurate."

"A boarding house is so common," Mrs. West said.

"If you want common, wrestle with four famished men at dinner with soda biscuits from the last war," I said. You have no idea."

"I watched you for five days, so I think I understand. Mrs. West said. "I had no idea how the poor lived."

"We are not poor," I said. "There are students here, and we earn a living. You want poor; I can take you to the Salvation Army shelter."

"No, thank you," Mrs. West said.

"You have no idea how most of Toronto exists?" I asked, but no answer. "You had a cook and butler?"

"Of course," Mrs. West said.

"Maybe the butler, did it? I asked.

"Certainly not," Mrs. West said. "You need to move from where you are living if you are to help."

"Where?" I asked. "After tax, I receive eighty-two dollars every two weeks. This place costs me one hundred dollars a month, so there is not much left over. I work forty hours weekly, but that can be fifty hours a week with the extra time, and I am not paid for that." There was a long pause before she spoke.

"I might have a solution. I have a safety deposit box with twenty-thousand dollars in it. It is at the Royal Bank on Front Street."

"You are dead, so I can't use your name," I said.

"Mr. Clark, my arrangements with my solicitor were that whoever provides a code and number would be given a key and access to my safety box at the Royal Bank. The box with the money did not flow into my estate since I kept it separate, and I did not tell my solicitor what was in it. My solicitor is George Montgomery Q.C."

"How do I know your solicitor will trust me?"

"I gave specific instructions, and he will," Mrs. West said. "However, he may tell my son, who is not pleasant. Remember, there are risks and rewards for everything. My solicitor has a mistress Miss Felicia Gordon, and I am sure he would not want this disclosed to his wife. Whatever you do, do not use your real name or address. I would hate for you to die before you started. There is one thing you can use. You will find photographs of Mr. George Montgomery and Miss Gordon in the safety box, along with the money. For that, you can buy a small duplex downtown and have money left over to purchase a car and decent clothes, and this busybody will not overhear us."

"If I show the pictures to your lawyer, isn't that blackmail?"

"I prefer to think of it as protection," Mrs. West said.

"You are careful," I said.

"I have to be," said Mrs. West.

"Are you Catholic, Mrs. West?" I asked.

"Is that relevant?" she asked.

"You mentioned when you wrote your will that it was the day of Our Lady of Sorrow," I said.

"I am glad you pay attention; now take notes. I am not Catholic, but my governess was Catholic and made me memorize the days for each saint. I wasn't writing my will; I was changing it, which is essential. My husband owned shares in several companies and was the major shareholder of an insurance company. When he died in 1950, I inherited his estate. I received ten million dollars along with the house. I managed to improve my investments, and based on the last statements in March, I was worth over twelve million dollars. That is money worth killing for."

"It is, and the question is, who would?" I asked.

"Yes, Mr. Clark, that is the question. Now you must find out the answer."

CHAPTER 4

Nothing but the Facts, Just the Facts

"What are you?" I asked.

"What do you mean, Mr. Clark?"

"Do you float?"

"I beg your pardon."

"Float, stand or sit? It's my first time with a spirit, so I have questions."

"Mr. Clark," Mrs. West said, "does that matter? I have no idea since I can't see myself. I am a... I don't know, but I can hear and see. The only person who can hear me is you, and you are the only person who can hear me or my sounds. As long as someone turns the pages, I can read. I don't watch television. I find it crass and designed for the common person. I have no idea how this happened, and I find it unsettling. I never believed in ghosts, so this whole thing is beyond my understanding, but I want to find out who did this to me, and that is where you come in. Let us begin, so ask your typical reporter questions?"

"I don't have typical reporter questions," I said. "Every case is different, and how I ask my questions depends on who I am with."

"Whom you are questioning since it is him or her and not, he or she," Mrs. West admonished me. "Where did you study?"

"The University of Regina," I said.

"That explains it."

"What do you mean? That's a great university."

"For Saskatchewan" Mrs. West said.

"You people in Toronto think you are so superior."

"We are. There are two kinds of people, Mr. Clark. Torontonians and those who wish they were, but we are digressing. Questions Mr. Clark."

"I suppose you attended private school?" I asked.

"Focus, Mr. Clark, but yes, I was a student at Havergal, and was Head Girl."

"Who is your killer?" I asked.

"Let me tell you about my family."

"So, you are not aware of who your killer is?" I asked.

"That is so crass. I prefer murderer and that is why I am asking for your help. Let me describe my family and stop talking. You are annoying."

"Me annoying?" I asked. "Annoying, really? How do you think I feel since only I can hear you? But you need me" I waited and took satisfaction that I irritated Mrs. West. She was a snob, and I was upset with her remarks about my university.

"My oldest son William was born in 1912 and was a wonderful gentleman. He became a lawyer and was an officer with the Queen's Own Rifles of Canada. William was a captain who was killed two days after the Normandy landings. William Junior, his son, was born in 1942. They live in Montreal, but he comes with Marie every Christmas and for a month each summer. I love them, they are lovely, and they are not under suspicion. Is that clear?"

"Yes" I said.

"My daughter Madeline was born in 1914 and is married to Gordon, a stockbroker. Her married name is Morton. They have three children, and they are selfish and inconsiderate. Madeline and Gordon drink too much and live beyond their means. Each Christmas, I pay them five thousand dollars to subsidize their lifestyle. Are you writing this?"

"I am Mrs. West" I said and avoided saying sheesh.

"My youngest child, Douglas, was born in 1915 and is married to Marigold, with two sons. He worked as a vice president for my husband's insurance company. Once I sold my shares, he was let go and is looking for work. He lives in Forest Hill which is an expensive part of Toronto, and his boys are in private school. He drives a Bentley and has servants. I give them ten thousand dollars each Christmas to help with their expenses. I suppose you believe that I am a dreadful mother to prefer one child over the rest?"

"Mrs. West. I have met none of your children, but I am sure you have your reasons.

"I find the whole thing distasteful. My first will divided my estate equally, but when I changed my will, I left eleven million dollars to Marie in trust for William junior. I divided the remaining one million dollars and the sale of my house and furniture between Madeline and Douglas. Douglas and Madeline are contesting the will, so the executor did not pay anything out and has not sold my house. I expect Douglas has borrowed money to pay his lawyer and living expenses. Start with Douglas and then Madeline."

"How do you know they are contesting the will" I asked.

"I don't know so you will have to check" Mrs. West said. I have no idea why I know that."

"I can't just make an appointment with him. What would I say?"

"You just left your position as a butler. Douglas goes through a butler every several months. Since he has a cash flow problem, I am sure he is without one."

"You want me to be his butler?" I asked.

"Yes" Mrs. West said.

"I have no idea about being a butler," I said.

"I will teach you, but you must purchase the proper attire and for that, you need money. I will dictate reference letters that you will type since I assume that your machine works. The references are in England and Douglas will never bother to check. I am afraid you will have to take time away from your employment, but you will have at least six thousand dollars left over once you buy a duplex."

"What is the code for the lawyer and the number?"

"George Montgomery Q, C. The number is 44332299," Mrs. West said.

"Let me guess," I said. "The code is 'Georgy Porgy pudding and pie, kissed Felicia and made her cry.' "

"Reginald, your attempts to be funny are inappropriate, so stop."

"Yes Mrs. West," I said.

"The code is " 'Oh, East is East, and West is West, and never the twain shall meet till Earth and Sky stand presently at God's great Judgment Seat.' "

"Kipling," I said.

"Yes, Mr. Clark, it is, and you can see why I chose it since I am West. And since you will be Douglas' butler, it is imperative that he not have any suspicions about you. If he murdered his mother, he would think nothing of doing the same to you. You must wear a disguise when you meet with George Montgomery, Q.C. Then you don't need to involve yourself with something as distasteful as blackmail. There are papers and documents you will need and photographs in my desk and Wallace has the key."

"Hasn't the executor assembled everything?" I asked.

"My desk has a secret compartment, but you need the key. The photographs are useful."

"For blackmail?" I asked.

"A loathsome word, Mr. Clark. They are a resource for you to use if required. Once I realized my children's nature, I needed to ensure my safety. I failed, but you won't. At least, I hope so. I am just getting to appreciate you, and if something happened, I would have to find someone else and start all over. I am beginning to like you, and it would be unfortunate if you were murdered."

CHAPTER 5

The Look

"Unfortunate, my death would be unfortunate?" I asked. "It would be a bloody tragedy, and my family and friends would be inconsolable."

"I doubt that, and there is no need to be melodramatic or swear, Mr. Clark," Mrs. West said. "You must realize that gentlemen never show emotion." Facing death, I bloody well would do ungentlemanly things like swearing, yelling and hiding. There was no point discussing this with Mrs. West. I was a means to her end, and I didn't think saying "bloody" was swearing. But I wasn't chaste and refined like Mrs. West, a proper Victorian lady. I bet she referred to underwear as unmentionables.

"Why don't you use a private detective?" I asked. No answer, then a sigh.

"Mr. Clark, I doubt you have ever used one," Mrs. West said. "My husband did, and it was not pleasant. After watching you, and you exhibit faults, but most young men do, you are what I want. I do not wish to be connected to a private detective. They are so common and uncouth, and what do people call them, a gumshoe?" I could add dick, shamus, and snoop, but she wouldn't be interested. She had no interest in learning slang or colourful expressions, which were the lifeblood of reporters.

"No Reginald, I will not associate with a gumshoe." I was Reginald, not Mr. Clark, so maybe she was warming to me. I am a pretty good fellow when you get to know me. I enjoy a sense of humour, pay for drinks, read a fair amount and am working on my first book. Or at least I was until Mrs. West's unfavourable remarks, but what would she know? I make my bed, polish my shoes and sort books by authors. At university, I studied English and began working for the *Cricket*, our university newspaper. I attended my first Canadian University Press Conference, where I witnessed heavy drinking and learned great stories.

It was my summer job for the *Leader-Post* in Regina, where I got the big scoop that brought me to Toronto. Instead of working my way up as a news reporter doing assignments like interviewing mothers of girls killed by accidents, they placed me in the crime section of the *Toronto Mirror*. That caused a few problems since I hadn't done my time in the grunt section.

But I was lucky to get a major scoop on the Larson kidnapping case. And because of that, my contacts increased, due to subsidizing bar tabs for Buddy and Trainwreck, two retired cops. Let me tell you, no one can drink like a cop, and that is when they are working. Retired cops are the worst and never want beer. Seagram's rye and ginger ale is Buddy's and Trainwreck's choice, and each was always a double. That was where my money moved, but those two were excellent sources as long as they were not drunk. Once drunk I couldn't understand them.

The best time for information was the first two hours before the rye took over. It was a world where everyone read a newspaper and drank at home or in a bar or a restaurant. Having a few after work was what everyone did, along with smoking. By five, cigarette smoke filled my favourite bar, the Country Tavern on Queen Street West, where Big Fish and his band sang beginning at eight. Big Fish was another excellent source, but I had to stay after midnight and buy him rum and coke.

That is a popular drink if you are from Bible Hill, Nova Scotia. I wasn't sure if he was pulling my leg when he said he was from Bible Hill. Big Fish said Bible Hill was dry, so he had to go to Truro to buy booze. Saskatchewan is where I come from, and many a tale has been told about the place, some true and others fanciful. If you want roads, we have them since there are more roads per person than the rest of Canada. Growing up I wore my Halloween costume over my snow suit, and I still froze. Stephen Leacock wrote "the Lord said, 'let there be wheat' and Saskatchewan was born but I think he forgot about the dirty thirties and the drought. We have strange names in Saskatchewan with a town called Biggar. The townsfolk love to say, "New York is big, but our town is Biggar." And never forget Moose Jaw, Dilke, Eye Brow, Smuts, Climax, Big Beaver and Urin like Urin Saskatchewan. Not much happens in Saskatchewan towns; curling and politics are about it, along with talk about wheat, fertilizer and freight prices. A famous Saskatchewan politician, John Diefenbaker, became prime minister today. Not bad for a lawyer from Prince Albert.

Big Fish, whose real name is Ira, runs a service to set up speakers, receivers and high-end record players for rich folks in Forest Hill and other affluent parts of the city. He listens and has a wonderful memory, which is essential. That is where he gets the goods, not playing country and western songs at the Country Tavern. With the noise he churns out, he couldn't hear anything, even if someone were yelling next to him. He's not called Big Fish because he drinks like a fish. Big Fish likes to fish and is from Nova Scotia. He hates the name Ira and blames it on his mother's favourite Uncle Ira. Big Fish told me his mother's other favourite uncle was Clarence, so his mother doomed him to receive a horrible name. I heard fingernails on a blackboard and looked around.

"I am still here, Reginald, but I am not sure. When I am here, I expect you to pay attention and not drift or whatever that was. Do I make myself clear?"

"Yes, Mrs. West. May I call you Alicia?"

"Certainly not," Mrs. Wests said. "You will address me as Mrs. West. Really Reginald, this business of young people and their familiarities. In my day, we learned how to behave and address our seniors."

"You mean our betters," I said.

"There is no need to be caustic. I will expect you to be dressed and alert so you can take a bath and enjoy breakfast. There is much to do and little time. Goodbye." I waited a couple of minutes before I said "Mrs. West," but no answer. I hated not knowing when she would appear, but that was not the right word. Her presence would be heard.

Saturday at the rooming house is noisy since everyone is there, unless they work a shift. I took the first bath and spent a few minutes scrubbing the dirty ring around the tub. I was the first at breakfast to enjoy bacon, eggs and pancakes. My fellow boarders spent Friday night drinking, so they were late. I ate alone, and in the bathroom brushed my teeth, and ascended to my room. I made sure I had a ribbon for my typewriter and paper and made sure I had pens that worked. When I heard Mrs. West say, "good, you are alert and ready," I checked my clock.

"How was your sleep?" I asked.

"I don't sleep," Mrs. West said.

"What do you mean, you must sleep?" I asked. There was silence.

"Mrs. West, are you here?"

"Yes, I am. You asked me where I slept. There is a problem with my situation. Once I chose you, I am connected."

"What does that mean?" I asked.

"Ten feet," Mrs. West said. "I think it is ten feet, but I have not measured it."

"What does that mean?" I asked, worrying about what she would say.

"I can be ten feet apart from you and no more."

"Where were you last night?"

"On your window box, and it was lovely," Mrs. West said. "The moon and stars were out, although the traffic noise was unbearable. However, your window box is filthy and needs to be cleaned. I think while this connection lasts, you must be celibate. I will not succumb to your immorality while I am connected with you. It makes me feel I am part of it."

"You can be outside my room with the door closed."

"Since you are not permitted guests, where will this take place?"

"None of your business," I said.

"You have no idea, do you?" Mrs. West asked but I remained silent since she was right, I didn't have a clue.

"This is a subject I will not mention again," Mrs. wets said. She was harsh but accurate. I was not good at dealing with ladies since I was too busy.

"You are my Jiminy Cricket," I said.

"I beg your pardon," Mrs. West said. "I do not know what you are talking about?"

"You know, the talking cricket with a top hat and umbrella in the Pinocchio cartoon, his conscience," I said.

"Reginald, I don't watch cartoons, so I do not understand your reference to a parrot."

"Jiminy Cricket was a cricket, not a parrot, and Pinocchio's conscience."

"Really, Reginald. A Parrot can talk, but crickets cannot. Reginald, focus; we must do many things today and discussing a cricket who talks is not part of it. Now the reference letters. One is from Lady Felicia Godwin, who is the niece of Major Horace Chesterton, and the other is from Major Chesterton. These will be letters of refence for you as a butler, and it is important that you have faithfully served them for four years after your promotion from a footman."

"Do you know them?" I asked.

"Yes, Lady Chesterton, the major's sister was at school with me, and I know the family. My children are aware of the family with Christmas cards and birthday messages. They live in Bath."

"Mrs. West, I have never been to Bath," I said. "I presume it is in England."

"It is," Mrs. West said.

"I have never been to England," I said.

"I thought everyone had," Mrs. West said.

"People who are rich travel," I said. "Toronto is the furthest that I travelled."

"How interesting" Mrs. West said. "The house is at 19 Cotswold Road. The major served with the artillery in the First World War, is retired, smokes a pipe and drinks scotch. Lady Felicia is an art historian of the renaissance."

"Mrs. West, I need more information," I said.

"Why?" Mrs. West asked. "My son-and daughter-in-law never question the staff. They are too caught up with being too important to bother. We will find a map of Bath and you took the Queen Mary from New York. That is all you need to know."

I spent the next two hours writing the letters of reference, and the problem was the signatures, which took an hour to get right. I prepared the envelopes, which were addressed to prospective employers of Edward Chambers.

"That is my name?" I asked.

"Yes," Mrs. West said.

"I need identification."

"Wallace will get it for you for a price."

"Who is Wallace?" I asked.

"My former butler who seems to be able to handle anything."

"Won't your son want to hire him?"

"Wallace has thrown him out of my house on several occasions. When Douglas demanded I fire Wallace, I called him into the room where Douglas glared at Wallace. I told Wallace I was increasing his salary by an extra twenty dollars a month. Wallace will not work for Douglas and Douglas cannot stand Wallace."

"I need Wallace's address and phone number."

"It is in my purse," Mrs. West said, "and I will give it to you."

"What purse?" I asked.

"Never mind, it will come to me," Mrs. West said. I was

connected to a spirit that was not connecting, but I would wait to find out if this was a minor mistake, or the beginning of something worse.

"What next" I asked.

"You require suitable clothing and footwear," Mrs. West said.

"I have two suits, shoes, a sports jacket and a blazer."

"One of your suits is a horrible check pattern and the other brown. One pair of shoes are brown and the other is black with no laces."

"They are called loafers," I said.

"I know what they are called, footwear for those too lazy to tie laces" Mrs. West said.

"I hadn't thought of that" I said.

"Reginald, a butler never wears loafers. They wear black oxfords. The suits are charcoal grey with stripes, dark blue with stripes or black with stripes."

"That is what a funeral director wears."

"Exactly. They are there to serve a bereaved family with decorum and respect. You are to wait on a family, also with respect. We are going to Cadburys on Bloor Street."

"Is that a chocolate store?" I asked.

"They are a men's fine furnishing establishment and tailors, where my late husband shopped. You need the look."

"The look?" I asked.

"Yes, the look as if you could be presented to the Queen at an afternoon tea."

"Maybe when I go to London, I will look her up" I said.

"That was an analogy," Mrs. West said.

"I know" I said. "I always shop at Eaton's when there is a sale," I said.

"Reginald, you must give your clothes away. They are not appropriate. Today we can outfit you with one suit, one shirt, one tie, cufflinks and black oxfords. How tall are you?"

"Six foot two inches."

"How much do you weigh?"

"One hundred and eighty-five pounds."

"Shoe size?"

"Eleven."

"I believe you can purchase something on the rack with adjustments, since you need the clothes for Monday" Mrs. West said. "How much money do you have?"

"Two hundred and fifty dollars, which I am saving for a trip to Europe" I said. "Most of it is from Christmas presents over the years."

"That will do for a suit, shirt, tie, cufflinks, belt, socks and a good pair of oxfords."

"I can get a suit on sale at Eaton's for thirty dollars. For two hundred and fifty dollars, I can buy a used car."

"I am sure you can, but you must look the part. Find your money and we need to move."

"It's a good thing the money is here." I took the streetcar to the subway, and the train traveled north to Bloor Street. Before we entered Cadburys, Mrs. West told me to ask for Mr. Richards. I was to tell him my grandfather was a friend of Mrs. Alicia West, who recommended the store, and that Mr. Richards would take care of me. I did as she asked, but whatever I explained would not overcome what I wore. Mrs. West said I would obtain a pair of Crocket & Jones.

"Why would I buy a pair of aircraft engines?" I asked.

"Shoes" Mrs. West said.

"You are right, I was thinking of Pratt & Whitney" I said.

"You were not and that was an attempt at humour which failed" Mrs. West said. Mr. Richards was there, but he took one glance at my suit and shoes, and I could swear he sighed. Once he heard my story, he looked at me and asked if I could afford to shop here. Before I could reply, Mrs. West told me to tell him I had come into an inheritance. I told him if he didn't treat me with respect, I would go to Cheswick & Martin down the street. Once I told him that, he changed and got down to business. I told him I needed the suit for Monday. He stared at me.

"Tell him you pay an extra ten dollars to get it done," Mrs.

West said, which I did. Whenever he asked me about positioning the pockets, cuffs, and the drape Mrs. West instructed me. By the time I was finished, Mr. Richards had thought of me as a young protégé. When it was time to choose a tie, Mr. Richards brought out four. As I was choosing, Mrs. West told me that the dark red tie in the display case was the one. I said this to Mr. Richards, who smiled and told me it was pure Italian silk and very expensive.

Three hours later, I had a pair of Crockett & Jones black oxfords, three ties, a belt, socks and a couple of cufflinks with a promise that my white shirts and dark blue suit would be ready for eleven o'clock on Monday. I paid two hundred and twenty-three dollars. For that, I could buy a six-year-old Nash Rambler. Outside the store, it was two in the afternoon. Mrs. West told me she would stay out of my life until Monday morning on one condition.

"You will attend church service on Sunday." My after-life detective was like my mother, but I said I would go.

"One other thing next week you must return to see Mr. Richards for two more suits and formal wear. You will have my money to spend."

"When are you going to teach me how to be a butler?"

"I forgot about that. Tomorrow."

"So, no church," I said.

"There is a choice. You will go to church, or I will spend the day with my fingers on a blackboard."

"Church it is," I said.

"I think I can spend time this afternoon to get you started since we must meet Wallace after he has his lunch on Sunday. How much money do you possess?"

"Twenty-three dollars."

"Take a taxi."

"I can walk."

"Time is of the essence" Mrs. West said. She had taken over my decisions, but what was the point of arguing?

"There is a Yellow Taxi; call it" Mrs. West said.

“Yes, Mrs. West” I said and resisted saying, yes mother.

CHAPTER 6

Butler Lessons and Annoying Mrs. West

We were back in my room, where I sat in my chair with a notepad and pen and attempted to look intelligent.

"Did your family employ a butler?" Mrs. West asked.

"No," I said. Regina was not the place for butlers and making it in our neighbourhood was having a twelve-foot fishing boat and a cleaning lady.

"Have you been with a family who employed a butler" Mrs. West asked.

"No, but I saw William Powell in *My Man Godfrey* play the butler. The socialite Carole Lombard picks him up in a city dump. It's a funny movie. I read P. G. Wodehouse and about his butler Jeeves. Have you read P.G. Wodehouse? He is a swell author."

"Reginald, butlers never say swell and never use slang. Butlers never demonstrate a sense of humour and never smile. A butler is there to serve and remains silent unless asked a question. If that occurs, he will reply with the least number of words. He will enunciate and open his mouth so no one will ask him to repeat what he has said. If it is my son Douglas, who drinks too much and is a fool, it might be necessary to speaks several times."

"Was your son switched at birth?" I asked.

"Reginald, I would appreciate it if you would not attempt humour. I want to find out who murdered me, which is a serious matter. Tomorrow when we visit Wallace, I am sure he will explain more." She didn't like her son so that was a decent question, but mothers are like that.

"About that. I can't just show up and say hello, Wallace; Reginald Clark here. I need to have a little talk."

"Leave that to me," said Mrs. West. "I left Wallace money to buy a small house last Christmas. Wallace had served us for forty years, and I felt I had to do it. I wasn't worried about anything happening but wanted him to have something."

"You weren't worried that something might happen to you last Christmas?"

"No, I wasn't."

"You said that you told your family you had changed the will. What did you say and when?"

"Really, Reginald, why bring this up?"

"I am a reporter," I said. "It is important."

"It was at my birthday party when I overheard Douglas talking to my daughter" Mrs. West said. "He had been drinking and talked about my health."

"Isn't that good? A son worried about his mother?" I asked.

"He was complaining I was in good health and wanted that to change for the worse so he could get his third of my estate. When he and Madeline came into the living room, I am afraid I lost my patience and told him what I had done. I said that I left eleven million dollars to Marie in trust for William. I added that I had divided the remaining one million dollars and the sale of my house and furniture between Madeline and Douglas. Let me say that the reaction from my children was not pleasant."

"Mrs. West, that was most unwise," I said.

"Reginald, you think so? I have regretted that since I said it but what I did is done."

"You waived a red flag in front of a bull," I said.

"Enough Reginald, I made a mistake and now you must

discover if it was Douglas or Madeline."

"I forgot Madeline's married name?"

"Morton" Mrs. West said.

"Who heard Mr. West say that to Mrs. Morton?"

"Only me. Their spouses were drinking at the bar, and the children were downstairs."

"Did you tell this to anyone else?" I asked.

"I was mortified, so no."

"Are you sure?" I asked.

"I told Wallace the next day, although I think he overheard it. He was making drinks at the bar."

"What did he say when you told him?" I asked.

"Wallace was upset and suggested I not allow Mr. West to visit again, but Douglas is my son."

"Your children forgot the first rule about money" I said.

"Which is?" asked Mrs. West.

"Always be kind to a rich relative before they die" I said.

"A little late now since I am dead" Mrs. West said.

"Glad I got that out of the way" I said.

"I wish you would not annoy me" Mrs. West said.

"That is what I do best" I said. "Don't take it personally, I do it to everyone."

"Stop that, now," Mrs. West said.

"Yes, Mrs. West," I said. "I don't think Mr. West hired someone to kill you."

"Why would you say that?" Mrs. West asked.

"Two retired policemen give me advice. They told me never to assume the obvious before an investigation. I would put your children as suspects and I will keep an open mind, but I don't think your son hired someone to murder you."

"Explain?" Mrs. West asked.

"The problem with hiring someone to carry out a murder is you contacted a person you don't want to annoy. You pay them and later they show up and say, gee about that murder, I am a little short of money and it never ends. Goodbye murder and hello blackmail. Mr. West would require a few stiff ones to hire this fellow. Anyone hired would see your son as a drinker who is talkative and at risk so they would not take the case. That is why I don't think he hired anyone. You understand."

"I do unfortunately," Mrs. West said. "I find it distasteful."

"Murder always is" I said. "When was your birthday?"

"March 18."

"This year?"

"Every year."

"I meant the one when you told them about changing the will."

"March 18 of this year."

"Did you hear any other threats from your son?" I asked.

"Only his wish for me to die."

"A jury would not find that as a threat on its own. If there was something else, perhaps. And besides, he didn't wish for you to die." I looked at my notes, "he said 'you were in good health and wanted that to change for the worse so he could get his third of my estate.' I accept that was a warning, but we must be exact."

"That is why you must be a butler in Douglas' home."

"What else does a butler do?" I asked.

"Think of the captain of a ship except instead of passengers, it is a family" Mrs. West said. "A butler is like a church deacon with the ability to handle anything. Laundry, keeping the wine cellar stocked, ensuring clothes are clean and ironed, shoes shined and the ability to organize a formal table. Now we will work on the items for a formal table. You will cut from paper knives, fish knives, spoons and forks. Then we will work on the wine and water glasses." Which we did until six, when I went to dinner.

I had the evening free, but Mrs. West was ten feet from me and watching. That cramped my style and at dinner I ate slowly and chewed with my mouth closed. My fellow boarders grabbed everything before I did and left me wishing I had been a little more assertive since I was still hungry. I left the table wondering if I had tapeworm.

The following day after breakfast I made notes, then at

eight, I changed.

"Mrs. West, are you there?"

"Yes, Reginald."

"Where did you go to church?"

"The Anglican Church," Mrs. West said. "Where are you planning to attend church service?"

"My family is United Church, but I keep hearing the hymns from the Baptist church nearby. I like "Are You Washed in the Blood" and "We Shall Gather by the River."

"You are not serious?" Mrs. West asked.

"I will try it, and they have lots of singing." When I or should I say we, arrived at the church, I sat at the back. It was a little loud, but I liked the tambourine that accompanied the piano. The minister was unique with his shouts, walking down the aisle and asking if we had accepted that we all were sinners. A few came forward, exclaiming they were. Mrs. West's commentaries continued through the service, so I knew she was not amused. In fact, she said it was not the way a proper church service should be. But I had never gone to an Anglican service so I could not make any comment. I must admit it was nothing like the United Church back home, but at least the Baptists liked to sing.

"Next Sunday, I will go to a Pentecostal church," I said. "They speak in tongues and get raucous." I gave it a few seconds.

"Or I could try the Salvation Army." This time Mrs. West didn't speak. Back in my room, I sat down at my typewriter and wrote "Mrs. West Demands", a story for the Saturday Evening Post.

"You wouldn't?" Mrs. West asked.

"Hello, Mrs. West," I said. "Are you talking to me? I thought you had an atmospheric black out?"

"You irritated me," Mrs. West said. "Next Sunday, you will go to Grace Church-on-the Hill in Forest Hill near my home. It is an Anglican Church, and our priest has the most wonderful homilies."

"Something to put me to sleep," I said.

"There are consequences to that behaviour," Mrs. West said.

"Fingernails on a blackboard?" I asked.

"Reginald, how nice you remembered," Mrs. West said.

"Unfortunately, yes," I said. "You lived in Forest Hill?" I asked.

"I did until my unfortunate passing."

"If I don't go to your church, there will be fingernails on a blackboard, or F.O.B.," I said.

"Reginald, F.O.B. is Freight on Board. The buyer assumes responsibility for the freight."

"How do you know that?" I asked.

"My husband was in the insurance business and liked to talk to me. Even if the topic was not that interesting, I felt it my duty to listen and ask questions. I enjoyed it when he was at home and not at his club. My life was full, and I enjoyed many things. Now I am anchored to a young man whose idea of enjoyment is hearing dreadful music with a band called Big Fish and drinking. Next Sunday we will go to my church, and next Thursday night you will go to *The Magic Flute* by Mozart. It is a wonderful opera, and I do not know where my season tickets are so you will buy one. In this state of being, I have decided to enjoy myself, and you will escort me. Once you get a haircut and obtain your suit, you will be respectable. You will discover young ladies with their mothers or female friends at the opera. There are intermissions; some of them might talk to you if you act appropriately."

"What do you mean, act properly?" I asked.

"No slang, no discussion of your music, and focus on asking questions. Discuss current events and books. Under no circumstances mention that you live in a boarding house ot discuss cartoons."

"You want me to be someone else? I asked.

"For the moment, yes," Mrs. West said. "You have potential but need guidance. Wallace can give you advice on drinks. Douglas drinks Scotch, and his wife Marigold drinks a vodka martini, which is two ounces of vodka, then sprinkle the vermouth on an ice-cold glass with an olive. When Marigold is in one of her moods, give her three ounces but cut back, she doesn't handle her martinis. Douglas drinks single malt, three cubes of ice and requires a double unless he demands a proper drink. If he does keep pouring until he says stop. Do the liquor run each week. You will require white gloves, six pairs and hold the tray out of reach of Douglas, who uses his hands when he tells one of his dreadful stories. Make sure he has a supply of Romeo and Julieta cigars, which is what Winston Churchill smokes. Be prepared to stamp out small fires since he has a cigar in his hand as much as in his mouth and he is careless."

"Hold on, I am writing this," I said, but Mrs. West continued.

"Now, once Douglas has finished more than three drinks, he becomes hard to understand, and when he has a cigar in his mouth, it is impossible. It is rather simple: ignore what he is saying and observe. If his glass is empty, pour him another. If he does not have a cigar, open the cigar box, wait until he takes one, use scissors to cut the end, hand it to him and light it. If he is still talking, turn to Marigold and ask her what he said. At six at night, turn on the television for the news but keep the volume low since they will ignore it. It is quite simple." I was making notes and wondered what I had gotten myself into. I went to lunch where a few of my boarders remarked I was wearing a tie, but Mrs. Brown thought I looked nice.

After lunch, we took the Queen streetcar east to meet Mr. Wallace at his house. I got off near Elmer Avenue. Ten minutes later, I knocked at 55 Elmer, but no one came to the door. After five minutes, Mrs. West told me to find a pay phone. There was one on Queen Street and she told me he was at her house and gave me a number to call. I put in a dime and dialed. On the third ring, someone picked up the phone.

"The West residence, whom may I say is calling?"

"Is this Mr. Wallace?"

"Yes, it is. Whom may I say is calling?" It was Mr. Wallace, only butlers use whom.

“Reginald Clark.”

“Thank heavens. Is she with you?”

“Who?” I asked.

“You mean whom, Mrs. West?”

“Yes” I said.

“Good. Bring her to her house. I have important information for her,” and hung up.

CHAPTER 7

A Visit to the West Residence

"You gave your name?" asked Mrs. West.

"He asked my name, said thank heavens, and asked if I was with you. I told him, yes, so he told me to bring you to your house since he has information for you."

"Good gracious, that cannot be," Mrs. West said. "He asked if I was with you?"

"Yes," I said. "Does he know you are dead?" I asked.

"He must," Mrs. West said. "Wallace was my butler, and I observed him leave for his vacation, but he would have come back. John Williams is my executor and would publish a notice of my death in the *Globe and Mail*. No use discussing this. Call a taxi."

"Mrs. West, this is a Sunday in east Toronto, and it is hot but not raining. There are no taxis."

"Call one at that pay phone." A Queen Street streetcar was heading to a stop, and I ran, climbed the stairs in the car and paid the fare. I walked to the back, where there were no passengers.

"I told you to go to that telephone booth to call a taxi," Mrs. West said.

"First, I would make the call, give the address and go back to wait. Second, it is Sunday in hot weather, so the fleet is down to half. I might get a taxi in thirty minutes and in twenty minutes on the streetcar I will get off at Younge Street, where there are cabs. If I had debated that with you, I would miss this streetcar, which runs every twenty minutes on Sunday. Trust me." It was when we were at Jarvis Street that she spoke.

"I will try." We got off at Yonge Street, and I asked her for the address. She told me 149 Dunvegan Road, and I grabbed a cab. The traffic was light, so we were there in twenty minutes. I paid the cab and walked up to the door, but it opened before I rang the bell. Mr. Wallace looked in his seventies, tall and thin with white hair. I would call him Mr. Wallace as befitted his age and found addressing servants by their last names degrading.

"Mr. Clark, I assume. Please come into the living room. There is tea and a notebook. Is Mrs. West with you?" as he closed the door.

"She is," I said.

"Please sit, sir," Mr. Wallace said. Once I sat, Mrs. West asked me to ask Wallace how he was aware that she was with me.

"Mrs. West wants to understand how you knew she was with me?" Mr. Wallace looked sad and then spoke.

"I connected to her for two days, and I suggested she use you," Mr. Wallace said. "She forgot this."

"Tell him I have no idea how I died or when, but I am aware of the date of my funeral, April 23, 1957," Mrs. West said.

"Mrs. West told me she knows nothing about how she died or when, but knows the date of her funeral, April 23, 1957," I said.

"Curious," Mr. Wallace said. "She has hired you to find out who murdered her?"

"Yes," I said.

"I have followed you at the *Toronto Mirror* and your investigative stories," Mr. Wallace said. "I am glad she found you."

"Why are you in her house?" I asked.

"You mean the house in which she lived until her unfortunate passing," Mr. Wallace said.

"I am going to take notes; I love your butler-like expressions," I said.

"Indeed sir," Mr. Wallace said. "Then you should enjoy Mountjoy's book, *Rules for Butlers*."

"Where can I buy one?" I asked

"They are rare" Mr. Wallace said, and I observed his serious expression, but he had a twinkle in his eye.

"You made that up?" I asked.

"Indeed sir, I did," Mr. Wallace said. "Glad to observe that you are on the ball. The executor, Mr. John Williams, hired me to take care of the house over the strong objections of Mr. West. The first thing I did was change the locks, since I believe Mr. West had a key."

"Ask Wallace what information he has?" Mrs. West asked, which I repeated to Mr. Wallace.

"Every evening, Mrs. West's maid would grind up her sleeping pills and medicine and place them in her tea at ten at night. Mrs. West preferred that method. I have the medical report and two pieces of information," Mr. Wallace said. "Mrs. West died on April 13, 1957, between ten and eleven on Saturday night. Mrs. West's maid found her dead when she brought her breakfast in at seven thirty Sunday morning. When the police suggested an autopsy, Mr. West objected and called the police chief so there was no autopsy. I spoke to Jenkins, Mr. West's butler who is leaving. He said that on April 13, 1957, the night Mrs. West died, Mr. West was out." Mr. Wallace stopped to look at me.

"I was on vacation, and I feel terrible that I wasn't there" Mr. Wallace said.

"It appears Mr. West had the opportunity and access to the house," I said. "If he was there, no one saw him."

"Indeed, sir," Mr. Wallace said.

"Is it possible that someone else administered a drug to Mrs. West in her tea?" I asked.

"I don't know, sir," Mr. Wallace said.

"Did the maid observe Mrs. West drink the tea?" I asked.

"I don't know, sir," Mr. Wallace said.

"Where is the washroom for the master suite?" I asked.

"Adjoining the suite," Mr. Wallace said.

"Did the maid close the door when she left?" I asked.

"She usually does," Mr. Wallace said.

"Is it possible Mrs. West went to the bathroom before drinking the tea?" I asked.

"No idea, sir" Mr. Wallace said.

"Neither do I," Mrs. West said. "My mind is blank for that night."

"Is it possible someone hid in the room and administered a drug in the tea after the maid left?" I asked. "I would need an autopsy for that, and we are too late."

"Thanks to Mr. West," Mr. Wallace said.

"There are three pieces of evidence that are incriminating," I said. "Mr. West was out that night, he had a key to the house, and he refused an autopsy."

"Reginald, that was why I needed to hire you," said Mrs. West. "This is the perfect murder scene."

"It is, with no clues and only suspects" I said.

"Mr. Clark, what do we do now?" Mr. Wallace asked.

"Find out if anyone saw or heard a stranger near the house, then find out what types of drugs can kill," I said. "It is hypothetical, since there was no autopsy." I made notes, then waited, and I heard Mrs. West crying for the first time and I had no idea she could do that. Then she stopped.

"Mrs. West, this is difficult, but what do you recall of that night?" I asked.

"As I told you, nothing," she said. "I tried, but I can't. "Please tell Wallace thank you and now to take you to my desk." I told that to Mr. Wallace, who looked at me.

"What did she say about that night?"

"How do you know I was listening?" I asked.

"As a reporter, you would. One minute with you looking straight ahead and concentrating. I was with her for several days, so I have an understanding."

"She recalls nothing," I said. Mr. Wallace brought me upstairs to a door and opened it. It was both an office and library, and in the center was a large roll-top desk.

"Reginald, ask Wallace for the key to my desk," which I did. Once he found it, he gave it to me.

"Turn it to the left, and the top will open," Mrs. West said. "At the back, a wooden box is attached to the writing surface. Turn the box left," which I did. The writing surface opened, and I found an accordion folder at the back, which I took out. Wallace watched me as I pulled out letters, journals, photographs and a document I opened. It stated it was a bearer bond for the Northern Ontario Uranium Company for twenty-five thousand dollars.

"What is a bearer bond?" I asked Mrs. West.

"It is a debt owed by the company with interest to whoever has the bond. There is no name and no registration, so it is like cash. They issued this bond on April 25, 1946, and was due April 24, 1957, with interest payable each year at four percent. My husband bought and paid far less than the face value since it was offered at a discount. I do not know if it is worth anything. You may keep that bond since I doubt if it is worth anything and if it is, it will help you with your inquiries. Tell Wallace to call Stirling," which I told Wallace.

"Tell Mrs. West it is Sunday, the Lord's Day of rest," Wallace said. He forgot Mrs. West could listen to him.

"I heard," Mrs. West said, "and I am not impressed. Tell Wallace I am aware of that. I once had and now my estate has close to twelve million dollars with Stirling, our broker. Remind Stirling of this when Wallace calls and ask him to ask if the Northern Ontario Uranium Company is worth anything." I told this to Wallace, who called Stirling and talked. Wallace said he would call back. Five minutes later, he did and spoke to Wallace, who took notes. After he put down the receiver, he spoke.

"The Federal Government has a uranium project at Chalk River with contracts with the Northern Ontario Uranium Company," Mr. Wallace said. "The company is solvent and is an excellent investment."

"Reginald, there are ten years of interest worth ten thousand dollars and the bond is worth twenty-five thousand dollars," Mrs. West said. "Sell the bond and invest the money in the Toronto Stock Exchange. Take the file and everything in it to study in your room while I explain my plan; then you tell Wallace." Which I did.

"Is Stirling his first or last name?" I asked.

"His first name," Wallace and Mrs. West said together. "Archibald is his last name," Mr. Wallace said.

"Mrs. West gave me the bearer bond to support the costs of my inquiries," I said.

"Mrs. West is most generous sir," Mr. Wallace said.

"Mrs. West will now tell us her plans," I said. I looked at Mr. Wallace. "This is awkward having to explain it each time," I said.

"Indeed, it is sir," Mr. Wallace said in his most butlery voice.

"Mrs. West is the most intelligent woman I have ever met," Mr. Wallace said.

"She is," I said.

"Mrs. West is kind," Mr. Wallace said.

"I am aware" I said.

"She is also devious, so don't annoy her," Mr. Wallace said, but I didn't reply. "Did you understand what I said?" asked Mr. Wallace.

"Yes," I said.

"She is also ruthless," Mr. Wallace said.

"She is dead, so what can she do to me?" I asked.

"Knowing her, if you upset her, she will come back to life to teach you a lesson" Mr. Wallace said. I felt an involuntary shudder.

"Reginald, I just might," Mrs. West whispered.

"I will do what you want, Mrs. West," I said.

"You will Reginald," Mrs. West said. "You will." The diary was on the desk and was for this year. I opened it and looked to April 14. There was a note, *meeting M. at 8:30.*

"Mrs. West, your diary has a note for April 14, meeting M. at eight-thirty. Do you know about the meeting and who is M.?" There was a long pause.

"I have no idea, Reginald" Mrs. West said. "Another little task for you to solve."

CHAPTER 8

Mrs. West's Plan

I noticed Mr. Wallace had a pained expression and his hands trembled.

"I find it distressing to wait for information. Sir, you must tell me everything and don't hold back."

"I won't" I said. "There is an entry in Mrs. West's calendar for April 14 was for a meeting with M. at eight-thirty. Mrs. West does not recall the meeting or who is M. Do you know who M. is?"

"No sir, I was on vacation," Mr. Wallace said. "I have no idea."

"If someone killed Mrs. West, was it done to prevent her meeting M.?" I asked. "I am still not sure Mrs. West was killed."

"Murdered" Mrs. West said, "and I was."

"Someone murdered Mrs. West," Mr. Wallace said. What was the difference, murdered, killed, eliminated, assassinated, eradicated, bumped off or dispatched, they all meant the same thing. Maybe I could use dispatched, since that was more genteel. At least she wasn't defenestrated since she wasn't thrown out of a window and there was always deaded, but only if you were Bluebottle in the *Goon Show*. I wondered if I could use deaded, but when I looked at Mr. Wallace decided not to. Making a joke about the manner of death would not go over well.

"We shall see," I said. "Was Mrs. West murdered to prevent

the meeting with M? Did M. telephone or write Mrs. West? We need to search for letters and ask Bell Telephone for a list of telephone numbers."

"Reginald, that is brilliant," said Mrs. West. "I am afraid I don't know who M. is or why I didn't write out the full name."

"Don't worry, we can still search," I said.

"I will look for these letters once you leave," Wallace said. "I am not sure what I can say to Bell Telephone on Monday, but I will think of something."

"My plan," Mrs. West said. "I want Reginald to assume the identity of Edward Chambers. My cousin was Raymond Chambers, and we were very close growing up in Toronto. Tell that to Wallace," which I did.

"Raymond became a lawyer in Toronto but moved west to Regina just after Saskatchewan became a province in 1905. He did well and formed his own firm. We often wrote, and I have his letters. His son William died, leaving one son Edward. Edward was raised in Regina and left for Australia in 1955. That year was in a car accident and never survived his injuries. Some of Raymond's letters mention Edward. Tell this to Wallace," which I did.

"Raymond died last year, and I have his letters. Tell Wallace to get them. They are in the basement in my boxes." I explained this to Wallace.

"I need Wallace to create an identification for Reginald as Edward Chambers, living in Toronto and living with Wallace at his house. He will require a driver's licence, library card and membership in a club. I need them by noon on Monday. I think the fact that Edward lived in Regina assists in my plan. Tell Wallace." which I did.

"When you meet with Mr. George Montgomery, you can mention this as the reason for my gift. If he asks, tell him that Wallace can provide the letters. I don't think he will, and your profession is a butler recently returned from England, having worked for Major Chesterton. Tell Wallace," and I told him.

"You will work as a butler for Mr. West with the letters

of reference and, if required, Raymond's letters. I would like Wallace to train you today. Inform Wallace," which I did.

"Excuse me, Mrs. West, but first I need to arrange for Mr. Clark's documents," Mr. Wallace said. "Please wait while I get my camera and I can train Mr. Clark tonight." He left, returned, and took three face shots.

"Mr. Clark, you will need to pay for the documents, but I will tell the amount once it is done" Mr. Wallace said.

"Tomorrow, Reginald will take a leave of absence from his employer," Mrs. West said. "He will call Mr. George Montgomery and Mr. Stirling Archibald to make appointments. For Mr. Montgomery, he will be Edward Chambers, and for Mr. Archibald, he will be himself. Do not call from a pay box; you cannot hear traffic sounds. You will have a haircut and obtain your suit and his new identification as Edward Chambers. You will meet with Mr. Montgomery in the afternoon and get the key. When you meet with Mr. Archibald, hire him and give him the bond to sell. You can't have an account with a false name, but tell him to call Wallace, who can verify I am the grandson of an old friend. Explain this to Wallace," which I did.

"Buy Seagram, Bell, and the banks and ask Stirling what is doing well. Go to the Royal Bank, obtain your money and the photographs and return to the house for Wallace to put them in the safe. Take out five hundred dollars for expenses, enjoy a dinner with Wallace, and stay at my house. Tell Wallace." Which I did.

"Pack your bags and end your lease, or whatever it is," Mrs. West said. "The following day, call my son about a job and find a house. Explain this to Wallace." When I did, he smiled.

"I take it there is money at the Royal Bank?" Mr. Wallace asked.

"Twenty-thousand," I said, "thanks to Mrs. West."

"She is generous if she likes you or the expenditure is required for her schemes," Mr. Wallace said. "I don't think she has reached the point of liking you, so this is part of her plans. You are the prospective buyer of my house. I expect to live here in the West's residence for the next two to three years. Our courts take time, then there may be an appeal. I plan to move to Hamilton to be near my sister, so I was about to sell my house at 55 Elmer Avenue at the Beaches. It is a three-bedroom semi-detached. I had it appraised at sixteen-thousand five hundred, but if I don't have to pay a real estate agent, I will sell it for sixteen thousand. You can use my furniture until I move to Hamilton." I didn't know what to say, but it made sense. The Queen Streetcar was close to the Beaches.

"I will look at the house, and if I like it, I will buy it. Will cash do?"

"Yes, Mr. Clark, cash will do, and you will have to hire a lawyer to do the paperwork."

"Questions about my plan?" asked Mrs. West.

"Mrs. West wants to know if you have questions about her plan?" I asked.

"No, she seems to have it worked out," Mr. Wallace said. "Do you?"

"No question, but what is your first name?"

"Cedric" Mr. Wallace said.

"May I call you Cedric?" I asked.

"Certainly not, sir" Mr. Wallace said. "I dislike the name. I will show you the house and if you wish to purchase it, you should stay there until you take ownership. If all goes well, you will soon work for Mr. West. One other thing, someone is watching this house. Every night for the past week a 1954 four door Ford is parked across the street."

CHAPTER 9

Mr. Wallace

"Did you report it to the police?" I asked.

"No sir, I did not," Mr. Wallace said.

"Did you talk to the driver? I asked.

"No, sir," Mr. Wallace said. "That is your job. With respect, sir, you are a reporter, and I am not. I believe you can convince your editor that this is an important story for which you must be in disguise. You will speak to this fellow once they authorized you to do the story. If I may be so bold as to suggest this, sir, that you will tell this person who you are doing a story on the death of Mrs. West. I think the expression is on reliable sources and you will tell this person you believe it was murder. You will wear glasses, a hat and a moustache. It will be dark, so I don't want you to be recognized if you work for Mr. West, since I think Mr. West has hired this fellow."

"If you are correct and this fellow works for Mr. West, he would learn of my investigation."

"Indeed, sir," Mr. Wallace said. "That is the intent. You are dealing with an alcoholic who will feel the pressure and make mistakes."

"Including having me killed," I said.

"There is always danger in life, sir," Mr. Wallace said. "A streetcar could run you over, but there is the Grey Ghost."

"Who is the Grey Ghost?" I asked.

"He is a former policeman who served with the commandos in the war and is very good at protecting people. I think four hundred dollars for two weeks would do."

"What is his real name?" I asked.

"You don't need to know, but he is good, and I trust him. Mrs. West is not aware of this, but her husband used the Grey Ghost and was very pleased with the result. I have his contact."

"Why did my husband use him?" Mrs. West asked. "Tell Wallace." I noticed Mrs. West never said please, but I told Mr. Wallace what she wanted.

"Mr. West swore me to secrecy," Wallace said.

"Tell Wallace my husband is dead," Mrs. West said, which I did.

"I am aware your husband died. You are placing me in an impossible situation since I gave my word to your husband. A young lady asked for help, and Mr. West gave her money. He paid by cheque, and the lady later claimed he paid her for an illicit relationship. Your husband did not have a relationship, and I can confirm where he was on the dates she claimed. He was a gentleman and loved you, and the Grey Ghost resolved the situation and we never heard from her again."

"Where did you find the Grey Ghost?" I asked.

"I served in the First World War in France. A fellow sergeant was a wonderful friend, and the Grey Ghost is his son."

"You are aware of his name?" I asked

"Yes, but he asked that I keep it secret, which I will," Mr. Wallace said.

"Reginald, hire him; you possess enough money," Mrs. West said. I said, "yes" and what else could I say? I had lost control over my decisions; told what to wear, when to get a haircut, when to take a leave from my job, ordered to leave my boarding house and risk death. Added to the list was to act correctly, no slang and to go to church, and not any church, the Anglican church. But it was a great story, and I was rich so long as I stayed alive, and for that, I would trust the Grey Ghost.

My life had become complicated. I needed to ask Mrs. West a question and was concerned about what she might say.

"Is your son dangerous?" I asked Mrs. West.

"Reginald, I hope he's not," she said, "but I have no idea My decision to change the will infuriated him, and he is not well because of his alcohol consumption. He did not serve in the last war but knows how to shoot. I think I am the only person he would hurt since we don't enjoy a good relationship. Five hundred thousand dollars is a lot of money. Properly invested, that would return twenty-five thousand dollars a year, far more than most people make. Knowing Douglas and Marigold, they would spend it in less than five years. He hates me, but whether he is a threat to you, I am not sure. That is why you must employ the Grey Ghost. I am not sure how he will react to learning you are doing a story about my death. He is not stupid and will recognize he is a suspect. He had potential since he is intelligent, but he is also lazy and spoiled. I suppose you must tell Wallace what I said," which I did.

"Right then, let us go to my house," Mr. Wallace said. "Ask Mrs. West if I can use the Buick Roadmaster," I asked her, and she said she would be delighted. In the garage was a light-yellow convertible with a brown roof and white wall tires. I asked Wallace how old it was.

"That is a classic, a 1939 Buick Roadmaster Phaeton with a 320 cubic inch straight eight engine" Mr. Wallace said. "I insured it and may drive it, but I haven't since it was Mr. West's pride." He opened the garage door and drove the car out, then closed it as I got in the passenger's side and Mr. Wallace in the driver's side.

"I take it you want to be in the back?" I asked Mrs. West.

"Hush now, Reginald; I want to enjoy the ride," Mrs. West said. As Mr. Wallace turned onto the front driveway, I asked if the Ford would follow us. Mr. Wallace smiled and told me to open the glove compartment. I did and saw a Browning pistol.

"What is that?" Mr. Wallace asked.

"A Browning," I said.

"Have you used one?" he asked.

"During my first and second year in officer training with the Canadian Officer Training Corps, I used one. I resigned before my third year to work on a newspaper."

"Mr. West licenced me after a break in, and I am only to use it at the house," Mr. Wallace said. "For now, this is part of the house." It didn't matter; the Ford did not follow us. After checking out the house on Elmer Avenue, I asked about the adjoining neighbour.

"Mrs. Murphy is a widow and very nice," Mr. Wallace said. "Sweep her leaves and shovel her snow and she will treat you to her cooking."

"Did you ever consider renting you house?" I asked.

"Right now, the number of people renting in Toronto is thirty-five percent, so there is an enormous demand," Mr. Wallace said. "The house is near the Queen Streetcar line and the beaches so I could get top dollar. If I rented the house, I could receive two hundred dollars a month. I want to buy in Hamilton. For sixteen thousand, I can get a detached house and let my sister live there, which is why I am selling."

I told him I would buy it if I liked it, then we drove to my rooming house to get my stuff where I gave notice. I had paid until June 30, so I was sure Mrs. Brown could rent it with extra income. She was a little upset, but I told her it was an emergency. We stopped to buy groceries, and at the house, Mr. Wallace helped me bring in my suitcases and boxes of books. There was a washing machine in the basement and fresh sheets on the bed. There was no point in training until I had a job. Mr. Wallace shook my hand, gave me the keys and drove off. I closed the door and stood there, staring at the living room.

"Reginald, you are very fortunate. Time for you to unpack, enjoy dinner, and go to bed. There is a shower, not a bathtub, which you don't need to share."

"Mrs. West, I don't know how to cook."

"Important things are happening, so that is not essential," Mrs. West said. "The fact your mother failed to teach you is not my problem. Within a few days, you will be Douglas's butler.

He has a lovely cook unless she has given notice." In Regina, no boy was taught how to cook. My job was to take out the garbage, mow the lawn, shovel the driveway, chop wood, clean the gutters, take off the storm windows, and fix dripping sinks. Mrs. West would say that was not her problem if I mentioned this.

"I don't," I said.

"Reginald, everyone knows how to cook," Mrs. West said. "I find that hard to believe. Tomorrow purchase cookbooks, and tonight, toast and eggs. The following day, buy canned tuna and see if there is a restaurant nearby."

"I have no idea how to cook an egg," I said. "Explain."

"I am sure it is quite simple," Mrs. West said. Turn on the burner, drop an egg in a pan, and wait until it is cooked."

"I take it I break the egg first?" I asked as Mrs. West snorted, another thing she could do.

"Do I use butter? And how high should I set the burner?"

"I am not sure," Mrs. West said.

"You don't know how to cook, do you?"

"I always had cooks."

"I thought so" I said. "I will put my clothes away and call someone who knows, Mr. Wallace."

"An excellent idea," Mrs. West said. Once I put my clothes away, I called Mr. Wallace and received his instructions. Maybe my egg and toast were burnt but it was my first time working a pan and toaster. I didn't swear, but if I did, I would upset Mrs. West. She would insist I create a swear jar. What was the point? I was alone, but that was not entirely accurate, Mrs. West was here. She would be on my case if I was not her idea of a perfect Victorian gentleman, and my problem was that I was born a hundred years too late. No top hat or calling cards. The phone rang and I was tempted to ask Mrs. West to pick it up but I answered it. It was the wrong day to annoy her. I had a scale for her reactions, a rebuke, a reprimand, a dressing down, an admonishment and a proper scolding, and the trick was to inflict my humour on Mrs. West every two to three days.

"Sorry to bother you sir," Mr. Wallace said "but the parked Ford has left and three other things I should tell you. Mrs. Murphy will be over at seven with a banana cake or an orange cake. She will think I am back. Invite her in and explain you are the new owner, and you will take care of her yard work. It is worth it since she is an excellent cook. At Mr. West's residence, when you take a shower, bring you wallet and cash with you to the shower. The staff are trustworthy, but Mr. West has a habit of taking money from his employees, so don't keep a lot of cash with you. The Grey Ghost will be back in Canada on Monday. He had to travel to Africa to extract a man from a hostage situation. Two weeks ago, he accomplished that, but celebrated in Paris. He wrote to his father about discovering a superb Grand Cru. Good night, sir and enjoy pleasant dreams."

"Thank you, Mr. Wallace," I said and hung up. Great, my protector needs to dry out, and I would stay with a kleptomaniac. That was wrong since kleptomania was a mania to steal, and Mr. West did not suffer from that affliction. He was a thief and possibly a murderer.

"Reginald, what did Wallace tell you?" asked Mrs. West, so I told her.

"Douglas should know better," she said. "He is a wretched man. My favorite Grand Cru was the 1934 Saint-Èmilian. It would be best if you went to Carstairs on Front Street, they sell the best French wines. I think you should go to bed Reginald, since tomorrow is a busy day." I should write to my mother to tell her she was replaced, turned off the lights and went upstairs Once I changed, I did my thing in the washroom and lay in my bed. I was almost asleep when I heard Mrs. West.

"Reginald, your prayers," she ordered, which I performed.

CHAPTER 10

Carrying out Mrs. West Plan and a Leave of Absence

At seven o'clock Monday morning, there was a knock on the kitchen door.

"Cedric. It is Martha. I have a little something," which I assumed was Mrs. Murphy. I opened the door, and she stepped back. She was attractive, with brown hair and blue eyes, and was in her forties.

"Who are you?" she asked.

"Reginald Clark, who is buying this house," I said.

"Cedric didn't tell me," Mrs. Murphy said.

"We arranged it last night on the condition that I rake your leaves, shovel your snow and help. Mrs. Murphy, is it?" I asked. "Do come in. Would you like coffee?" That was the one thing I did without making a mess. She stepped inside, closed the door, and put a basket on the table. Mrs. Murphy picked up the pot of coffee, smelled it, then made a face and put it down. She saw the burnt eggs in the frying pan and looked at me.

"You don't know how to cook, do you?" She walked to my toaster, turned a knob to the left, and picked up my frying pan.

"I don't know what Cedric was thinking," Mrs. Murphy said. "You need a new frying pan. Come to my kitchen, and I will cook you a decent breakfast. You can enjoy my banana bread for dessert tonight." Inside her kitchen, a small dog raced over to sniff me, then returned to a mat and lay down. Mrs. Murphy said that Trixie, a street dog she found, stayed with her. After a breakfast of toast, not burnt, eggs not burnt, and bacon, Mrs. Murphy said she was going to Eaton's after school to buy some curtains and buy me a frying pan.

"I am a teacher, Mr. Clark. I bought *Betty Crocker's Cookbook for Boys and Girls* for my niece, so I will see if they still have one. You can pay when you see me. My upstairs sink drips, and would you fix it when you have time?" I said I would tonight. I may not know how to cook, but I understood dripping sinks and would have to call Mr. Wallace to find where he kept his tools. After taking the streetcar to work, I went inside my building and met my boss in his office.

My boss, Bill Wise, looked like W. C. Fields with his prominent nose and he talks out of the corner of his mouth. We call him W. C. behind his back, which made Arthur smile. He was from London, England, where the initials W.C. are a water closet or a crapper. Mr. Wise came of age in the twenties, so his slang was from that era. He was tough and tried to be one step ahead of the other newspapers. My story intrigued Mr. Wise. He took the cigar out of his mouth, told me to take three weeks off, and wanted all rights to the story. Mr. Wise was very magnanimous when he told me it would be without pay unless I could prove, in his words, who "bumped off the old dame." Mr. Wise was aware of the West family and their wealth. I knew that when I was alone, Mrs. West would give me a piece of mind about my boss. I don't think she knew about the newspaper business's roughness.

"Really, Reginald," she exclaimed, but I ignored her.

"Mr. Wise, I need to make a few private calls," I said. "Is there anywhere I can do that?" I can't use a telephone booth because of traffic noise." Wise said he was going to the dentist, and I could use his phone. Once he left and closed the door, Mrs. West let me have it.

"Bumping off the old dame," Mrs. West said. "The very idea, indeed. That man is not a gentleman."

"He's an editor in a cutthroat business, and I couldn't say anything since he is my boss."

"You should work at the *Globe and Mail*," Mrs. West said.

"They didn't offer me a job. I must make some calls." I made an appointment with Mr. Montgomery at one and Mr. Alexander at four. When I called Mr. Wallace, he told me to meet him at the house at noon. My next call was to Big Fish.

"Big Fish, can you call Fred and see if he can buy a 1939 Buick Roadmaster Phaeton convertible?"

"Sure, but I'm not sure he can find one," Big Fish said.

"If he can't find one in Toronto, have him make calls to Hamilton," I said.

"Might be tough, and what Fred finds will need work."

"I'll pay as long as the total is only six hundred dollars," I said.

"For six hundred dollars, Fred can find you a three-year-old Chevrolet," Big Fish said.

"I want the Buick convertible," I said.

"Ok will find out; call you later," I explained my move and gave him my new number.

"I hope you are not planning to spend all your money on cars," Mrs. West said.

"I may die or be driven insane acting as a butler for your son," I said. "A used car is six hundred dollars unless it is cheap, and I like the 1939 Buick convertible. If I was to go out with a proper young lady, which would she prefer, a tiny Nash Rambler or a classic car?"

"Fine, Reginald, I see your point. Now for what is important, you need a haircut." She was a no-nonsense boss. I went out of the building to Mario's barbershop. I hopped in the chair, and once he covered me, I told him to give me the usual.

"A short haircut, Reginald, and your neck must be trimmed," Mrs. West ordered.

"Mario, today I want it short and my neck trimmed," I said.

"Ok, boss, short it is," Mario said, and once Mario finished, I looked like an army recruit. After I paid Mario, my hat was too loose. Outside, I headed to the Yonge Street subway to go north to Bloor when I heard Mrs. West.

"Very nice, and you need a new Fedora." Mr. Richards had my shirts and suit ready at Cadbury's, and I tried them on. I wouldn't wear them until home, so he placed them on hangers in a garment bag. I told Mr. Richard I would return tomorrow for two more suits and a formal suit."

"And two hats and another pair of shoes," Mrs. West said.

"And two hats and another pair of shoes," I said to Mr. Richards. I took a taxi to Mrs. West's house, and once I paid the driver, I looked around for the Ford, but the street was deserted. Mr. Wallace opened the door, and I walked inside the kitchen and placed my purchases on a chair.

"Coffee, sir," Mr. Wallace asked, and I nodded. Once he poured the coffee, he showed me the documents for my identification which looked authentic. As I drank the coffee, I asked Mr. Wallace about his tools, and he told me they were in the basement. He said I should come by at seven tonight for more lessons, and I paid him the money for my identification. I went to the basement for the toolbox, then returned to the kitchen.

"When will I meet the Grey Ghost?" I asked.

"Today is Monday, June 24, and I expect he may be free tomorrow," Mr. Wallace said. "Once you begin as Mr. West's butler, he will expect you there twenty-four hours a day with Sunday off. I suggest you inform Mr. West that your mother is ill and you must be away on Saturdays and Sundays. That will leave time to meet with witnesses and review documents. You cannot leave anything at Mr. West's home."

"Mrs. West, do you have anything you wish to ask Mr. Wallace?" I asked.

"No, but I realize I have made a colossal error," Mrs. West said. "I will be with you at my son and daughter-in-law's house, and I cannot stand them."

"It was your idea so that you could suffer too," I said.

"A little chat with Mrs. West, I presume?" asked Mr.

Wallace.

"Yes, she is not looking forward to being in her son's house," I said.

"It was her idea," Mr. Wallace said and called me a cab. "Before you go, here is the bond, and treat it like cash," Mr. Wallace said. "Good luck."

At home, I changed and ate banana bread. I organized my wallet and took a briefcase with the bond inside. The street car was half full at this time of day, and I got off at Bay Street. I was there early for my appointment, and Mr. Montgomery arrived at ten after one. I stood as he walked in. He looked at me, with short hair, in an expensive suit and shoes, and smiled.

"Mr. Chambers?" Mr. Montgomery asked.

"I am, sir," and he shook my hand.

"Come in," and he opened the door to his office, which faced Bay Street, and once inside, he closed the door. I sat in one of the two chairs facing Mr. Montgomery.

"My secretary did not explain why you wish to see me."

"I have been in touch with Mr. Wallace, the butler to my late third cousin, Mrs. West," I said. "She was my grandfather Raymond Chambers' first cousin, a lawyer in Regina. He died last year but told me that Mrs. West had a gift for me." I took out my identification and showed it to Mr. Montgomery. "I do not know what it is, but Mr. Wallace told me he knew of my grandfather and believes there is correspondence from my grandfather to Mrs. West." Mr. Montgomery made a note.

"I am to tell you the number 44332299 and the code 'Oh, East is East, and West is West, and never the twain shall meet, till Earth and Sky stand presently at God's great Judgment.'And you are to give me a key." Mr. Montgomery looked surprised and said wait a moment. He picked up his phone and asked for the Mrs. Alicia West file.

"I did not expect this, Mr. Chambers, but we will see." An older lady walked in with the file, gave it to him, left, and closed the door. Mr. Montgomery opened the file and asked me to repeat the number and code, which I did and made a note. Mr.

Montgomery asked me to sign a receipt, gave me a key and the address of the Royal Bank and shook my hand. At the elevator, I pressed the down button, got in it and the door closed. I was alone in the elevator.

"That went well, but we shall see," Mrs. West said.

"See what?" I asked.

"We shall find out if Mr. Montgomery checked the deposit box." It took some time at the bank since I needed to show my identification and sign forms. Once we opened it with both keys in the vault, the clerk placed it on the table and left, closing the door.

"There should be money in hundred-dollar bills. Open the envelope." Inside were pictures of Mr. Montgomery and a lady and Mr. West and a lady.

"That is Douglas, my son, and the lady is not his wife," Mrs. West said. "Her name is Miss Eunice Walker. Put the money and the photographs in your briefcase and off to my house." Once I put them in my briefcase, I knocked, opened the door, and thanked the clerk. On Front Street, I took a cab to the house, and once I paid for the taxi, I walked to the entrance, where Mr. Wallace opened the door. Once inside, he closed the door, and we went to the basement, where I opened my briefcase and took out two thousand dollars. I told Mr. Wallace to take sixteen thousand dollars and what the lawyer required for the transfer.

"Why so much money, Reginald?" Mrs. West asked.

"Suits and shoes, eight hundred, the Grey Ghost, four hundred and my car, six hundred. That leaves me with two hundred dollars."

"Quite right, you need that money," Mrs. West said. "I am pleased. Mr. Montgomery is an honourable lawyer, but that does not excuse his affair with Felicity. Please tell Wallace to destroy Mr. Montgomery's photographs and keep those of Douglas and that woman," which I told him to do. At three-thirty, I called a taxi and headed to Mr. Archibald's.

At his front area, his secretary brought me into his office and closed the door. I was told to sit. I told him I was the grandson of a friend of Mrs. West and he could call Mr. Wallace. He asked for my identification, which I gave and the bond. I set up an account, and Mr. Archibald said the money should arrive in ten days. He asked what did I intend to do with it? I told him to buy Seagram, Bell telephone and the banks.

"I may need to take out thirty-two thousand dollars," I said.

"Why would you do that since that is a lot of money?" Mr. Archibald asked.

"The purchase of two homes to rent out," I said. He nodded. We stood, and he shook my hand. Outside, as I waited for a taxi, I heard Mrs. West.

"If you buy the houses near the beaches near the street car, you will receive four hundred dollars a month less insurance and taxes," Mrs. West said. "Your return will be around four thousand dollars a year, and you still have three thousand invested."

"Better than seventeen hundred and fifty dollars a year," I said.

"Yes, it is," Mrs. West said. "I am impressed."

"You should be," I said. I took a taxi home, and inside I changed. I took the tool chest and knocked on Mrs. Murphy's door. She opened wearing a black dress and makeup. Mrs. Murphy wasn't bad looking and told me to sit and have some wine. I told her I had to be with Mr. Wallace soon but would love to spend another night with her. Mrs. Murphy was disappointed and took me upstairs to the bathroom. It took me twenty minutes to fix the leak. I paid for the frying pan and recipe book in her kitchen. She gave me part of a casserole since I wouldn't have time to enjoy it with her over a glass of wine to know each other. I paused at the door, imagining feeling her leg pressed against mine under the table, and hesitated to leave.

"Reginald, remember what I told you," Mrs. West said. "You must leave now," I said goodbye. I returned to my kitchen, where I ate the chicken casserole and read the introduction to *Betty Crocker's Cookbook for Boys and Girls.*

"Reginald, Mrs. Murphy has designs for you," Mrs. West said. "You must exercise extreme caution."

"Me," I said. "She is twenty years older."

"I saw how you looked at her, like a child in front of a cookie jar," Mrs. West said. "She will keep having problems with her plumbing, and then she will invite you for dinner and make sure you drink enough wine before she makes her move. Be careful with her; she is a hussy." That was the first time I had heard someone say hussy, and I nodded.

"Reginald, that is just a nod," Mrs. West said. "Repeat after me; I will stay away from Mrs. Murphy." There was no way I would say that, not in a million years. The sound of fingernails on a blackboard forced me out of my idyllic dreams. I repeated that I would stay away from Mrs. West, but I had my fingers crossed behind my back and was already thinking of her as my little sweetheart. This was the first time I might get close to something I had always wanted, a woman. And not just any woman, someone near and desirable who wished to be with me and next door. It was a fantasy come true.

When I arrived at the West residence at seven at night, I asked Mr. Wallace about Mrs. Murphy.

"She is a delightful woman," Mr. Wallace said. This was awkward since they must be good friends. He looked at me and smiled.

"The black dress and the wine, always a temptation," Mr. Wallace said.

"Mrs. West is connected to me and ten feet from me," I said.

"Mrs. West and Mrs. Murphy should declare a truce," Mr. Wallace said. "We never discuss Mrs. West in her present situation. As long as you and Mrs. West are connected, you will be as celibate as a Trappist monk." Mr. Wallace instructed me on the fine art of being a butler by showing and explaining things. He told me that Mr. West's butler was leaving on Friday and that the advertisement would be in the *Globe and Mail* tomorrow. Applicants would reserve a time for an interview.

I returned home at nine and noticed Mrs. Murphy's lights were on, and I thought maybe I could have a glass of wine with her. That would be neighbourly, and she was alone and maybe needed company. I heard Mrs. West's voice as I turned the knob on my kitchen door to go outside to visit her.

"Reginald, you should go to bed," Mrs. West said.

"Is this to keep me from wandering next door?" I asked. "You want me to resist temptation."

"For her, you must," Mrs. West said. "Go upstairs and read a book."

"Here we go again, Jiminy Cricket, my conscience," I said.

"The talking parrot' Mrs. West said.

"He was a cricket, and you want me to remain inside," I said.

"Yes," Mrs. West said.

"Gunsmoke is on television," I said.

"Gunsmoke," Mrs. West asked. "Like a police siren or car horn."

"Those are auditory, and it is the name of a television show," I said.

"Gunsmoke?" Mrs. West asked. "How strange."

"A western," I said.

"As opposed to an eastern," Mrs. West said.

"You are having me on," I said.

"Yes, when the stars are correctly aligned with the moon, I am permitted to be whimsical," Mrs. West said.

"Are the stars aligned with the moon?" I asked.

"I have no idea," Mrs. West said.

"More whimsy?" I asked.

"Yes," Mrs. West said. "This confuses me since you don't have a television set."

"I should buy one," I said.

"That would be unfortunate? Mrs. West said. "They are in such large cabinets, and where would you put them?"

"In the living room," I said.

"You wouldn't dare," Mrs. West said.

"You don't like furniture that can talk," I said.

"I suppose I don't," Mrs. West said.

"That wasn't me; it was Fred Allen," I said.

"What was Fred Allen?" Mrs. West asked.

"The quote about talking furniture," I said.

"A friend?" Mrs. West asked.

"He was on the radio," I said.

"Allen said television is for people who haven't anything better to do to watch people who can't do anything."

"He sounds like a wise man," Mrs. West said.

"Every time I watch television, fingernails scrape on a blackboard?" I asked.

"Yes," Mrs. West said.

"You're no fun," I said. "Maybe there is opera on television?"

"I doubt that and not a reason to buy one," Mrs. West said. "If they did, they would ruin it by adding animals and clowns to make it more entertaining." I resisted asking what was wrong with that.

"I could watch it across the street; the curtains are open," I said.

"You wouldn't hear anything," Mrs. West said.

"It's pretty simple; a crime is committed; Miss Kitty sidetracks Marshall Dillon in her bedroom, so Doc solves it," I said.

"If you know what will happen, it is a waste of time," Mrs. West said.

"I have fun making up dialogue," I said. "You would be shocked with Miss Kitty's suggestions to the marshal."

"Not really," Mrs. West said. "If you are to help, you require a good night's sleep," Mrs. West said. It tempted me to argue, but what was the point? There was always another day or another month, and I was not in the mood for fingernails on a blackboard, so I headed off to bed. This time I said my prayers without being told.

CHAPTER 11

Meeting the Grey Ghost and an Interview

On Tuesday, I walked to the shop on the corner and bought the Globe and Mail, found the ad and called. I spoke with Mr. Jenkins, and gave my name as Edward Chambers.

"Mr. Chambers, you are the first who has called, and it would please me to meet you at the house at four this afternoon. I am speaking from the library since Mr. and Mrs. West are still asleep. I am a friend of Mr. Wallace, who has filled me in. Once I have interviewed the applicants, I will hire you. When you arrive, I will give you a list of the do's and don'ts; the don'ts are much larger." He gave me the address and said goodbye. This was much easier than I expected, which concerned me, so what was I missing?

Mr. Wallace called and told me I would have lunch with the Grey Ghost at Morton's Steak House this afternoon at one on Richmond Street, near Bay Street.

"I made a reservation last night," Mr. Wallace said. "Go to the last booth, wear a suit, and the bill might be as much as fifty dollars, which you will pay."

"My lunches are less than two dollars, including soup, the main course, coffee and dessert, including the tip," I said.

"This isn't a luncheonette at a five and dime," Mr. Wallace said. "You will eat at one of the top restaurants in Toronto, where they have expensive wines. This is Mrs. West's money for you to spend to solve her death. Enjoy yourself," and hung up.

I took a taxi to Cadburys and decided I only needed one suit, which I bought along with formal wear, a raincoat, shoes, ties, and hats. It was not straightforward since Mrs. West couldn't decide between dark charcoal with stripes or black with stripes. The dark charcoal won, and all three ties were Italian silk. I bought six pairs of white gloves, and when Mr. Richards looked at me, I explained that I was careless. It was close to seven hundred dollars, and I called Big Fish from the store.

"Fred has looked, but no 1939 Buick Roadmaster convertibles," Big Fish said. "Fred found a 1941 Buick Roadmaster convertible. It is red with a light brown top but needs a paint job, a new roof, brakes, clutch and tires. Three hundred dollars, and Fred thinks it will be two hundred dollars for parts and labour. He should have the parts, and everything will be done in two weeks."

"Did Fred check it?" I asked.

"He did and drove it, so that is why he knows what it needs," Big Fish said.

"Meet you in twenty minutes, and I will bring the money, including ten for you and Fred." I took a cab and told the driver to wait until I arrived. I paid the money to Big Fish and Fred and told Fred that if he found some other problems to call me. After watching Fred drive it to his garage, I realized I didn't have insurance. Back in the cab, I stopped at an insurance agency, but they refused to sell me insurance until I had the title.

I took the streetcar to the theatre to buy tickets for the opera. All the inexpensive seats were sold, so I had to pay ten dollars. I arrived at Morton's Steak House at ten to one, and the maître d' seated me at the last booth. The waiter, dressed in formal wear, filled my water glass and left. My table had a white tablecloth and white napkins. The waiter returned with the menu and left. With the dim lights, it was hard to read the menu.

I looked at the separate wine list to see the price of a bottle of wine. For some bottles, I could buy a ten-year-old car and made a note never to eat in a restaurant where the waiters wore formal wear. A man stood at the end of my table and removed his hat.

"Mr. Clark," he asked.

"Yes," I said as he sat in the booth across from me. He was in his thirties, dressed in a black suit. He was clean-shaven with a small scar near his eye, and when he looked at me, I recognized that I should do nothing to annoy him. I am not sure if the right word was menacing, but he had the look.

"We have a mutual friend," he said. "You will call me Mr. Grey. You will give me your phone number, and I will call you. I never provide my phone number or address; you pay me in cash, no cheques. Are we clear?"

"Yes, sir," I said, wrote out my telephone number, and gave it to him.

"Knock off the sir; it is Mr. Grey." I was petrified, so this time, I nodded. The waiter rushed over and asked Mr. Grey how he was. Mr. Grey said okay, he would have his usual. A few minutes the waiter returned with a red French bottle of wine and opened it. He poured a small amount into a glass and asked Mr. Grey to try it. Mr. Grey did and nodded. The waiter put down the bottle in a silver container, returned with new glasses and poured us each a glass. Once we ordered, he looked at me.

"You are six foot two, maybe one hundred-eighty pounds. Ever box?" Mr. Grey asked.

"No, but I played hockey. I was on the officer training course for two summers," I said.

"Take up boxing," Mr. Grey said. "You seem like you could handle yourself. They taught you to solve problems and get along with your other officer cadets. Mr. Wallace has talked to me, and until we find out who this fellow is in the 1954 Ford, I am not sure you will need me. The price quoted does not include expenses." We stopped while our food was served. Mr. Grey ate like he hadn't eaten in a while and never looked up to engage me in conversation. As a reporter, I had hunches about people, and my impression was not to ask him about his war experiences or work. When we finished the bottle, I asked if he wanted another one.

"Very generous, but no," he said. "I need you to get old pants and a shirt and get a bicycle with a light. Tomorrow night, after dark, you are the distraction. You will weave back and forth on the bike, heading towards the Ford. You will act drunk, and when you arrive near the Ford, you will fall against the car. Try not to have your bicycle hit the car. It will be hot so the windows will be down. At that moment, I will reach in and grab the driver and then we will find out what we are dealing with. Have fifty dollars to pay him if there is damage to the car. After that, we decide and thank you for lunch." He left the restaurant. Mr. Wallace was wrong; the tip was sixty-five dollars even. It was three, so I walked to a five-and-dime luncheonette for coffee to try to sober up. I stopped in a drug store for breath mints and took a cab to the Douglas West Residence.

Mr. Jenkins met me at the door and took me to the library. He was thin and tall in his thirties and told me to sit and close the door. He asked questions from a list and wrote the answers. I gave him the two letters of reference and watched as he opened the envelope and read the letters. He raised one eyebrow and told me they were the worst reference letters he had ever read and to destroy them.

"Mr. Jenkins, they are from my former employer," I said.

"I don't think so," Mr. Jenkins said. "What a potential employer requires is whether you won't steal the silver, pour a drink, handle a dinner service and ensure dresses, suits and shoes are ironed and polished. There is nothing in those letters that deals with that." Mr. Jenkins returned the letters, which I put in my pocket. He took my telephone number, said he would call me on Friday, and handed me a list.

"These are the dos and don'ts. Be aware they are spoiled, selfish and petulant," Mr. Jenkins said.

"The children?" I asked.

"Oh no, sir," Mr. Jenkins said. "Mr. and Mrs. West. The

nanny deals with the children when they are fed and not tired; they are manageable. I am sure you will be fine, Mr. Chambers, and you are what Mr. and Mrs. West require." We stood; he shook my hand and escorted me to the front door. As I stepped out, he closed the door, and as I walked down the steps, I could swear I heard laughter.

CHAPTER 12

The Mutt, the Finer Things in Life and Dinner with Mr. Wallace

Wednesday started with a knock on my kitchen door at seven, and I wondered if it would be banana cake or orange cake. I opened the door to see a distraught Mrs. Murphy.

"She's gone," she said. "I have looked everywhere. Have you seen her?"

"Who?" I asked.

"Trixie silly, whom did you think I was talking about?" asked Mr. Murphy. I had forgotten the dog's name. It could have been a rabid squirrel since it was a little early, and I hadn't had my coffee.

"The dog, oh no," I said. "I will search for her."

"I bet you will," Mrs. West said.

"Oh, Mr. Clark, you are so wonderful, and I didn't know what else to do," as she looked at me. I tried to appear huggable, and it worked. She came over and embraced me. Our hug might have extended more than required, but I enjoyed feeling her body against mine. She stood back, said she had to go to school, and handed me a leash. Once I closed the kitchen door, I waited, and sure enough, I heard Mrs. West.

"Dismissed with the leash," Mrs. West said. "Is that for the dog or you? I am surprised she didn't say fetch."

"That's not fair I said.

"And that look you gave her," Mrs. West said.

"What look?" I asked.

"Really?" Mrs. West said. "Reginald, you invited that hug, which was far too long, and now you are Sir Galahad," she said. "I expect she shoved the dog out this morning."

"That's unfair to suggest Mrs. Murphy let out the dog," I said.

"We shall see, and now she has you where she wants you, connected," Mrs. West said.

"I am aware of how that feels," I said

"Reginald, with respect, I am connected to you for a greater purpose, to find out who murdered me," Mrs. West said. "That woman is a schemer and a manipulator." I thought it takes one to know one, but I finished my coffee.

"Well, time to find Trixie," I said.

"Who?" Mrs. West asked.

"The dog," I said.

"You are not planning to do this, are you? The city has dog catchers."

"They do, but I said I would."

"For a cheap embrace," Mrs. West said.

"I had no idea she was going to do that," I said. "It wasn't cheap, it was…."

"Cheap," Mrs. West said, and with that, I locked the door and went to the sidewalk. It was a cloudless day and hot as I walked down the street, calling, "Trixie, here, Trixie."

"A car ran over it," suggested Mrs. West, who never owned a dog. Dogs have names; if you don't recognize the name, it is he or she but never it. Trixie decided we were up for a game called a chase, which did not end well for me. It took half an hour, but I found Trixie munching on a bone. After two hours, I gave up and returned home, and as I opened my door, Trixie bounded up the steps into my house. I had had enough; I put her in the basement with water and papers and closed the door. The howling began, so it was time to buy a bicycle downtown. If all went well, I would return by four when Mrs. Murphy should be back from teaching school, and I would be the hero. I was sure that would get me another embrace and maybe a kiss, and for what I had done, perhaps a passionate one.

It was almost twelve when I picked up my clothes from Cadbury's and took a cab home, arriving at twelve twenty. I was opening my front door when Mrs. Murphy ran up.

"That's Trixie's bark; you found her," Mrs. Murphy said. "Thank you so much. May I call you Reggie?"

"Of course," I said. "May I call you Martha?" I asked, thinking that if we were on a first-name basis, more hugs would come, and she nodded. I told her to follow me inside and closed the door. I put down my clothes as she approached me, and she said I needed a reward. She kissed my lips and put her arms around me. As I became excited, Trixie howled. Martha stopped, ran to the basement door, and opened it as Trixie jumped into her arms. She put Trixie down and reached into her pocket.

"If Trixie does this again, you can put her in my house," Martha said. She handed me a key. "Thanks so much, Reggie, you are an angel," he opened the kitchen door and left with the mutt that disturbed our embrace. I watched her through the kitchen window as she turned and blew me a kiss. I thought that was more like it; maybe tomorrow, I will use the key to let Trixie out.

"Reginald, you are hopeless, and now you have the key to her house," Mrs. West said.

"Only if Trixie escapes," I said.

"Horsefeathers," Mrs. West said. "You do not understand the trap she is setting. I expect she will soon buy you a toothbrush and pyjamas when you stay in her bedroom."

"Oh, I don't think so," I said, but thinking, yes, yes, yes.

"Young man, that is not a woman for you," Mrs. West said. "Once she ensnares you in her web, it is difficult to leave. And you will, but it will be too late. I have had dealings with Jezebels, and it never turned out well. And if you don't understand what a Jezebel is, read a dictionary, and I am not referring to the one in the Bible."

"I don't think she is," I said.

"Really, Reginald? Mrs. West asked. "Assume you solve my problem, so we are no longer connected. You have your affair with Mrs. Murphy but end it. Mrs. Murphy is devastated and very hurt. You find a nice young lady, fall in love, and set the wedding day. On that day, the minister asks if anyone in the congregation objects to the marriage. In the back row, Mrs. Murphy stands, dressed in white, and points to you. She says that you had shared her bed for months, that you were her love, and no one else can have you." That did it, a bucket of water over my wishes, and I decided not to say anything. What could I say?

I need to gain culinary skills to decide between two choices: hot dogs, a la mustard or grilled cheese on the pan. I chose the grilled cheese sandwich and made sure it did not burn. After lunch, I put on old chino pants, Clark's desert boots, which my friend called brothel creepers, and a short-sleeved blue shirt.

"If you want to know why I am dressed this way, I am buying a bicycle," I said.

"I am aware of that," Mrs. West said. "My memory is fine. I want you to be careful tonight."

"You will be there with me," I said.

"Yes, but I am concerned," she said.

"So am I," I said. "I am going to the garage before I buy the bicycle." Once I paid for the cab, I walked inside the garage since the large door was open. There were four cars, and mine was at the back. Fred had painted it, and it had new whitewall tires. Fred came out to shake my hand.

"We removed the rust, rebuilt the body, and painted it," Fred said. "I've ordered new bumpers, and Ralph will redo the seats and put down new floor mats. He will start on your roof this week. The brakes are done, and I am waiting for a new clutch. You owe me seventy-five for the bumpers and seats." I reached into my pocket and counted out seven tens and a five.

"Who has the title, Ira or you?" I asked.

"Me," Fred said. "Don't let Big Fish know you used the

hated name," I told Fred to transfer the title to me so I could get insurance.

"Once I am finished, this will be just like new and may be worth a thousand," Fred said. "If you want to sell, I can find someone to buy it."

"Nope," I said. "This is my dream car, and I am not selling it." We shook hands, and I caught the streetcar on Queen Street to a bicycle dealer. I bought a three-speed Raleigh bicycle and a light they would assemble, and I gave the West Residence address. I called Mr. Wallace and said I was having my bike delivered. He told me to be there at four, and I would have dinner with him. I asked if there was a lane behind the house, and Mr. Wallace said there was. Outside, I found an alley and told Mrs. West what Mr. Wallace had told me.

"You have a couple of hours," Mrs. West said. "I believe it is time to learn about art. Tomorrow you will go to the Art Gallery of Toronto. Please go to my favourite gallery to purchase a painting. It is also time you became educated in the finer things of life. Make a reservation for one in the afternoon tomorrow at La Chaumiere Restaurant at 77 Church Street. They serve marvellous French food and leave a generous tip after lunch. Take the special and what wines they recommend. After lunch, speak to Monsieur Jean, the owner, and explain that I was your godmother and that I often spoke of the restaurant and for Monsieur Jean to recommend wines. Do not forget to take notes and ask for the names of the wine stores. Now let us go to Bentleys on Adelaide. It is a wonderful gallery, and I want you to choose art you enjoy that will go up in value. You can leave a deposit and pay when you pick up the art and tell them I was your godmother."

When I mentioned that Mrs. West was my godmother, the owner, Mr. Bentley, became excited and said two Lawren Harris paintings came in today and were in the back. He sent an assistant to bring them out and put them on a desk.

"Douglas," Mrs. West said. "How could you? Last Christmas and the year before, I gave him these gifts." I asked how much the two paintings were, and Mr. Bentley told me one thousand dollars. I asked to use the washroom, and I waited once I locked the door.

"Reginald, you must buy them," Mrs. West said.

"It is a lot of money," I whispered.

"They are wonderful paintings, and I could sit for hours looking at them," she said. "They will go up in value."

"You can only watch them when I am in the living room," I whispered.

"Does that mean you will buy them?" asked Mrs. Yest.

"I will, but who is the artist?" I asked.

"Really, Reginald?" Mrs. West asked. "He is one of the Group of Seven, one of the most famous Canadian painters, so they are an excellent investment." I came out of the toilet, paid a one-hundred-dollar deposit, and said I would provide the balance tomorrow. I liked the paintings, asked to use the telephone, and made reservations at La Chaumiere. Outside, I said I was spending too much, but Mrs. West told me those paintings were worth it.

"You must tell Wallace that you are my godson in case anyone asks," Mrs. West said. "Tomorrow, you must buy a set of couches, end tables and a coffee table for your living room and place Wallace's furniture in the basement. An excellent furniture must surround the Harris paintings. There is a gallery with exceptional furniture we will visit tomorrow." I wondered whose life I was living and decided it wasn't mine, but I was learning to enjoy it. Not bad for a boy from Saskatchewan.

I took a cab to the West Residence and paid the driver. Mr. Wallace was riding the bicycle on the driveway. He stopped and got off as I walked over to him.

"I have found three references to M." Mr. Wallace said. "The Morton's are Mrs. West's daughter- and son-in-law, Mrs. Mildred Foster and Mr. Anthony Maurice. Here are the addresses for you to interview them."

"Great," I said. "How was the bicycle?"

"You know what they say about bicycles?" he asked.

"You always remember how to use them," I said.

"Well, yes, but they can get you killed," Mr. Wallace said.

"Are you referring to tonight?" I asked. "Who told you what will happen?"

"The Grey Ghost," Mr. Wallace said.

"I hadn't thought about that," Mr. Wallace said. "I was referring to me, this bicycle and my brush with death."

"The worst that could happen was you would fall on the pavement," I said.

"Ten minutes ago, I was on the street, and the large truck driver didn't see me," Mr. Wallace said. "That was what I was referring to." As we walked into the house, I told him I was Mrs. West's godson, Mr. West, selling Mrs. West's Christmas presents and my purchasing them.

"Come inside," Mr. Wallace said. "You will enjoy dinner with me, and I want to show you how to make crepes suzette."

"Why," I asked.

"A skill every butler must have," Mr. Wallace said.

"Mr. West sold the Lawren Harris?" Mr. Wallace asked."

"Two of them," I said.

"I forgot about the other one," Mr. Wallace said. "Mrs. West must be upset."

"She was but is happy that I have them so she can look at them," I said. "She also wants me to learn about wine."

"I will teach you to cook crepes suzette and then review wines for you," Mr. Wallace said.

"What are crepes suzette, and why do I need to learn to cook them?"

"Pay attention," Mr. Wallace said. "You need to learn about them as a butler and something to take your mind off your impending death." He must have noticed the effect of that remark and raised his eyebrow.

"You are what, twenty-four?" Mr. Wallace asked.

"Twenty-five," I said.

"I was twenty-five in my first year in France with the 15th

Battalion, the 48th Highlanders of Canada. Death was all around me; over ten million people died in that war. By Christmas of 1915, most of my battalion was dead or invalided home. I never understood why I was still alive. A few years later, I read a poem by Alan Seeger, who died the following year in France. This is the first stanza; 'I have a rendezvous with death, at some disputed barricade, when Spring comes back with rustling shade, and apple-blossoms fill the air, I have a rendezvous with death when Spring brings back blue days and fair.' " He stopped to look at me.

"Perhaps, sir, my sense of humour was ill-advised, but you do not have a rendezvous with death," Mr. Wallace said. "Perhaps a scrape, but the one who bears the risk is the Grey Ghost. Once you fall against the car and see that the Grey Ghost controls the man in the 1954 Ford, you get on your bicycle, turn off your lights, and peddle away. Come, sir, there is much to teach and little time." I tried the bicycle and put it behind the house. Inside, I joined Mr. Wallace in the kitchen.

"I need money, perhaps another fifteen hundred," I said. Mr. Wallace said I was getting low on funds, and I told him Mrs. West had expensive tastes.

"She always did, but she never concerned herself with how much things cost," Mr. Wallace said. "I will be back." He returned a few minutes later and handed me the money.

"You are a large man, so you can have three glasses of wine tonight to maintain sobriety. Here is a chilled Chardonnay since we have chicken tonight. Now let us start by how to address Mr. and Mrs. West," Mr. Wallace said.

"The horse's ass and the dreadful woman," Mrs. West said.

"Did you hear me?" Mr. Wallace said.

"Mrs. West spoke with what she believes are the correct names for her son and daughter-in-law," I said.

"Don't tell me what she said; I need to maintain my composure," Mr. Wallace said. "Mrs. West, with great respect, it is important that Mr. Clark learn how to address Mr. and Mrs. West."

"I suppose so," Mrs. West said. "Listen to Wallace."

"You will address Mr. West as sir and Mrs. West as madam. In a proper house, we address the butler as Mr. and his last name. Unfortunately, the family never understood that and always called me Wallace. You will be called Chambers."

"I wasn't aware of that," Mrs. West said. "Wallace never told me."

"Too late now, so I think you can stay with Wallace," I said.

"It seems Mrs. West learned something, but it is fine; I am used to it," Mr. Wallace said. "Mr. Clark, at ten minutes to ten, you will head out the back gate to the laneway with a fisherman's cap and a moustache. No glasses in case you fall; they may injure your eye. How is the wine?"

"It's fine," I said.

"With an excellent wine, you must use words like superb or outstanding," Mr. Wallace said. "Fine means mediocre; what you just drank is an expensive wine and superb. Now let us talk about Mr. West; when Mr. West says something and looks to you for a comment, you may say, indeed sir or really sir, or my word, sir, depending on what he said. If it is a long story and Mr. West wishes an acknowledgment, you might say, excellent sir, or very droll sir. You cannot show emotion and no smiles or frowns, even if Mr. West has lit his pants on fire. Your job is to extinguish the flames, treating them the same way you serve a drink as if it happens all the time. Never express surprise, but you may raise an eyebrow in exceptional situations. Are we clear?" I nodded. Then there were more butler tips and a review of wines. I made notes, then dinner in the dining room with the magnificent silver and elegant wine glasses. During dinner, Mr. Wallace played Glen Miller and Arty Shaw.

"Another thing," Mr. Wallace said. "Mrs. West adores the opera and loves listening to the Italian composers Puccini, Donizetti, Verdi and Bellini. She also enjoys Mozart's operas. You must purchase a record player and albums. This is my record player from my house. Mr. West removed the record player that was there. It was in a cabinet, and he brought a man to assist.

I told him he was not allowed, but he took it anyway. He said he gave it as a gift to his mother, and since she no longer was around to enjoy it, he took it."

"If Douglas was drinking, I am sure it was an ugly scene," Mrs. West said. "Ask Wallace what he said."

"What did Mr. Douglas West say?" I asked.

"Does she want to know?" Mr. Wallace asked.

"She does," I said.

"Mr. West was inspecting the house and asked for a drink which I served him," Mr. Wallace said. "It was after his third drink that he looked at the record console and said he would take it. I told him he couldn't. He said, 'watch me since I bought that; since mother is dead, she won't care if I take it' and brought a man to help. I notified the executor, who said he would deduct that from Mr. West's share of the estate, which will be greatly reduced because of legal fees."

"That's my Douglas," Mrs. West said. "He is getting worse, and I do not know what to do."

"Not much you can do, Mrs. West, since you are no longer here," I said.

"Mrs. West can't do anything, and that is why we have Mr. Clark," Mr. Wallace said. "Go to Bloor Street to the Gerrard dealer. They sell high-end record players and buy the 301 model. Then go to Mendelson's Classical Record store on Bloor. Mrs. West will tell you which operas she wants but do that before you arrive at the store." It was nearly ten when Mr. Wallace put on my moustache and gave me my cap. He told me to get on my bicycle and do my bit.

"Good luck, sir," Mr. Wallace said. "Trust in the Grey Ghost and your good fortune, and I will see you soon."

"I hope so, Mr. Wallace," I said." I hope so."

"Take care, Reginald," Mrs. West said, but I was too nervous to reply.

CHAPTER 13

A Decoy and a Surprise

As I mounted my bicycle, I told myself to breathe and remain calm. The overcast sky blocked the moon as I turned onto Dunvegan Road. Once, I was on the road, no one was out, and no cars passed me. It was hot, so whoever was in the 1954 Ford would have his windows down. I wove back and forth, heading towards the Ford. The bike fell, and I got up, pushed the bike and jumped on.

I turned off my lamp and headed to the next intersection. The driver had parked the Ford in the shade, so I couldn't see him. My last weave caused me to fall against the car as my bicycle fell onto the pavement. I stood up to see the Grey Ghost beside the driver's open window. On my bike, I looked back and saw the Grey Ghost had his arm around the driver's neck. Once I was behind the West Residence, I got off and opened the gate and pushed the bicycle to the patio and knocked on the rear door. Mr. Wallace opened it and took me to the living room with the lights out, and the curtains closed.

"Open the drapes a bit and watch," Mr. Wallace said. "Here is a set of binoculars" I used to watch the Grey Ghost. He was in the passenger side of the Ford and appeared to be laughing. About ten minutes later, he opened the car door and walked down the street. A few minutes later, his car drove into the driveway, stopped, and the Grey Ghost shut the engine. He came to the door, and Mr. Wallace answered it. Once he was inside, Mr. Wallace closed the door, and the Grey Ghost looked at us.

"You will never believe it," the Grey Ghost said. "He was a gumshoe checking on the activities of his client's husband, visiting a divorced lady at 147 Dunvegan, next door. Can you believe that? Time for a drink," and walked towards the kitchen as we followed.

This time it was scotch. The Grey Ghost took off his hat and began talking once he had a drink. I knew he was talking to Mr. Wallace, but he told the story of Africa and the rescue. After an hour, he looked at me and said I should go home and there would be no charge.

"I did this for my dad's old friend, and I want to have some time with Mr. Wallace," the Grey Ghost said. I shook his hand and thanked him. It was eleven thirty when I paid for my taxi and noticed lights on in my house, and I couldn't remember if I had left them on. After I closed my front door and locked it, I heard a voice from the kitchen.

"Is that you, Reggie? I am in the kitchen making pancakes for our breakfast," Martha said. "I couldn't sleep, and I thought you wanted company. I just had to try out this recipe."

"Oh, fiddlesticks, that hussy," Mrs. West said. Did you give her a key?"

"No one says fiddlesticks anymore," I said.

"I do," said Mrs. West.

"No one says hussy anymore," I said.

"I do," said Mrs. West.

"No, I didn't give her a key, and besides, you have been with me within your ten feet," I said.

"Our ten feet," Mrs. West said.

"I can handle it," I said.

"What did you say, Reggie?" Martha asked.

"I said you are so beautiful."

"That is so nice, Reggie," Martha said. "You are a sweet guy."

"Really, Reginald, that is handling it?" Mrs. West asked.

"Shit," I said.

"What did you say?" Martha asked.

"I said hit. When I came in, I hit myself."

"It didn't sound like that," Martha said. "It was a naughty swear word."

"I saw a cockroach," I said.

"Much better," Mrs. West said.

"Kill it, Reggie; I hate them," Martha said. "Where is it?"

"The living room," I said.

"You should have said kitchen," Mrs. West said as I ran around the living rooms pretending to look for a cockroach.

"Did you find it?" asked Martha.

"Not yet," I said.

"The pancakes are in the refrigerator, along with some Aunt Jemima maple syrup," Martha said. "I can't stand cockroaches."

"Where did you get the key?" I asked.

"Cedric, he is such a sweetheart," Martha said. She looked at me and blew a kiss. "Okey dokey, Regiekins, nighty night, don't let the bed bugs bite." She closed the kitchen door, and I shook my head.

"I didn't expect that," I said.

"I don't think you did," Mrs. West said. "Things are seldom what they seem; skim milk masquerades as cream."

"What?" I asked.

"It is a song from Gilbert and Sullivan from *H.M.S. Pinafore,* " Mrs. West said. "Well, Reginald, you handled it. That was very good."

"Do you think she had a thing with Mr. Wallace?"

"Of course not, but never ask him," Mrs. West said. "He is entitled to his dreams, even if it is with that woman." It was time for bed, I was exhausted, and when I was finished in the bathroom, I said my prayers.

"Good night, Reginald," Mrs. West said. "Well done on your bicycle as a decoy and tonight."

"Good night Mrs. West," I said. "Thank you."

"Two things, Reginald," Mrs. West said.

"Yes? I said.

"Change the locks once you take ownership," Mrs. West said.

"Will do," I said.

"Under no circumstances tell that woman you have killed the cockroach."

"Agreed," I said.

CHAPTER 14

Fulfilling Requests and the Magic Flute

Thursday morning, I woke with one of those; how did I forget that thought? Had any neighbour witnessed the person entering the doors of the West's residence? I called Mr. Wallace and told him it was late to do this, but could he talk to neighbours to find out if they had noticed anyone going in the back gate around eleven the night of Mrs. West's death? He could explain there had been a break-in that night and hung up. I also needed to find out about M.

I called Fred and told him I needed two guys he used for chores to come to my house to take furniture to the basement and put new furniture in the bedrooms and main floor. I would leave a list, and I needed them for two days.

"Pay them each five dollars a day and give me five to arrange it," Fred said.

"Fine, how's the car?" I asked.

"Roof needs to be finished, and the clutch," Fred said. "A piece of advice. Keep the car in a garage and store it in the winter. It is a classic."

"Thanks, Fred. I'll think about it," I said. "Send them to 55 Elmer at 9:30, and I will pay them for the streetcars. Tell them to take the Queen Street east car, and I am at the beaches." I could take another thousand from the bond sale, but that was it; I would have to be careful with my money. The house, the clothes and the painting left me with one thousand six hundred and twenty-five dollars.

Once a butler, I would have minimal expenses and an income, so things would be fine. I put on my charcoal suit, white shirt, blue tie and black oxford shoes. The boys arrived at nine, and I told them what to do. I took a streetcar to Queen Street West to an antique store and bought a dining room table, six wing-back chairs, two armoires, a roll-top desk, a desk chair and a bookshelf. The dining room table, chairs and armoires were light pine. Mrs. West informed me they weren't her style but were for me. Negotiating took a while, and I paid two hundred dollars, including delivery.

I found a real estate office and met with an agent. I told him I was interested in two houses in the Beaches, near the streetcar line, in good condition to be rented out. He asked me how much I would pay, and I said up to sixteen thousand dollars a house. He took my name, and I said I could only call in the morning and visit on Saturdays. The agent, Mr. Foster, said he had several listings and would check on them.

I, or perhaps it would be more correct to say we, attended Mrs. West's furniture gallery, which was filled with Danish furniture. It took a while to appreciate them, and I bought two couches, two chairs, two end tables, two lamps, a coffee table and three rugs. They gave me ten percent off and delivery, but it cost me three hundred and fifty dollars. We were at the Bentley gallery, where I paid for the pictures and bought an A. Y. Jackson's painting was worth three hundred dollars. They said they would deliver, and outside I told Mrs. West we needed to go to Eaton's, where I bought a bed, mattress, tables and lamps for my bedroom, sheets, pillowcases and towels. The total was just over one hundred dollars, and Eaton's said they would deliver.

"I have around thirteen hundred dollars left," I said.

"You forgot one thing," Mrs. West said.

"The record player and the records," I said.

"Do it after lunch since it is almost one, and you have to get to La Chaumiere," Mrs. West said. With my introduction as Mrs. West's Godson and perhaps because I was well dressed, I had the royal treatment. It started with the hors d'oeuvres cart, followed by French soup, a salad, Scallops Normandie and dessert. The wines were superb, and after lunch, the owner talked about wines and where he purchased them in Toronto. It was three when I took a cab to the Gerrard dealer and bought the 301 model for seventy-five dollars, and they said they would deliver it to my house.

By now, I was tired and still slightly drunk when I entered Mendelson's classical music store. I told Mr. Mendelson I wanted operas by Mozart, Donizetti, Bellini and Puccini. He looked at me, pulled out his pipe, lit it, took a puff, and smiled.

"It depends on what we have in the store, but possibly thirty records," Mr. Mendelson said. "Have you listened to them?" he asked.

"No," I said.

"Do you want them?" he asked.

"You will tell the amiable gentleman that you do," Mrs. West said.

"I do," I said and was tempted to add amiable gentleman, but if I did, my admonishment would be lengthy, and what was the point? I would save witty responses for another time. I had to be in the right mood to receive a telling-off.

"Let me start slow, give me the most popular of each of them and then I can return for more," I said.

"A wise decision," Mr. Mendelson said. Twenty minutes I was outside with five records and called a cab to take me home. Inside the house, the antique furniture and the delivery from Eaton's had arrived, so they were busy setting up my bedroom and office. The dining room table and chairs were in the dining room. The doorbell rang, and when I opened it, the man from Bentley was there with my pictures and offered to help hang them. We placed the two Harris' in my living room and hung the Jackson in my dining room. He declined a tip when the doorbell rang, and the furniture store man was there and carried in the furniture, and we set it up in the living room and turned on the lights. He helped me place the three rugs in the living room, office, and bedroom, then left. George and Manny were downstairs when Gerrard's delivery arrived, and I put the record player in the living room. After he left, I paid my helpers and said I wouldn't need them tomorrow.

Mrs. West asked for Mozart, which I put on the record player, then asked what I would cook. I said pancakes and walked into the kitchen. On the back counter was a can, and when I picked it up, it was marked D.D.T., which Martha had left. The label warned me not to get any on my skin, not to breathe, and to keep it away from animals. I put it back on the counter and opened the refrigerator when I heard Martha on the other side of the door asking if I had killed the cockroach.

"Hi Martha, how are you," I asked in a neighbourly fashion.

"Did you use the D.D.T.?" she asked.

"I just got in the kitchen and found the can, so no," I said.

"Use it," Martha said.

"I need to cook dinner, and I will do it before I go to bed," I said.

"Just spray it now," Martha said. "I want to come inside and visit."

"Not yet; the label says not to breathe it," I said. "I worry about your gentle disposition."

"My, what, oh, don't be silly, use it," Martha said. "I'm tougher than you think."

"Of course, you are," Mrs. West said.

"Shush," I said.

"What? Martha asked.

"I beg your pardon? Mrs. West asked.

"I named him Archy," I said.

"What?" asked Martha.

"I named the cockroach Archy," I said.

"What on earth?" asked Martha.

"From Archy and Mehitabel, the short stories and books by Don Marquis," I said. "Mehitabel was the alley cat, and Archy was the cockroach."

"Bye, Reggie," Martha said and walked down the steps.

"Archy?" asked Mrs. West.

"From Don Marquis' books," I said.

"Archy," said Mrs. West. "I never know if you are serious, but I take it that can is for things you want to get rid of," Mrs. West said. "Perhaps you can use it on Martha?"

"She means well and is a nice person," I said. Mrs. West's laughter was prolonged, but I decided not to say anything. Martha would remain next door while I was connected to Mrs. West until I found out who murdered her. Who knew how long that would take; a week, a month or until all her suspects died? I decided not to explain the characters of Archy and Mehitabel to Mrs. West since I didn't think they would interest her. I cooked the pancakes, cleaned up, and took a taxi to Massey Hall for the Mozart opera. I liked the opera and, at the intermission, smiled at two young ladies.

"That is Miss Young and Miss Taylor. Ask them what they thought of the production," Mrs. West said, which I did.

"Introduce yourself and shake their hands," Mrs. West said, which I did.

"Now ask them which books they are reading," Mrs. West said, which I did. They both started discussing books, and I listened.

"Ask them if you could have another opportunity to talk, perhaps a meeting for a coffee," Mrs. West asked, which I did. They said yes, and one wrote out their names and telephone numbers. After the opera, I took a taxi home. I made the bed, used the washroom and said my prayers. I realized that Mrs. West was an asset for clothes, operas and young ladies, then drifted off to sleep in my new bed.

CHAPTER 15

The Interview and Something Unexpected

On Friday morning, June 28, a telephone call woke me at seven. Mr. Wallace asked me to go to the West Residence Friday night to safeguard it for the weekend. He planned to go to Hamilton to check out houses and said he would be back by four on Sunday. I would be paid twenty dollars, and he had arranged this with the executor. Mr. Wallace told me to stop by the residence after my interview with Mr. West.

"You talked with Mr. Jenkins?" I asked.

"Indeed, sir, I have," Mr. Wallace said. "It is all part of Mrs. West's plan. Mr. Jenkin has some advice for you, lock your bedroom door at night."

"To prevent Mr. West from stealing my money?" I asked.

"He did not say, sir," Mr. Wallace said. "Have a pleasant interview." I was at the Douglas West residence for my eleven o'clock interview. Jenkins took me to the library, and I noticed his non-butler-like smile. Once inside, he closed the door and handed me a book.

"This is your Bible. The list includes dry cleaners, liquor stores and lists of wine and telephone numbers. The most important is the alcohol and make sure you have enough, or Mr. West will be unhappy, and Mrs. Marigold will have an unpleasant reaction. I have included insurance, when they come due, the garage for the Bentley and the names of the staff. Birthday dates, shoe sizes, dress sizes and suit measurements with a list of stores. Good luck, you will need it," Mr. Jenkins paused and laughed.

"I was led to believe that butlers never show emotion," I said,

"This is a butler-to-butler discussion and, for me, a celebration," Jenkins said.

"And what may I expect?" I asked.

"I think it best not to say anything to you," Jenkins said. "You may be the right butler."

"Do you think so?" I asked.

"Of course not," Jenkins said, then laughed. "But miracles can happen."

"You raised my hopes," I said.

"Get over it," Mr. Jenkins said. "Mr. and Mrs. West are a challenge, and the sooner you understand, it will make your job easier. This envelope has the name and picture of Mr. West's mistress," Mr. Jenkins said. "I never used it, but it is your protection." He handed me the book and envelope, shook my hand, and left the library.

"Bravo, Jenkins," Mrs. West said. "I never guessed you had it in you." I put both in my jacket.

"How old is your son?" I asked.

"I told you his birth date; he is forty-two," Mrs. West said. Twenty minutes later, Mr. West came in and frowned. He looked older than his forty-two years, around six feet and held in his belly. That was before he sat, and once in the chair, his stomach was over his belt. He had a double chin and bags under his eyes. Mr. West was not in good shape, but excessive drinking and too much rich food can do that.

"You are young," said Mr. West.

"Yes, he is," said Mrs. West. "What has that got to do with the price of tea in China?"

"Yes, sir," I said.

"I am told you have experience," Mr. West said.

"Yes, sir," I said.

"I require three things," Mr. West said. "Can you cut and light a cigar?"

"Yes, sir," I said.

"Can you mix drinks?" he asked.

"Yes, sir," I said.

"Can you make crepes suzette?" Mr. West asked.

"Yes, sir," I said.

"I am not sure I should hire you," Mr. West said.

"Why is that, sir?" I asked.

"You are well dressed, young and handsome," Mr. West said.

"If you say so, sir," I said.

"I said so, and stay away from my wife," Mr. West said.

"I assure you, sir, I will," I said. Mr. West scowled at me.

"My goodness," Mrs. West said.

"Do you know those mystery novels where, in the end, the butler did it?" Mr. West asked.

"Yes, sir," I said, becoming nervous.

"If I discover that my butler did it to my wife, it will not end well," Mr. West said.

"I can assure you, sir, nothing will happen," I said.

"I am not to be trifled with," Mr. West said. "I am a crack shot, and I would hate to put a bullet in your head."

"Goodness gracious," Mrs. West said.

"If you feel that way, I will refuse your offer," I said.

"Damnit, I need a butler, so I must hire you with reservations," Mr. West said. "I have warned you, and I only give warnings once." he looked at me, still scowling.

"I understand, sir," I said. "My mother's situation requires me to be away Saturday and Sunday, but the rest of the time, I will be available whenever required." Mr. West looked apoplectic.

"Damn, Jenkins didn't tell me," Mr. West said. "Is this necessary?"

"Yes, sir," I said.

"I will pay you twenty dollars a week, not twenty-five," Mr. West said.

"Very good, sir," I said. "I will be here at eight on Sunday to move in," I said. "Will that be satisfactory, sir?"

"He was always frugal with his servants," Mrs. West said, "but now he is getting worse. Make sure you drink his good scotch. I paid Wallace two hundred and fifty dollars a month with weekends off and gave him a generous Christmas bonus worth one month's pay. Douglas gives a turkey to his staff at Christmas, with a voucher they use to pick them up. Too bad you won't be here at Christmas; you could read Dickens, *The Christmas Carol.*"

"Are you paying attention?" Mr. West asked. "You are not giving me much choice but to be here at eight Sunday night."

"He will not offer you dinner in the kitchen even if they are still eating," Mrs. West said.

"Is there anything else, sir?" I asked. He sat there and said nothing.

"Sir, is there anything else?" I asked again.

"What, no, you can go, Jenkins." It was not appropriate to correct him. Was Chambers a hard name to remember? It wasn't, but I wasn't Mr. Douglas West. I would find Mr. Jenkins' address and give it to Mr. West. Perhaps I could leave notes around the house that stated *Jenkins did it with you know who.* I stepped out the door and asked Mr. Jenkins to call me a taxi. Outside, watching for the taxi, I waited for Mrs. West to comment.

"You don't look like Jenkins, and you don't have Jenkins manner, but who knows what Douglas has been up to," Mrs. West said. "He threatened you, but there are no witnesses. Reginald, you must get a tape recorder, and that is a requirement. I wonder what my daughter-in-law has been up to with Jenkins, and I believe he gave his notice." The threats rattled me enough, and wondered if I should resign before I started. The taxi arrived, sparing me answers to Mrs. West. Once inside the taxi, I gave my address and sat back to attempt to relax.

"Reginald, have courage," Mrs. Alicia West said. "I need you there to solve this case." Great, I would be a butler, but I knew I would be out of there at the first sign of a threat.

"You haven't met Marigold, my daughter-in-law," Mrs. West said. "Mrs. Marigold West is thirty-six, insipid, pale and tall. Although she never lived in England, she talks with an English accent. She has too much red lipstick on her pale face, which makes her appear like a ghost attempting to look alive. Marigold is greedy, self-centred and drinks too much, but this is the first time I have heard of marital problems because of an affair. I believe Marigold felt marital duties were not her cup of tea. She put up with them to produce children, but perhaps I was wrong. I detest immorality at the best of times, but I find it appalling in my family. Reginald, make sure you lock your bedroom door at night."

First, Mr. Jenkins and now Mrs. West gave me this warning. I would follow their advice and lock my door. It tempted me to keep it unlocked to find out what would happen, but then I remembered Mr. West's threats. When I arrived at Mrs. Alicia West Residence, Mr. Wallace was waiting for me outside, and when I got out, I paid the driver.

"Sir, let us retire to the kitchen to discuss something," Mr. Wallace said.

"What?" I asked.

"You should come with me and hear me out," Mr. Wallace said, so I followed inside the front door, which he closed and to the kitchen. I sat as he poured me a coffee and waited until he made his own and sat.

"I will travel to Hamilton to check out houses on Saturday, and I will catch the early bus," Mr. Wallace said. "I have a plan which I think is rather good. I am convinced there is something in this house which I cannot find. I suspect that Mr. West left it, whether he panicked or ran out of time. I spoke to Mr. Jenkins and told him I was leaving this afternoon for Hamilton and would be away until Sunday at four. I asked him to tell that to Mr. West so if he came to the residence, he would assume no one was there. Your thoughts, sir?" I let out a sigh.

"A trap, how delightful," Mrs. West said.

"I wish you had consulted with me," I said. "Mrs. West, your son just threatened me. How do you think he will react to finding me here?"

"Oh, my goodness, Reginald, I hadn't considered that, but won't it be exciting?" Mrs. West said.

"Exciting for you but not so much for me," I said.

"A little chat with Mrs. West," Mr. Wallace said.

"She thinks the trap is exciting," I said.

"Mrs. West never understood what her servants went through," Mr. Wallace said.

"That is most unfair," Mrs. West said.

"She disagrees," I said.

"Of course, she does," Mr. Wallace said. "What else is new? Mr. Clark, I called you yesterday and left a message with a man who answered the telephone. Did he not relay the message?"

"No," I said, regretting hiring brawn but not brains.

"What was his name?" I asked.

"George," Mr. Wallace said.

"Ah ha," I said and time to chat with Fred.

"Why didn't you discuss it this morning?" I asked.

"It surprised me you didn't mention it, but your fellow George said he would tell you," Mr. Wallace said. "You should get rid of disposable items at your house, pack and be here at four. You will cook dinner under my guidance, then once it becomes dark, we wait. We will take shifts and no lights. Once Mr. West has what he is looking for, we apprehend him."

"He would know who I am," I said.

"You will have a face mask," Mr. Wallace said.

"Will you call the police?" I asked.

"Perhaps, depending on what we find," Mr. Wallace said.

"And what happens if Mr. West breaks in Saturday night when I am alone?" I asked.

"In the kitchen, there is a large container marked brownies," Mr. Wallace said. "Inside is my Browning, loaded with blanks. I am sure you will know what to do. If Mrs. West has retained you, she has every confidence in you."

"And you?" I asked.

"Who am I to disagree with Mrs. West," Mr. Wallace said. "Although occasionally she has made errors. If it does not go according to plan, you know where the back gate is. I am sure you can outrun Mr. West; he is a poor shot, and I expect he will be drinking.

CHAPTER 16

The Break-In at the West Residence

How can I describe my life with Mrs. West? I did nothing or watched anything alone; it was always with her. Sometimes it was the royal we. I never knew when she would jump in with a comment or direction to do or not do something. I was Captain Hook, she was the crocodile, I was Holmes, she was Watson, I was Abbot, she was Costello, I was Nick Charles, and she was Nora from the Thin Man movies. We were inseparable, and once in a while, she would remind me when I forgot about her.

We visited the art gallery, picked up wine and visited Stirling Archibald, my broker. He told me he would have the thirty-five thousand seven hundred and fifty dollars in his account the following Monday. I told him to have a cheque for me for seven hundred and fifty dollars since I needed money. He told me he would give me a cheque, and I signed various papers. With the cheque, I deposited it in my bank and changed my address to Fifty-Fve Elmer Street. I called Mr. Wallace, who told me to go to my lawyer to sign papers. When I was there, the lawyer told me I was most foolish to have paid the seller before obtaining the title, but the property had no encumbrances. I should have the title in my name in three to four days.

I was back at the West Residence at four, where I paid the

driver, and Mr. Wallace and I carried my bags and the garment bags for my suits. Once inside the residence with the door closed, Mr. Wallace took me to the guest room, and I hung my garment bags in the closet.

"You searched everywhere in the house, and you think something is hidden?" I asked Mr. Wallace. "It has to be medication or drugs," I said.

"Exactly, sir," Mr. Wallace said.

"Powerful enough to kill?" I asked.

"Yes, sir," Mr. Wallace said. "Mrs. West was five foot four and of the delicate build. She weighed one hundred pounds, so any medication would affect her.

"Blue lips, dilated pupils, the smell of almonds on her breath," I said.

"If you say so, sir since I am not acquainted with signs of poison," Mr. Wallace said. "Let's go to the kitchen, have a glass, and continue this discussion." In the kitchen, he poured us each a glass of red wine and asked me what I knew about Mrs. West's death.

"It is based on what you told me," I said. "The maid brought in her breakfast at seven-thirty and found her dead," I said. "Mr. West told the police she was not in good health and objected to the police performing an autopsy. He had a key to the house, and he was out of his residence Saturday night, April 13th, before Mrs. West's death. He also had a motive."

"Reginald, you are building a case," Mrs. West said.

"The police never made inquiries of Mrs. West's doctor, nor did they ask the staff about the state of her health, which was excellent," Mr. Wallace said. "I was unaware she had a heart condition. I asked Mary and Grace, the maids if they administered any heart medicine. They said no, and I never picked up any at a drugstore. They provided the medications and ground-up sleeping pills in Mrs. West's tea. Putting aside the possibility that she died of natural causes, I am left with a nagging suspicion that an intruder administered something which caused her death."

"You think there are pills in her room that need to be removed?" I asked.

"Yes, sir, and I believe that may happen tonight since Mr. West knows no one is here," Mr. Wallace said.

"Telling Mr. West would make him suspicious," I said.

"He is desperate," Mr. Wallace said.

"Ruin, and desperation and dismay, who durst so proudly tempt the son of God," Mrs. West said.

"Who was that?" I asked.

Paradise Regained: The Fourth Book Mrs. West said.

"Who was what? Mr. Wallace asked.

"Mrs. West is showing off her Milton," I said. "I am sure she will refrain from continuing since I have important work to do."

"Fine, Reginald," Mrs. West said.

"What about the maids? I asked.

"Sir, I believe they have nothing to do with it," Mr. Wallace said.

"They put ground-up pills in her food or tea," I said. "Maybe they added something."

"Impossible," Mr. Wallace said.

"I will need their addresses and phone numbers," I said.

"I will provide them, sir," Mr. Wallace said.

"Sir, how is the wine?" Mr. Wallace asked.

"Superb," I said, which was true. I liked it.

The next few hours were exciting, shoe polishing and ironing, which in my case was a refresher followed by instruction in the fine art of dining by that famous chef, Monsieur Wallace. He gave me a camera and gloves in case I found the evidence. I wore black pants, a black shirt, soft desert boots, and a face mask and took the first shift from ten until two in the morning. The drapes in the living room were closed, and I sat in a chair near the entrance by the stairs. There were two ways into the house: the front door or the kitchen door. My assignment was to stop Mr. West and grab what he took. I expected he would come in and leave by the kitchen door.

Nothing happened on my shift other than occasionally; Mrs. West asked if I was awake. Mr. Wallace replaced me at two, and I went to bed. In the morning at seven, he knocked on the door and told me nothing had happened, and he was taking a taxi to the bus station. After a shower and changing clothes, I had breakfast and decided to search Mrs. West's bedroom. I started up the stairs when Mrs. West spoke.

"It would be delightful if you brought the record player and my records to play while you are there." Several trips later, I began with Donizetti, "Lucia de Lammermoor." I opened the windows, and Mrs. West directed me where to search. I put on Rossini and Bellini, then Mozart. It was noon when the doorbell rang. I opened it to see a woman in her seventies in a dress looking at me.

"Where is Mr. Wallace?" he asked.

"That is my good friend Miss Thompson," Mrs. West said.

"Hello Miss Thomson, Mr. Wallace is in Hamilton until tomorrow," I said. "May I help you."

"How do you know my name?"

"I am Mrs. West's fourth cousin, and she often spoke of you," I said and smiled, which caused a blush.

"These are Mrs. West's favourite composers," Miss Thompson said.

"I know," I said.

"This is strange. Are you sure we never met?" Miss Thompson asked.

"Tell her that it was at my garden party in June, five years ago where she wore the yellow dress," Mrs. West said.

"It was at the garden party in June, five years ago where you wore the yellow dress," I said.

"Yes, that is where we met," Mis Thompson said. "Well, goodbye; nice seeing you again," and turned, so I closed the door.

"It was so wonderful to see her," Mrs. West said. "Lunch and then back to work." After I finished eating, I continued in the bedroom but found nothing. After supper, I turned off the lights and moved to the living room to wait.

"Reginald," Mrs. West said, "there is someone at the back door." I had fallen asleep and looked at my watch with my flashlight. It was two in the morning, and there was scraping at the back door; then it opened. Whoever was there waited, then I heard footsteps heading up the stairs.

Half an hour later, the creaking floorboards alerted me, so I put on my face mask and gloves. I was at the entrance to the living room near the stairs. I could see the outline of someone at the bottom of the stairs, and I leapt forward and tackled the intruder to the floor. He was thin and short, and I grabbed a bag out of his right hand when he hit my upper right arm with a metal rod. There was enough light for me to determine he was right-handed. He scratched my face and struggled free. When I took the metal rod, I received a kick to my private parts, which doubled me over. Still holding the bag in one hand, I pushed his chest to force him to the floor and touched breasts.

"Bastard" a deep female voice said.

"Sorry" I said, always the proper fellow. "I didn't know you were a woman.

CHAPTER 17

The Evidence and the Police

She stayed on her feet, so I kicked out and grabbed her. She screamed and squirmed through my grip, ran to the back door, opened it, and left. I was in too much pain to pursue.

"He is getting away," Mrs. West said.

"That's a she, who kicked me in my private parts, and it hurts," I said.

"Reginald, he kicked you in your..., ladies don't do that," Mrs. West said.

"This spitfire did and scratched me," I said.

"It had to be a man," Mrs. West said.

"Didn't you hear her calling me a bastard and her scream?" I said.

"Ladies, don't swear," Mrs. West said.

"She wasn't a lady, but definitely a woman," I said. "I accidentally touched her breasts."

"Goodness, who was she?" Mrs. West asked.

"No idea, but I want to check what I have," I said. "She was one tough woman who knew where to kick, and I wished she had worn sneakers. Maybe she works in a bar or a circus." An image came of her with a whip, chasing lions and men she disliked around the floor of a large tent. I went to the kitchen and put on the lights. I removed one pill, wrapped it in a napkin, and put it in my pocket. The package had a bottle with large tablets. The metal rod was a grappling thing that you could tighten from the top and was flexible. I took a picture of the pillbox and grappling thing, then called the police.

"No wonder Mr. Wallace couldn't find the bottle of pills," I said. "They were down the heating vent."

"I suspected something was in the house," Mrs. West said. Ten minutes later, two policemen arrived. I met one constable and explained who I was and the details of the break-in and gave them the bag, the container of pills and the metal rod.

"What's that?" Constable Jones asked, pointing to the metal rod.

"The official term is thingamabob," I said.

"Clark," said Constable Jones.

"Or maybe a whatchamacallit," I said.

"Clark," said Constable Jones.

"It is a metal rod for extracting things, and I have no idea what its name is" I said.

"Why were you wearing gloves?" Constable Jones asked.

"I thought you never would ask?" I said. "I was expecting a break-in."

"Why did you expect a break-in?" Constable Jones asked.

"To remove the pills that killed the owner of this house, Mrs. West," I said.

"Are you working on a story?" Constable Jones asked.

"Yes, but until now, I had no proof," I said. "Once you find out what those pills are, there is a case."

"Clark, have you ever worked with horses?" Constable Jones asked.

"No," I said.

"I have," Constable Jones said. "Those are horse tranquillizers, when ground up, can kill. Those might be murder weapons, but we will have to examine them. Are you busy tomorrow morning? I need to call this in, and you need to come to division fifty-three to meet Sergeant Rifkin. It is station fifty-three, not your normal one, but we will give you coffee. It will be where we ask questions for a change." Ten minutes later, they were gone.

"Reginald, well done. Go to bed, and don't forget to say your prayers."

Once I woke, I showered and put on my chino pants and a short-sleeve shirt. After breakfast standing and listening to Puccini's *Tosca,* I walked to the stop and caught the bus to division fifty-three. I remained standing, although the bus was empty. At the station, I introduced myself and was told to wait outside the counter. A man sat there bruised and cut and kept muttering threats but never looked at me. I stood since it was painful for a particular part of my anatomy. I leaned against the counter until the sergeant opened it and led me to the interview room. Sergeant Rifkin sat in his uniform shirt, looked up at me, nodded, and told me to sit. He looked in his late forties, with brown eyes, a bulldog face, a crooked nose, and spoke in a deep voice. I told him I would rather stand.

"Suit yourself," the sergeant said. "Constable Jones states you wore gloves because you expected a break-in. You told him that you set a trap to catch a person removing pills that killed Mrs. West, the owner of the house." He stared at me and made a note.

"Constable Jones knows you and says you have treated the Toronto Metropolitan Police Force fairly in your stories. He says you are working on a story where you believe someone murdered Mrs. West with those pills. The break-in was to recover the pills that killed her. Am I getting this?"

"At last, an intelligent policeman," Mrs. West said. "I was worried when they abolished our Forest Hill Police last year."

"Clark, are you paying attention?" Sergeant Rifkin asked.

"Yes, sergeant? I said.

"You were waiting for the break-in, correct?"

"Yes" I said.

"It happened at two in the morning on Sunday June 30?"

"Yes sergeant," I said.

"You had a suspect, didn't you?" the sergeant asked.

"Mrs. West's son, Douglas West," I said.

"Why do you suspect him?" the sergeant asked.

"He was told that the house would be vacant this weekend," I said.

"Did you tell Mr. West this?" the sergeant asked.

"No," I said. "Mr. Wallace, the former butler for Mrs. West, called Mr. West's butler to give him the message." The sergeant made a note and then looked at me, and I didn't like his look.

"I am going to give you advice, off the record," the sergeant said. "I met Wallace, who said that Mr. West murdered Mrs. West, and that Mr. West had a key to the house. According to Wallace, Mrs. West was in good health. I met with Mr. West in his large house, with servants and a butler. Do you know he has a Bentley? Mr. West told me that his mother was ill, and he was worried she might die at any time. Wallace said that the motive for the murder was Mrs. West changed the will. Instead of receiving four million dollars, Mr. West would receive half a million dollars." Sergeant Rifkin shook his head and smiled. I didn't like how this was going.

"Clark, what do you make in a year?" the sergeant asked.

"I cannot see the point?" I said.

"This policeman is not getting it," Mrs. West said.

"How much?" the sergeant asked.

"Twenty-four hundred dollars," I said.

"After twenty years' service as a sergeant, I make sixty-two hundred dollars. And Mr. West is getting over half a million big smakeroos," the sergeant said.

"He is disputing the will," I said.

"So, what?" the sergeant said. "Mr. West told me that this butler Wallace hated him and threw him out of Mrs. West's house frequently," the sergeant said and smiled.

"It was twice, you nincompoop," Mrs. West said.

"This is the case of a resentful butler taking revenge on a rich man, so the file is closed," the sergeant said. "There is no way I would recommend digging up the grave of a respectable lady in High Park. The reason I am here is to get information on the break-in."

"Sergeant, I think there was a murder committed," I said.

"Look sonny, write your damn story and see if you editor will publish it when we have closed the file because we have no case," the sergeant said. "I know Mr. West will sue you for defamation. Tell me what happened last night," so I did. Once I finished, the sergeant gave me an evil smile.

"Right in the old nuts, was it? That must have hurt?" the sergeant said.

"It did," I said. "She had hard pointed shoes?"

"Let me make a note of that," the sergeant said.

"The hard pointed shoes?" I asked.

"No, that she kicked you in the nuts," the sergeant said, then laughed. "Of course, it was the hard pointed shoes, although it seems every dame has them. No idea who the lady was?"

"None, but you have the pills," I said.

"We do, which will be in our evidence locker to be used if we find this lady and charge her with break and enter under the *Criminal Code*. I will have them checked for finger prints, but I expect she wore gloves?" the sergeant asked.

"She did," I said.

"Well, that's it, you can go," the sergeant said.

"Reginald, make him listen," Mrs. West said. There was no point, so I shook the sergeant's hand and left the station, knowing I would be on the receiving line of a very upset Mrs. West.

"Reginald, is there anything you can do?" Mrs. West asked.

"Nothing and I bet your son gave the dear sergeant the best scotch and a cigar," I said. "The chance of a defamation case is high unless I get more evidence."

"Well, get it," Mrs. West said.

"Is your son's mistress slender and short?" I asked.

"I only have her picture, but I have her address," Mrs. West said.

"I will give the camera to Fred and tell him to hire

someone with brains," I said. "I would love to hear her say bastard."

"Reginald," Mrs. West said.

"This is part of the case," I said.

"I suppose so," Mrs. West said. At the house, I found the address and told Fred to take a taxi to my place. I took out the roll of film and put in another roll. Once Fred arrived, he looked around, but I said I was working on a story.

"The pill is in the paper bag, and could you have your cousin at the pharmacy verify that this was a horse tranquillizer" I said. "I will pay twenty dollars for the report." I gave Fred ten dollars for helping and another twenty dollars to take photographs.

"I won't use George. He is a little slow," Fred said.

"Now you tell me" I said.

"I promised his mother I would help him" Fred said.

"Is his mother your aunt? I asked.

"Maybe" Fred said.

"Maybe? I asked.

"Ok, she is my aunt and George is my cousin" Fred said. "I hate your tough reporter questions."

"Question not questions" I said. "That was my scintillating cross examination at work."

"I withered, didn't I?" Fred asked.

"Folded like a cheap handkerchief" I said.

"I will use Manny and forget about a cab; I will take a bus" Fred said and left.

"What was that?" asked Mrs. West.

"Our sense of humour" I said. "You should it see when we insult each other."

"No thank you" Mrs. West said.

"We have nicknames" I said.

"I have no interest in learning them" Mrs. West said. "They probably are scatological."

"How did you know that?" I asked. "I admit they are slightly obscene with a hint of toilet humour." Fred is the only fellow I know who can string swear words together without repeating one. I think it comes from serving below decks in the navy."

"That is enough" Mrs. West said. She was right, my experiences were inappropriate for her, and I wasn't going to change her and the only one changing was me. I took taxis to two addresses Mr. Wallace gave me to inquire about M. They knew nothing about any meeting with Mrs. West and I decided not to visit Mrs. West's daughter or son-in-law. I was going tonight as a butler for her son, and I did not know how often they met. I had a key to the West Residence and was back at four.

Mr. Wallace invited me to the kitchen, where I filled him in. No information about M. and reviewed the break-in, the woman, the kick and the police. He listened and shook his head, then told me he had bought a house for his sister to live in. We had dinner with me sitting on a pillow on a chair, and at seven-thirty, I was in a cab to the Douglas West residence. I still sat uncomfortably; the spitfire had hard shoes.

CHAPTER 18

The Douglas West Residence and a Dinner

After I paid the cab, I walked up the steps with my bags and garment bags. A lady in a uniform answered the door. She was in her twenties and not bad looking, but she looked like she was going to cry.

"Edward Chambers, the new butler," I said.

"Margaret, one of the maids, thank God you are here," she said. "I know nothing about mixing drinks, and they keep saying I am doing it wrong. Go to the servant's entrance at the side and get changed."

"I don't work on Sundays," I said.

"Neither do I, but please, sir, help me," Margaret said. She looked so upset that I said I would. I was there at seven-thirty, and Margaret took me to the servant's entrance and up the back staircase to my room. I changed and didn't bother ironing my shirt, but I didn't think it mattered and put on my white gloves.

There was a dinner party of eight in the dining room as I appeared at the door and bowed. Mr. West looked at his guests and at me.

"Hallelujah, my new butler," Mr. West said. "Jenkins, I need a scotch."

"Very good, sir," I said. He nodded as I took his empty

glass. At the bar, taking a clean glass, I put three ice cubes and poured four ounces into the glass. I put it on a tray, took it to the left side of Mr. West and put it on a new coaster.

"Douglas," his wife said. "Is our new butler also called Jenkins?"

"Makes it easier to remember the name," Mr. West said, then laughed.

"My son, the idiot," Mrs. West said.

"Jenkins," Mrs. Marigold West said. "I would like a drink."

"Very good, madam," I said, removed her glass, took it to the bar, took out another drink, and poured a strong martini. I put it on the tray and placed it on the coaster. She tried it and sighed.

"Perfect, Jenkins," she said. "The master martini maker makes martinis that make me mellow and mellifluous," and giggled. It surprised me that she could put the words together as the male guests laughed while the female guests looked at each other. I refrained from looking at Mr. West, who harrumphed.

"Marigold," one of the female guests said. "If he is a new butler, how did he know what drink you wanted?"

"Jenkins always understands my drink," Mrs. Marigold West said and hiccupped, this time slurring her words. The friend who had asked looked confused, which I understood. Which Jenkins was Mrs. Marigold West referring to, and in her condition, I was not sure she did.

"Marigold, the mistaken," Mrs. West said. "She played field hockey at private school, and sometimes I think a stick hit her head. Make the next drink weaker, much weaker." Mr. West called me over and told me to walk to the hallway. Once we arrived, he looked at me.

"My wife has had enough," Mr. West said. "The next drink will be water with a small amount of vodka and vermouth."

"Very good, sir, "I said and followed him back into the dining room. For once, mother and son agreed. The rest of the guests wanted wine, which was a simple task. At ten, the guests left, leaving Mrs. Marigold West holding her glass on her head.

In officer training, that meant to come to someone who put his hand on his head, so I approached her.

"You have had enough," Mr. West said.

"You drank more than I did," Mrs. Marigold West said, pouting at her husband.

"I can hold it, you can't, and time for bed," Mr. West said. She wasn't that bad looking if you like your ladies tall and thin with a face like a horse.

"Makes you want to neigh, doesn't it," Mrs. West said, which caused me to put my gloved hand in front of my smile. "Watch out for her squint." If I weren't careful, I would laugh.

'No, she doesn't," I said at the bar.

"What was that, Jenkins?" Mr. West asked.

"A delight, sir," I said.

"For what?" Mr. West asked.

"To assist you, sir," I said.

"Good show Jenkins," Mr. West said. The politeness of private school education.

"I think I may throw up," Mrs. West said.

"Jenkins another martini, and this time with actual vodka and vermouth," Mrs. Marigold West said.

"Jenkins, you will not serve my wife another drink," Mr. West said.

"Yes, sir," I said.

"This is getting good," Mrs. West said.

"Jenkins, I told you to get me a proper martini," Mrs. Marigold West said.

"Now, what are you going to do?" Mrs. West asked.

"Indeed, you did, Madam, but your husband has forbidden me to do so," I said, throwing it back to Mr. West.

"Reginald nicely played," Mrs. West said.

"Oh Doughy, Woughy, mama wants a little drinky winky," Mrs. Marigold West said and winked her eye at her husband, who sighed.

"Disgusting," Mrs. West said. The evening ended with more drinks and helping Mr. West and Mrs. Marigold West upstairs to their bedroom, where I closed their door. I returned to help take the glasses, dishes and cutlery to the kitchen, where I met the other maid, Jane and the cook, Mrs. Carruthers. I returned to organize the bar then I retired to use the washroom. I locked my door and put my clothes away. It was twelve-thirty, my first evening as a butler.

"Reginald, they need help," Mrs. West said.

"Mrs. West, I am here to find out if they had anything to do with your murder," I said. "I know one thing. Mrs. Marigold West was not the one who kicked me in my private parts. She is too tall. How can I help them?" I asked. "If I attempt to comment on their drinking, they will fire me."

"I know, but it is sad," Mrs. West said.

"I agree," I said. "Many things in this life are."

"Well then, say your prayers and go to sleep." I decided not to write *Jenkins did it* on notes, now that I was Jenkins.

CHAPTER 19

The Elusive Mr. West

Mrs. West interrupted my delightful dream, asking what did I require to solve her murder?

"What time is it?" I asked with my eyes closed.

"Six thirty, you slept enough," Mrs. West said. "Well, what is your next step?"

"I have no idea," I said. "It was twelve-thirty when I lay down. My bed is still calling me; not enough sleep; good night Mrs. West."

"It's morning, and the early bird catches the murderer," Mrs. West said.

"A reporter with adequate sleep can concentrate," I said.

"Oh, fiddlesticks, take a cold shower, change and have coffee," Mrs. West said. "I need a tape recorder, the druggist's report, and for you to find out about Douglas' mistress."

"While still anchored here working as a butler for your son-and daughter-in-law," I said. "I need house insurance, to change my telephone, to change the electricity, municipal taxes and fuel."

"You can call your insurance broker and Wallace can do the rest," Mrs. West said. "Call them. Were you aware that Douglas doesn't get up until eleven and Marigold at noon."

"You got me up this early while they still sleep," I said.

"They are your employers, and you are a servant" Mrs. West said.

"Pursuant to your direction" I said.

"Yes, Reginald but I have given up on them, and you need to take care of yourself," Mrs. West said. "After breakfast, take a brisk half-hour walk. It is a lovely neighbourhood; you need to learn about it and meet other servants. Then when you return, you can make your telephone calls, meet the staff and make friends with them, so time to get up." She was worse than my mother on chores day; if I didn't move, she would nag, nag, nag. I got out of bed, groaned, put on my housecoat and grabbed a shaving kit and my clothes.

"Reginald, groaning like Marley's ghost is most unappealing" Mrs. West said.

"I thought he wailed" I said.

"Maybe he did" Mrs. West said. "I like to be surrounded by happy individuals."

"You mean those who have slept well" I asked.

"You have things to do" Mrs. West said, and I went to the bathroom. She had a point, but I would not say anything to her. After showering and shaving I put on a check shirt, light chino pants and desert boots. Once dressed I asked Mrs. West if she approved of my outfit.

"Reginald, a butler wears a dark suit, black oxfords, white shirt and tie," Mrs. West said.

"I will later," I said. "What happens if I drop strawberry jam on my pants?" I asked.

"Really, Reginald," Mrs. West said.

"Think of me as representing a new generation of butlers," I said. "Besides, it is going to be hot and if I am to walk, I will not wear a suit," I said. I was in the kitchen at ten to seven and saw Mrs. Caruthers take something out of the oven. She put a sheet with rolls on the counter and looked at me.

"Taking the day off?" she asked.

"I will change later," I said. "If I was formally dressed, I might drop strawberry jam on my pants."

"That is most wise and thank you for replacing Margaret and helping take out the dishes," Mrs. Caruthers said.

"Anything I can do to help," I said. She told me to sit and place a cup, filled it with coffee, put down a plate and, with tongs, placed two rolls on it. She put butter and jam dishes on the table and asked how I would like my eggs. I told her, and as she cooked, I asked her how long she had been with the Wests.

"Five months, Margaret three months and Jane nine months," Mrs. Caruthers said. "This is confidential, but we are all looking for alternative employment, Mr. Chambers."

"You can call me Edward," I said.

"I thought we always called butlers by their last name" Mrs. Carruthers said.

"I am the new generation," I said.

"Reginald," Mrs. West said.

"Excuse me for asking, but if your name is Chambers, why did Mr. West and Mrs. West call you Jenkins?" Mrs. Caruthers asked.

"I have no idea but if they want to call me Jenkins, that is fine, so don't call me Mr. Chambers," I said. "I don't want to tax their little minds too much." Mrs. Caruthers laughed and served me my eggs with bacon.

"Edward, you are a bit of a card," Mrs. Caruthers said.

"Wonderful, an audience for your dreadful humour," Mrs. West said.

"They like to drink," I said.

"Don't get me going on that," Mrs. Carruthers said. "That is one reason we are leaving."

"What are the others?" I asked.

"Just wait and watch," Mrs. Carruthers said. After breakfast, I did a stroll around the mansion and then went for a walk.

"What do you want me to do?" I asked Mrs. West.

"Watch Douglas and listen," Mrs. West said. "If he goes out, follow him."

"I doubt he walks. He will use the Bentley," I said. "I

suppose I could lie on the back floor of the Bentley with a blanket on me, but I would have to know when he is driving."

"There is no need to be sarcastic." Mrs. West said. "You just have to be prepared."

"Like a Boy Scout," I said.

"What?" Mrs. West asked.

"I see your point. I will be ready," I said.

"Good," Mrs. West said. "I want you to follow him to his mistress."

"Which one," I asked.

"Reginald, that is not funny," Mrs. West said.

"Yes, madam," I said. If that annoyed her, so be it, but I continued my walk. At eight, I was back. I opened the garage and polished the Bentley. I opened the rear trunk to see if I could hide in it and open it, but I didn't see a button. I went to my room and changed and sat in the kitchen.

Mr. West was up at eleven when I brought in the paper and a coffee in the library. He was casually dressed but asking him what he planned to do was inappropriate. Maybe if I winked and asked if he was doing the nasty with his honey, he might confide in me but decided that would lead to my immediate termination. After I left him, I wondered if I should get the goods from the all-seeing and all-knowing cook but decided not to on my first day on the job. When I delivered breakfast on a tray to the library and served Mr. West, he continued reading. He told me he would be using the Bentley.

"Indeed, sir," I said. "I contemplated that was a possibility."

"What did you say?" Mr. West asked.

"The Bentley is ready and polished," I said.

"Jenkins why can't butlers speak so I can understand," Mr. West said.

"Indeed, sir," I said, to throw him off his tracks.

"You may go," Mr. West said.

"Excellent, sir," I said and took the tray. When I returned to take the dishes, he was gone. I heard the garage door open and ran out, the Bentley was heading down the driveway, so I closed the garage door and looked around. A Yellow Cab had stopped across the street, so I ran to catch it. He had dropped off a lady, and I asked if he was free.

"Nope, you pay," the driver said. He had a bow tie and a cap, so I got in the front seat wondering if there would be more wisecracks.

"Follow the Bentley," I said.

"You mean the big dark blue car?" the driver asked.

"Yes," I said.

"Ok, buddy, here we go," and he put the taxi in gear. The Bentley headed west, and we followed.

"Tell him to keep up," Mrs. West said.

"Step on it," I said.

"Listen buddy" the driver said. "No one uses that cliché and if I get too close, he will notice. I don't tell you what to do and you don't tell me what to do." Forty minutes later, the Bentley turned into the St. George, Golf and Country Club so I told my driver to take me back to my house. Once we arrived, I paid the driver. I did butler things, organizing dry cleaning, sampling the booze, polishing shoes and having lunch.

I heard the Bentley arrive at four, so I opened the garage door. I assisted Mr. West with his golf clubs and put them against the wall. He gave me his golf shoes to clean, and once I closed the door, I followed him inside and put the golf shoes in the back entrance way. I walked into the library to the bar and poured a scotch with three ice cubes. I put it on a tray and put it on a coaster on the table. Mr. West frowned when he walked in, so someone found him cheating. I contemplated asking if he wanted me to fluff up the seat cushion before he sat in the chair. I decided that fluffing cushions and pillows were a part of my job, but he sat down before I had the chance.

"Jenkins, did you follow me in a taxi?" Mr. West asked.

"Sir, would you like me to fluff your seat cushion?" I asked.

"Forget about that, did you follow me in a taxi?"

"A taxi?" I asked, seeing if I could draw this out so he

would forget the question.

“Yes, a taxi” Mr. West asked again, and I was tempted to ask what colour, but that would give it away.

“No sir” I said.

“Are you sure? Mr. West asked.

“No, sir. Would you like a cigar?” I asked.

“I asked if you were sure, and you said no” Mr. West said.

“Indeed sir” I said.

“Did you mean you were not sure?” Mr. West asked.

“No sir, I am always sure” I said.

“That you followed me in a taxi” Mr. West said.

“No sir, I did not” I said.

“Did not what?” Mr. West asked.

“Follow you in a taxi,” I said.

“I was sure you were behind me in a taxi,” Mr. West said.

“Indeed, sir, most strange for you to say that?” I said, taking his glass for a refill.

“Another scotch, sir?” but he didn’t answer for some reason.

“You were, weren’t you?” Mr. West asked.

“Were what, sir?” I asked, looking all innocent.

“You are rather obtuse, and you annoy me” Mr. West said.

“Indeed sir?” I asked.

“Yes, and let me start again. Were you following me in a taxi?” Mr. West asked.

“No sir, and I have no idea why you don’t believe me?”

“I just hired you” Mr. West said. “I don’t know you.”

“On the recommendation of your faithful butler” I said.

“Who is no longer working for me” Mr. West said. “And I am not sure he was faithful. He gave notice but never told me why?” I resisted raising my hand to say I know, your cheapness or Marigold on the prowl.

“How is Mr. Jenkins?” I asked. Mr. West stared at me.

“Stop changing the subject” and lowered his lip.

“I was concerned about his health since he has high blood pressure” I said.

"I never knew that," Mr. West said.

"Indeed, sir, but he didn't want to concern you" I said. "He was a resolute butler."

"Never mind him" Mr. West said. I could swear you were following me," then frowned. "Are you quite sure?"

"Yes, sir" I said.

"Positive?" Mr. West asked.

"Scouts honour," I said.

"Did my wife ask you to do it?" Mr. West asks.

"To do what, sir?" I asked.

"To follow me," Mr. West said.

"I thought we had agreed I did not follow you," I said and placed the scotch on the coaster on the table. Mr. West stared at me and sighed.

"Assuming you are telling the truth, my wife does not trust me," Mr. West said.

"Indeed, sir," I said, filling a fresh glass since this would be at least a three-glass complaint.

"Jenkins, I give her money; we are in a beautiful house" Mr. West said. "We have two wonderful children, and my wife never seems to be content. She seems to think I have a girlfriend. Me, the most loving husband in the world." The beginning of a heart-to-heart master-butler chat.

"Horsefeathers," Mrs. West said.

"Here is your scotch, sir," I said, removing the empty glass and replacing it with a full one. "It must be an awful burden on you, sir."

"It is Jenkins, it is," Mr. West said. "I give her everything, and what do I get, a back turned when I am in bed?"

"This is nauseating," Mrs. West said.

"Indeed, sir," I said.

"I get nothing, absolutely nothing" Mr. West said. "No affection not even a kiss." I decided not to say anything, this was too painful.

"Well, two can play this game" Mr. West said. "Perhaps I will get a girlfriend, but the very thought of that repels me. I am a moral man who does not sanction adultery."

"What is Douglas doing, trying to bring you onside for a divorce court?" Mrs. West asked. It seemed to me he was setting up a justification for a mistress, perhaps a second, so he could alternate, one week with Honey one and the other week with Honey two.

"It must be difficult, sir," I said.

"It is Jenkins, and I try to be the best husband I can," Mr. West said. "Well enough, I must see Marigold and find out how her day was." He stood and walked out of the library. I assembled the glasses to be washed.

"Reginald, I do not know what that was about, but he has a mistress unless he wants you to have a little heart-to-heart with Marigold," Mrs. West said

"Maybe he wants two of them, and this was the opening justification," I said. "Mrs. West, I hated lying to your son."

"It is for the greater good and you can confess the sin," Mrs. West said. "Sorry for you betraying your Scouts oath."

"I was never a Scout" I said.

"Really, I thought you were?" Mrs. West asked.

"Nope" I said.

With Mrs. West, my moral failings were irrelevant. She was an indomitable force, pushing me the way she wished. She had the power over me, and there was nothing I could do about it. I realized I didn't have time to do my errands, so I would do them tomorrow.

CHAPTER 20

Investigations at the Douglas West Residence

"Reginald, time to get up," Mrs. West said. I put a pillow over my head then heard fingernails on a blackboard.

"Can you lower the volume or use soft chalk" I said. "My alarm was for six thirty. What time is it?"

"If you had opened your eyes to look at the clock, it is six," Mrs. West said. "Birds are awake, the sun is out, and so should you. You can use the shower, have a coffee and be ready to be my sleuth."

"The crocodile never got Captain Hook up at six nor did Doctor Watson with Sherlock Holmes" I said. "A wide-awake detective is an alert detective."

"Nonsense, out of bed, and greet the day," Mrs. West said. "I have no idea who Captain Hook is, but I have heard of Sherlock Holmes. My late husband took me to a movie with Basil Rathbone who played Mr. Holmes." There was no use resisting her, I was up, so time to shower and change. I had finished breakfast at seven when Mrs. Carruthers, the cook, smiled.

"Welcome to an adventure," Mrs. Carruthers said. "Today Mrs. West is hosting a book club at four, so sandwiches, dessert, tea, coffee and you."

"Me?" I asked. "What do you mean me?"

"Drinks, Edward, and lots of them," Mrs. Caruthers said. "One chardonnay, one vodka and orange juice, one gin martini, one vodka martini. Mrs. Gibbs will want a single malt scotch and you know what that leads to?"

"Visits to the toilet to throw up and hangovers" I said.

"Probably, but since you are young and good looking, their excitement and they will watch you. Make sure you bend down for them to look at your behind."

"I beg your pardon," I said.

"Really," Mrs. West said.

"I thought this was a respectable house" I said.

"You would be surprised." Mrs. Carruthers said. "I don't make the rules, I just tell you what to expect. There will be four guests between the ages of thirty-five and forty-five and after a few drinks, they let loose, and this is their excuse to be unrestrained. The book club is what they tell their husbands, but it is an excuse to drink, smoke, gossip and carry on. And you, Edward, are the feature attraction. You are new and young and not bad looking. Mr. West will play golf, which means after he finishes, he will drink with his buddies, dinner at the club and be back at ten. After the ladies leave, you will be here alone with you know who?"

"The dog? I asked.

"There is no dog, as you know" Mrs. Carruthers said.

"Mrs. Carruthers, I need a favour?" I asked.

"I know what you want," Mr. Caruthers said. "You want Margaret, Jane, and I around until Mr. West returns home. Funny, the last butler wanted that, and we will be there."

"Thank you," I said.

"There you are, Reginald, your chaperones," Mrs. West said. "It was a good thing you helped last night."

"Mr. Jenkins always locked his door at night," Mrs. Carruthers said.

"Why?" I asked.

"The wandering lady of the house," Mrs. Caruthers said.

"As quiet as a mouse," I said, which caused Mrs. Caruthers to laugh. "Not to bother the spouse," prompting more laughter.

"You are such a card," Mrs. Carruthers said

"Lord, give me strength," said Mrs. West. "The last thing you need is an audience, Reginald." Now that I had Mrs. Caruthers relaxed, it was time to ask questions.

"I understand Mr. West lost his mother in April this year," I said. "That must have been a significant loss to him." I never expected a snort, but that is what Mrs. Caruthers did.

"You would think he would be upset, but not in the way you or I would be," Mrs. Caruthers said. "He was upset about the fact he would not receive one third of his mother's estate. Understand I am getting this second hand from Gilbert. Gilbert is Mr. Jenkins the first. I never served Mr. and Mrs. West. Gilbert was called around eight on Sunday morning, learning Mrs. West had passed away. Gilbert knocked on the bedroom door and told Mr. West that his mother had passed away. There was no reply, so Gilbert repeated the message. Mr. West said he heard him the first time and to go away. He remained outside the bedroom and heard Mr. West say, 'about time.' Mr. West never went to the house to pay his last respects. When the police came the next day Gilbert told me it was a bit of a party. Mr. West told the policeman his mother was in bad health and there was no need for an autopsy. Gilbert gave the policeman three glasses of scotch and a cigar. I was horrified, but that is Mr. West."

"Is Mr. West out of the house some nights?" I asked to see if I could prompt her recollections of April 13th.

"I am in bed, so I do not know," Mrs. Carruthers said. "I get up at five to serve breakfast."

"I may need to contact Mr. Jenkins to ask him questions," I said. Once I finished breakfast I took my plate, cutlery and plates to the sink, where Mrs. Carruthers said I didn't need to. Note to self to buy Mrs. Carruthers flowers. Outside the house I said "wait" until I was on the street.

"Yes, it is suspicious, but it is not clear that your son killed you," I said. There was no response, so I waited.

"You are right, but he could have been more kind and visited me, but he didn't," Mrs. West said. "That hurts me. And to have a party with the investigating policeman is reprehensible."

"I agree, but not every horrible person is a murderer," I said.

"But all murderers are bad people" Mrs. West said. "So let us keep digging. I don't like the odour and we are just getting started."

"Suspicion always haunts the guilty mind," I said.

"The thief doth fear each bush an officer," said Mrs. West, which was the following line from Shakespeare King Henry V1."

"I am impressed," I said.

"You shouldn't be, we had to memorize poems in my classes," Mrs. West said. I kept saying hello to people picking up papers and yelled, "practicing lines for a play" but I was not sure they cared. This was the wealthiest neighbourhood in Toronto and had its share of eccentrics, but I wanted to be careful. Back at the house, I changed in my bedroom, took out a notebook and made my first call to Mr. Foster, my real estate agent. It was nice to have my telephone, but I wondered if anyone else listened.

"Mr. Clark, I am glad you called. I have a new listing at 32 Elmer Avenue, a three-story house and basement, four bedrooms and one-and one-half baths."

"How much?" I asked.

"Nineteen thousand, which is more than you wanted to pay, but it is a detached house. Here is where it becomes interesting. I am aware of a large Italian family who are looking to rent a house. With the baby, there are ten, including the grandmother. The father and oldest son are bricklayers and bring in good money. I told them for a four-bedroom house it would be three hundred dollars and they are prepared to pay it. You have nothing against Italians, do you?"

"No, I just want good tenants," I said.

"This may go fast. Can you look at it this morning?"

"No, but a friend could," I said. I will call you back. I called Mr. Wallace, who said he would take care of the things required for the house transfer. He added he be available at nine if the agent wished to pick him up. I called Mr. Foster and said I would have the deposit to him today and gave him the address for Mr. Wallace. The deposit was one-thousand dollars.

I called Big Fish to talk about tape recorders, but he said it would not work and explained they were large, and the microphone was on a short cable. I called Fred, who said he had spoken to his cousin, and they needed to send the sample to a lab, which would cost twenty-five dollars. Fred said he would pay for it. I asked if he could use Manny to find out about Miss Eunice Walker and gave the address. I said I would pay five dollars a day, and I wanted her description, and next Saturday, I would pay a visit. At a quarter to ten, I called Mr. Wallace, who told me the house was in good shape and to buy it. I called Mr. Foster and said I would purchase it. I walked to the kitchen and told Mrs. Caruthers I had to go downtown to buy coveralls to work on the car.

I visited the real estate agent to sign for the house. Then I went to the Army and Navy for work pants, work boots, a shirt and coveralls. By eleven, I was back in the kitchen when Jane said Mr. West wished to see me in the dining room. I walked in and stood there.

"Yes, sir," I said. He stared at me with bloodshot eyes.

"I pay you to be here," he said.

"Indeed, sir," I said. "I was up before seven and was available, then realized I needed clothes and coveralls to clean your car. That was what I was doing. Is there anything I can do, sir?"

"I am golfing after lunch, so wash and dry the Bentley," Mr. West said. "Have you driven a car?"

"Yes sir," I said.

"The keys are on a rack in the garage," Mr. West said. "At four you will serve drinks at my wife's book club."

"Yes sir," I said. "Is there anything else?"

"Get me another coffee," he said.

"Very good, sir," I said and wondered if I should have asked if he wanted some brandy or scotch in it since he looked hung over. I brought the coffee, changed, and took out the Bentley. I washed it, dried it and then drove around the block three times to ensure it worked, put in in neutral and revved the engine, British technology at its best. Back in the garage I tried the radio, moved the seat back and forth, shut it off and returned the keys then had a wonderful lunch in the servants' kitchen.

Once Mr. West left, I called Fred to find out about the convertible. It would be another two weeks, so he offered me a motorcycle for two hundred dollars. It was a 1953 BSA, and I said I would give him the money. I spoke to Mrs. Marigold West and said I would have to do a liquor run, and she gave me thirty dollars and told me to take a cab.

Once I visited Fred to pay him the money for the services and motorcycle, I told him to check it out. I was back with the liquor and told Mrs. West about the tape recorder, that Manny would watch the mistress and get the lab report. I told her about the house and the tenants but refrained from telling her that the tenants were Italian. At three, I set up the bar, filled up the ice bucket and determined which rear profile was best for the book club ladies. I was in a pickle, and I hoped I would not be sliced or diced.

CHAPTER 21

The Book Club

For a group of society ladies, once they had drinks, they were loud, crude, and entertaining. They were like loose boards on a lumber wagon with their incessant gossip. I learned by serving drinks which lady had an affair, who was plump and who coloured their hair wrong since none of these ladies were present. By four-thirty, Mrs. Marigold West insisted it was too hot for me to wear a jacket and asked that I take it off.

"Madam, that would violate the code of the Guild of Butlers, so I must decline" I said.

"Jenkins, no one would know," Mrs. Marigold West said.

"It is a point of honour that we maintain our code at all times," I said. "I took a sacred oath before Queen and Country" and wondered if I had overdone it.

"Are you sure you are not confusing that with the Boy Scouts?" Mrs. West asked. "You are laying it on a little thick."

"Very well, Jenkins," Mrs. Marigold West said. "I would like another."

"Excellent, madam," I said.

"I just love how you say that" Mrs. Marigold West said as I left for the bar.

"Make it light," Mrs. West said. Mrs. West's running commentaries did not help. By five, the ladies would take my hand each time I provided a drink. It was Muriel, Grace, Lana and Celeste and no last names, but I insisted on calling Mrs. Marigold West, madam.

A few minutes later, when I was making a drink for Mrs. Lana Cartwright, she came in and stood, touching me. I had to move since I found her chest against my arm arousing, which was her intent.

"Mr. Jenkins, I know something you don't," Mrs. Cartwright said.

"Shit, she knows I am a reporter," I thought. "And what would that be, madam?" I asked, watching her step closer.

"You need a new employer," she said. "Mr. Fleming, our butler, is retiring, and we need a replacement. We pay one hundred and sixty dollars a month; your weekends are free. How much do the Wests pay you?"

"I should not discuss that madam," I said, stepping back. We were like dancing the tango. She moved, and I deflected.

"Oh, come on Mr. Jenkins, this is between you and me," Mrs. Cartwright said.

"Twenty dollars a week with weekends free," I said. Mrs. Cartwright giggled.

"You are getting four dollars a day, that is what we pay our dog walker," she said and giggled again.

"What is so funny," asked Mrs. Marigold West, "and why are you talking to my butler?" I hadn't heard her enter the library.

"And why are you so close," as I stepped back.

"I wanted to know if he would work for us since we pay a decent wage," Mrs. Cartwright said. "We pay one hundred and sixty dollars a month. It turns out you pay your butler four dollars a day, which is what we pay our dog walker."

"Reginald, you never discuss what you receive as pay," Mrs. West said.

"A little late now. I have a hurricane to contend with," I said. Mrs. Marigold West and Mrs. Cartwright said "what" simultaneously.

"There is a storm warning, and later I must deal with it," I said.

"Jenkins, you must have misunderstood what Douglas said and we always pay our butlers one hundred and sixty dollars a month," Mrs. Marigold West said.

"I am terribly sorry for the misunderstanding and regret the problem I created, madam," I said. "Will you forgive me?"

"Of course, Jenkins and I am sure that Lana is leaving, aren't you?" Mrs. Marigold West said.

"Bye Jenkins, bye Marigold, and you both behave," Mrs. Cartwright said and left.

"I don't know what has gotten into Mrs. Cartwright, so make her next drink weak," Mrs. Marigold West said.

"Very good, madam," I said and observed her leave.

"Make sure you remind Douglas of your new salary," Mrs. West said. "Whether those guests are ladies is in doubt, but you are here as a butler and a proper butler you shall be. No more showing your rear, and they are to be addressed by using their last names."

"Yes, Mrs. West, but how am I to serve drinks without bending over?"

"Use the tray and hand it to them," Mrs. West said.

"That is not what Mr. Wallace taught me," I said.

"Do it," Mrs. West said.

"Yes, madam," I said.

"You were having fun," Mrs. West said.

"Yes, madam, I was," I said.

"Don't and address me as Mrs. West" Mrs. West said. Back in the living room, I resumed a more formal manner which annoyed the book club ladies, but I had my orders. Mrs. West trumped Mrs. Marigold West since a Queen outranked a princess. As far as I was concerned, I had two queens, one in Buckingham Palace, whose face was on our stamps and coins and the other my afterlife director. By this time, Mrs. Marigold West was too drunk to respond to my subtle inquiries to find out who murdered Mrs. West, and she had her friends in attendance. Once they left, I would be in the staff kitchen with my chaperones and would bring Margaret or Jane with me if she wanted a drink. I wondered if I should teach the Book Club a song, "Little Brown Jug" but they probably knew it.

The party broke up at seven, and Jane and I helped Mrs. Marigold West to her bedroom. Once she sat on a chair, we left, closed the door and we returned to the kitchen. I enjoyed prime roast beef, baked potatoes and Yorkshire pudding with a five-year-old French wine. Dessert was chocolate eclairs, and then the four of us played cards until Mr. West came home. He wasn't hungry but wanted a couple of scotches and a cigar before he went to bed. He was not talkative, so once his glass was empty, I refilled it. I took out his box of cigars, and he nodded. I took one out, cut the end, gave it to him, and lit it. Then it was back behind the bar to wait.

"Remember what Wallace told you, never ask him how his day was or chat." Mrs. West said. "Speak only when spoken to and wait until tomorrow to tell him your new salary. Douglas, when drunk, is unpleasant."

"Can I ask him if he murdered you?" I whispered, but Mr. West was deep in thought in the library chair. I looked again, and his eyes were closed.

"How long should I wait?" I asked.

"Fifteen minutes," Mrs. West said. It was ten minutes before he opened his eyes and looked at me.

"Jenkins," he said. "I am going to bed."

"Very good sir," I said. "Do you require help?"

"No Jenkins, I do not," Mr. West said."

"Good night, sir," I said, but he ignored me. I followed to observed his progress, and he only missed two steps. He had told me he did not require help, so I remained in the hall as a dutiful and obedient butler, knowing my place.

"Reginald, you should have helped him," Mrs. West said.

"And ignore his specific instructions?" I said.

"Yes," said Mrs. West.

"I am a dutiful and obedient butler, knowing my place," I

said.

"You dislike him, don't you?" she asked.

"Yes," I said. "Putting aside whether he murdered you, he treated you horribly when you died. That was wrong."

"Thank you, Reginald," Mrs. West said. "You understand, and no son should treat his mother like that. Now clean up and go to bed, and I won't keep reminding you to say your prayers. You know what you should do." I washed and dried the glasses in the kitchen and returned to the library, where I poured myself a scotch and sat in a comfortable chair. Being a butler had advantages. Good food, driving the Bentley up and down the driveway and around the block, excellent wines and scotch. The downside was Mr. West and Mrs. Marigold West. I wondered where the children were. Had the parents misplaced them or were they kidnapped?

"Mrs. West, where are the children?" I asked.

"Summer camp," she said. I finished my scotch, washed and dried the glass, walked upstairs, changed, and used the washroom. I locked the door, turned off the lights and felt the bed. Marigold was here then realized one maid had placed more pillows on my bed.

"Good night Mrs. West."

"Good night, Reginald," and lay awake, thinking. There was something to be said about sobriety. I should have the lab report in the next few days. I had asked the report writer to find out if it was a horse tranquillizer and whether two or three pills ground up would kill a person. I needed to find the identity of the lady in Mrs. West's bedroom. That was the key to the case. I needed to talk to Jenkins to confirm Mr. West was out on April 13 at night. He told Mr. Wallace this, but I needed to speak to him. Once I did, he would know I was doing an investigation and may not talk to me, but I had to try.

Then I would work on Mrs. Marigold West when she was alone between sobriety and intoxication. That was risky, and I would end it if she became problematic. Mr. West would be a challenge, but I would watch and listen. I had two weeks before I returned to my job at the *Toronto Mirror* and had wasted the first week, but now, I was in my investigation. The best thing was that no one questioned my skills as a butler. Apart from serving drinks, doing errands, washing and drying the Bentley and polishing the silver, they expected me to be on call from eleven in the morning to midnight. I wondered if butlers had morning jobs, and soon, I was asleep.

CHAPTER 22

Fired and Rehired

The first I learned about the Montreal trip was at breakfast. Mr. West had left a note that on Wednesday. Jane and I would accompany Mr. and Mrs. Marigold West to Montreal for four days and stay with friends of Mr. West in Westmount. Mr. West had forgotten that I don't work Saturdays, but I was excited about seeing Montreal. I had learned French at university, but I was rusty. I was planning to interview Mr. West's mistress on Saturday, but I could do it on Sunday. I wasn't sure why they needed a maid and a butler, but what did I know?

In my room to change, I told Mrs. West I was going to Montreal for four days on Wednesday.

"I have never been to Montreal," I said.

"You won't see the city other than from the train station to George Weatherby's mansion," she said. "I assume you are travelling by train since Marigold does not like flying."

"I believe so," I said. "You lived in Montreal in 1907."

"Who told you that?" Mrs. West asked.

"You did," I said, and Mrs. West said she had forgotten she told me.

"Why does your son want to bring a maid and butler with him?" I asked.

"To demonstrate that he is rich and has servants which

very few persons have," Mrs. West said.

"Won't Mr. Weatherby have a butler?" I asked.

"I expect he will, and your job is to work under him and follow his direction," Mrs. West said. "Pack your formal wear and extra white gloves. You will pack Douglas' bags and I will tell you what to pack."

I made several telephone calls but learned nothing. I checked in with my real estate broker, who told me he would call Mr. Wallace since he had a house to show. It was a semi-detached house with three bedrooms, and one bathroom with a basement for fifteen thousand dollars on Waverley Road. I said to call him and added I was off to Montreal for four days, but if Mr. Wallace liked it, I would have a cheque for the deposit. I told him to come before noon and give the address.

"Why move so fast with the houses?" asked Mrs. West.

"Five hundred dollars a month in rental income, which goes to my broker, and there is no use waiting for that," I said. An hour later I spoke to Mr. Foster, who told me Mr. Wallace approved, and I told him the time to meet me.

My meeting with Mr. West did not go well. Cheapness was his way of life for servants. He fired me. Then he changed his mind, hired me, looked at me and fired me again. He relented only after I packed my bags and informed him the taxi was coming. I would have Saturdays and Sundays off to see my mother, and my salary was one hundred and sixty dollars. In between our negotiations, if you can consider being called a God damned thieving blackmailer, I paid a deposit to Mr. Foster. Negotiating with Mr. West was simple, his insults, my stoic silence, watching him stand up and sit down, and being fired and rehired.

When I was alone in my bedroom, I sighed. I knew Mr. West would think of ways to make me work, requiring me to take the Bentley apart and put it back together, then the television set. Who knows what evil lurked in his mind, but I was still employed, and he had met my demands. I couldn't wait for Mr. West to have a little chat with his wife about negotiating with me in his absence, and perhaps she had done this before. This demonstrates the perils of having a soused spouse.

"Douglas is frugal when paying servants," Mrs. West said.

"Frugal, he gives Scrooge a run for his money," I said. "Miserly is more like it, and the eighty dollars for my increased salary is nothing compared to what he spends on alcohol and wine."

"Yes, Reginald, but that alcohol and wine is for Douglas and his wife," Mrs. West said. "You are an expense like repairing a window. Douglas does not take pleasure from windows and servants."

"That pained me" I said.

"I detest puns" Mrs. West said.

"I was a waiting for a laugh" I said.

"Which will never happen" Mrs. West said.

"You started it by comparing me with a window" I said.

"And you finished with that dreadful pun" Mrs. West said.

"Since you love puns so much, how about this," I said. " 'Hanging is too good for a man who makes puns; he should be hanged, drawn and quoted.' "

"Spare me," Mrs. West said.

"I think I got that right," I said. "That was not mine it was Fred Allen's. I suppose your son will buy a large dog for me to walk three times a day," I said.

"Marigold does not like dogs," Mrs. West said.

"He will acquire a cat for me to walk," I said.

"Marigold does not like cats," Mrs. West said.

"He will purchase a parrot and I will have to teach it to say Mr. West is wonderful."

"Don't be ridiculous" Mrs. West said.

"He will think of something," I said.

"I am sure he will have you clean the furnace and heating vents," said Mrs. West. "He will get his money's worth."

Mrs. Marigold West did not come down for breakfast or lunch. Around one afternoon, their fight began, and everyone in the house and street heard it. As a domestic brouhaha over my increase in remuneration, it was long and loud, punctuated by accusations back and forth between husband and wife.

"It is like a Wagnerian opera," Mrs. West said. Eventually, husband and wife stopped, perhaps because of exhaustion or to check if their marriage warranty had run out. I was sitting in the servant's kitchen. Mrs. Carruthers and I had made a bet on the length of the disagreement, she said more than half an hour, and I said less. When Mr. West shouted my name, I was happily eating pie as Mrs. Caruthers opened the door and I paid her a dollar.

"I want a word with you," Mr. West said, but having heard him for the last forty minutes, I knew it would be more. Possibly three or four thousand if I was lucky. He glared at me as I followed him into the library and stood there.

"I suppose it is my fault dealing with a member of the younger generation who thinks the world owes them," Mr. West said as he sat. I decided to remain standing to make a quick exit. He was like my grade eleven vice principal, and I found keeping quiet the safest course. When someone was angry it was best to let them get it out and if he looked threatening, I could suggest he throw plates or stamp his feet

"I don't understand why you had the temerity to discuss your remuneration with a woman," he said. "That is a man's responsibility."

"I believe he means his wife, but Douglas gets confused when he is angry," Mrs. West said. I remained silent.

"I would have expected that if you had a problem you would speak to me," he said. "You have upset my wife, and I want you to apologize to get her out of our bedroom so you can pack my clothes."

"Very good, sir," I said. I walked up to the master bedroom, knocked and asked if I could come in. Mrs. Marigold West told me I could. I opened the door, and she sat in bed wearing a housecoat and drinking something out of a cup. She was pale but smiled at me.

"Madam, I am sorry for creating this difficulty between

you and your husband, and I apologize," I said. I tried to look penitent and bowed.

"What did you say, Jenkins?" she asked, raised her eyebrows and frowned. I repeated it.

"Why are you apologizing for my husband?" she asked, and I explained what her husband had asked me to do.

"Did he?" Mrs. Marigold West said. "The little snake. Would you be so kind as to ask my husband to see me?" Downstairs I found Mr. West in the library and told him his wife would like to see him. In the staff kitchen, I had a cup of coffee, and made another bet and this time I won. It wasn't until three when Jane and I could pack the luggage, which took me longer because Mrs. West provided instructions.

I returned downstairs to learn that Mr. West and Mrs. Marigold West had gone for dinner. I went upstairs to my bedroom, where Mrs. West instructed me to pack for the Montreal trip. That was assuming my boss and his wife spoke to each other and travelled together. In the kitchen I enjoyed a lovely roast chicken, mashed potatoes, green beans, salad, and pie for dessert. It was a superb chardonnay, and we played cards until ten awaiting the Wests. When they returned, they did not want drinks and went to bed. For some reason they did not speak to each other, maybe they had bad service at the restaurant. I was in bed at ten thirty, and we said our usual good nights and I lay there thinking of how to annoy Mr. West without being fired.

CHAPTER 23

The Trip to Montreal

"Reginald, time to get up," Mrs. West said.

"What time is it?" I asked.

"Five o'clock," Mrs. West said.

"I set the alarm for five-thirty," I said. "It is still dark."

"Yes, but I am bored," Mrs. West said. "What is the meaning of life?"

"Mrs. West I am just waking up," I said. I was tempted to say sex but was not prepared to be at the receiving end of a champion scolding. My problem was an immature twenty-five-year-old wisecracker connected to a proper Victorian lady. I decided that proper and Victorian ladies were a redundancy.

"I had been thinking about it and decided that tolerable acceptance is the meaning of life," Mrs. West said. "Don't you agree?"

"I guess so," I said.

"Reginald, simply saying 'I guess so' is indifferent," Mrs. West said.

"You mean namby-pamby" I said.

"I beg your pardon, what is that?" Mrs. West asked.

"Weak or indecisive" I said.

"Use words everyone can understand and not ridiculous words" Mrs. West said. "Say what you mean with the simplest words and take a position and decide" Mrs. West said.

"What if I am unsure?"

"Then say so" Mrs. West said. "Reginald there is much for you to learn, and I have no idea how long I will be here. Once you are at the station, you must count the bags, get them in the baggage car and get a receipt. Then help Douglas and Marigold to their car, which will be in first class then find your coach car. Ask the cook to pack you a meal. Get up, much for you to be done."

At least I was clear-headed as I put on my housecoat, grabbed my toiletry bag, and headed to the bathroom. At this time of the morning, the maids were still asleep, Mrs. Caruthers was in the kitchen, and I could wake up in the shower. Mrs. West had the advantage of never sleeping, and I wondered how she passed the hours at night. I had never thought about the meaning of life; I was too busy. Perhaps the answer is to be engaged and have a purpose. Mrs. West was a spirit with one goal, to discover who murdered her, and the only resource was me. I would not want to rely on me. As the hot shower descended, I felt sorry for Mrs. West since I needed to work on this more. The problem was I couldn't hang around outside the marital chambers waiting for Mr. West to talk. Maybe he would turn to his wife and say: "Marigold, my dear, I must confess something."

"Marigold would look at her husband and ask, "cheating at golf ?"

"Not that serious; I bumped off mother."

"She didn't die of old age?" Marigold would ask.

"No, my little sweety pie, I hastened her death," Mr. West would say.

"Yes, dear, but she had it coming," Marigold would say. "Your mother was getting on in years."

"That's what I thought, and the deed is done" Mr. West would say. Even if I managed to hang around outside the door, Mr. West would not confess when he and Mrs. West had problems in their relationship. My first job was to restore marital bliss, maybe suggest that Mr. West give Mrs. Marigold West a foot rub. Once dressed, I asked about the trip.

"Why are we going to Montreal to visit Mr. Weatherby?" I asked.

"I am not sure, but Douglas was a classmate of George Weatherby at McGill, Commerce Class of 1937. There was a group of them, John Faulkner from Ottawa in politics, David Boulton from Vancouver in business, Conrad Vaughn from New York in broadcasting, and Gerald McKenzie from Winnipeg in agriculture. It will be a reunion, so pay attention to what you hear."

"What do you know of Mr. West's mistress, Eunice Walker," I asked.

"I overheard Douglas, who has the subtlety of a drunken sailor, when he mentioned to his friend Walter he was 'having a bit on the side.' I didn't know what that meant, so I consulted Wallace, who was a little embarrassed to tell me. I asked Wallace to hire a private investigator, and I believe he consulted with the Grey Ghost. I would never have known about Miss Eunice Walker if Douglas were discreet. He has to be the center of attention and has to brag to his friends. Gentlemen must never discuss those things and not do those things."

"You mean affairs," I said.

"Yes, affairs," Mrs. West said. "A violation of the marriage oath. But apart from the name and address, I know nothing else. He didn't bring her to my residence, and I gave permission for Wallace to inform Jenkins of the name and an address, a butler-to-butler communication. It would keep Jenkins aware of the situation."

"Why tell Mr. Jenkins?" I asked.

"I didn't want a scandal," Mrs. West said. "If Jenkins was driving Marigold to a bridge party in the same building at the time Douglas was violating his marital commitments, Jenkins could claim a flat tire. I didn't approve, but the last thing I wanted was Marigold to learn of this and sue for divorce. It would be in the papers."

"If I succeed and write my story, it will be in the papers," I said.

"Douglas should have thought about that before he murdered me," Mrs. West said.

"Douglas or the spitfire who tried to retrieve the pills," I said.

"Yes, Reginald, you must find out who this spitfire is," Mrs. West said.

"I need to confirm if it was Miss Walker or someone else," I said.

"Why is finding a murderer so difficult?" Mrs. West asked.

"Not always, but in your case, it is," I said. "You realize if I am successful, they will examine your body to determine if someone poisoned you."

"Yes, but you will stay away from High Park that day," Mrs. West said.

"The awful stuff will be in the mortuary, and they will not allow me to be there," I said.

"Do your job," she said. During breakfast, I read a note with a five-dollar bill attached. I would take a taxi to Union Station with five suitcases, five clothes bags, and four hat boxes. There I would pick up the tickets and place the bags in the baggage car. Once I did that, I would be at the front entrance on Front Street at eight to meet them since the train left at eight-thirty. Mrs. Caruthers gave me a lunch bag, and at seven, the cab arrived. After I paid the driver at Union Station, I hired a porter who asked if my family was travelling to Vancouver. Montreal I said and he laughed. After I got the tickets, we went to the baggage car, and he helped me hand the baggage to the agent. I paid him two dollars and the agent one dollar since I would need his help in Montreal, gave him my lunch bag and he looked in it.

"Very generous, but they feed me on the train," he said.

"I need you to hold it until I return," I said and sat on a bench. I saw Bob Malone, who works for the *Toronto Telegram* and is a drinking buddy. He stopped and I stood, and we shook hands.

"Going to a funeral?" Bob asked, looking at my suit.

"No, to my wedding," I said.

"Congratulations, wait a minute. You don't have a girlfriend," Bob said and stared at me.

"You have a story," he said. "I think I will stick around." I looked to see when the next train would arrive, and there was one from Windsor.

"The train from Windsor arrives in ten minutes," I said.

"So," he said, but I noticed he touched his ear. When Bob was excited or worried, he did that.

"The Provincial Minister of Highways lives in Windsor," I said. "He might be on the train and travelling with Mr. Edwards, the owner of a major highway construction company. I keep hearing rumours about those two. Track four, let me go and see."

"All right, Reggie," Bob said. "Stay here, and once I publish the story, I will call you."

"Once I publish my story, I will call you, so go," I said.

"Deal," Bob said, and we shook hands. Bob headed down the ramp, and I resumed sitting. I met Mr. and Mrs. West and Jane at eight, escorted them to their carriage, and watched as the porter helped them up. Mr. West handed me a new note and told me to collect the bags in Montreal and to take a taxi to the address. I returned, collected my lunch bag, found my carriage, and took a seat across from Jane.

"Where is your lunch bag?" I asked.

"Mrs. West told me that maids never carried lunch bags when they were with important people." I told her I would share mine with her. She became upset, but I told her I would go to another car if she didn't. I had fifty dollars in small bills, and I could buy whatever we needed. There were two large roast beef sandwiches and two bags of potato chips in my lunch bag.

Before I fell asleep, I learned about Jane and her family. Around Kingston, we had lunch. I purchased two Coca-Colas from an attendant and read my book, *Carry on Jeeves*, by P. G. Wodehouse. If I was going to be a butler, it was best to find out what butlers did, and I learned about Jeeves, the valet, Bertie Wooster, Bingo Little and Sir Roderick Glossop. While Jane was asleep, I practiced saying, " 'oh, I say,' 'what ho,' 'cheerio,' and 'memories are like mulligatawny soup in a cheap restaurant.' "

"That is enough, Reginald," Mrs. West said. "I think you should read more serious literature and not nonsense from some ridiculous author." I remained silent, being insulted by my choice of authors; even if she was correct, but I would not admit that to her. I assumed she had never read P.G. Wodehouse.

I waited with a porter at the Montreal station who retrieved the bags. Outside, I paid him two dollars, and he smiled. He walked over to a Diamond Taxi and talked with the driver, who got out and looked at me. Then, between the two of them, they loaded the taxi in the back seat and trunk. I stood watching them when I heard a voice behind me.

"They left me, those awful people," the voice said. I looked around, and it was Jane. She sat with me in the front seat. When we pulled up to the mansion, I saw a tall and a short man in dark suits waiting at the entrance. We got out, I paid the driver and gave him a fifty-cent tip.

"Are you with us until the New Year?" the tall man asked in a Scottish accent.

"Until Saturday," I said.

"I am Mr. McGregor, butler for Mr. Weatherby," he said. "This is Mr. Ruskin, butler for Mr. Boulton. I understand you are Mr. Jenkins, but not Mr. Jenkins, who was here last year."

"Correct, and once I leave my employment with Mr. West, I am sure another Mr. Jenkins will replace me. Thank you for helping me, sir."

"It is Mr. McGregor, not sir," Mr. McGregor said. Where were you trained?"

"In Bath, but my butler was a little confused," I said.

"Incompetent, more likely," Mr. McGregor said.

"Who is the lady?" Mr. McGregor asked.

"Jane, Mrs. Marigold West's maid," I said.

"Tell her to follow us to the servants' entrance," Mr. McGregor said, which I did. We took in the bags, and once inside, at a long entrance, Mr. McGregor asked me to set aside my bags and Jane's, which I did. He, Mr. Ruskin and I took the bags for the Wests to their room. He introduced Jane to Marie and told me to follow him to a small office where he and Mr. Ruskin sat. I stood.

"Right, you are the last to arrive and the youngest, so you are in the basement on a cot. There is a shower, washstand and toilet down there along with Daisy."

"Who is Daisy?" I asked.

"An escaped snake, but not venomous," Mr. McGregor said. "Or I think so. Master Richard hides important information from me and let him out of his cage. As the third and last butler, you will fetch and carry, which means you can go downtown. On Friday night, formal wear since there will be a large party. In residence are the Weatherby's, and the guests are Richard Faulkner and wife; cabinet minister David Boulton and wife; investments, Conrad Vaughn and friend, broadcasting, Gerald Mackenzie and wife; grain futures and Mr. West and wife. Dress in a dark suit unless they ask us to do manual labour. The tents are behind the house next to the swimming pool. Do you know what happens when a tipsy guest meets a water hazard? A disaster so I employed a lifeguard there for Friday night. You know how to make drinks?"

"Yes," I said.

"Good, there will be two bars Friday night and I hired four waiters. The Commerce Class, McGill 1937, will be here on Friday night. Heavy drinkers. Well, most of them since a few are dead or are in the Kingston Penitentiary. Nothing serious like murder, just stock manipulation and fraud. The steps to the basement are off the kitchen. Relax and be ready at four for the first call for drinks. Sorry about the basement, but no waiting for a shower. Good luck and we will see you at four." That was very generous since it was three-twenty in the afternoon, and I had to take my suitcase and suit bag to the basement and hang my suits.

The one thing I could say about my new lodging was that they were immense. The downside was the narrow tall windows, the three light bulbs and the dank smell. Once I hung my suit, I found the toilet since I tripped over it. They set it up near the wall, giving me an excellent view of the furnace. The shower was near the two washing machines, and the laundry sink was on the other side of the washing machines.

"Hello, Daisy," I said. "I warn you to stay away from my cot, or it will force me to hire a mongoose, which never ends well."

"Reginald, I am sorry for putting you through this," Mrs. West said.

"Let me try the cot," I said and lay on it. The sheets, blanket and pillow were next to it on a table, along with a towel and hand towel. My feet stuck out four inches, but I could find boxes and put them at the end.

"I wonder if this was used to punish servants if they found them pilfering silver?"

"No, the employers dismiss them without a reference," Mrs. West said. "We can talk down here."

"Yes, we can between the hours of one to six when I am exhausted," I said. "Why don't you write out the things I am to do?" I asked.

"Reginald, there is no need to be snippy." Mrs. West said.

"Sorry, but I must go to serve drinks," I said. "Or fetch and carry as butlers do. Make sure you listen."

"My hearing is excellent," Mrs. West said. "It is you I am worried about, so stay focused." I put on my butler wear, my white gloves and was ready to perform butler like things and thinking butler like thoughts.

CHAPTER 24

In Service as Butler Three

I reached the top of the stairs and opened the door. Mr. McGregor stared at me.

"Do you always talk to yourself or are you off your medications?" he asked. Apart from Mr. McGregor, no one else was in the kitchen.

"Lines for a play," I said. "Ever act?" I asked.

"Around here, every day," Mr. McGregor said.

"How do you keep serious?" I asked.

"I imagine eating haggis," he said.

"What is that?" I asked.

"A pudding with a sheep's heart, liver and lungs with mutton, oatmeal and spices boiled in an intestine," Mr. McGregor said. "A famous Scottish dish, but the very thought of it makes me sick."

"Sounds worse than cottage cheese" I said. "They issued me the wrong size of cot," I said. "Mine is a small, and I need a large."

"Is this an attempt at humour?" Mr. McGregor asked.

"It is," I said. "You should be doubled over laughing and beg me to stop."

"A butler with excellent taste," Mrs. West said.

"That is most regrettable," Mr. McGregor said. "It would

be preferable to attempt your humour elsewhere, perhaps in Toronto. I understand they are more primitive. The educated class only read the comics in the newspapers."

"What a disagreeable butler," Mrs. West said.

"I was trying to be funny, but your remarks about Toronto are unwarranted," I said.

"They are warranted," Mr. McGregor said. "Montreal is larger, more cultured, and we have won more hockey playoffs."

"In Montreal, they sell tickets to watch the riots after a hockey game, and your favourite dish is French fries," I said. "With cheese on top. I found the toilet. I tripped over it; maybe paint it yellow."

"Reginald enough," Mrs. West said.

"You will note I am ignoring your humour as we all have our problems," Mr. McGregor said. "I am sharing my room with Mr. Ruskin, who snores. On the scale of one to ten he is off the Richter scale."

"I thought that was for earthquakes" I said.

"Precisely" Mr. McGregor said. "This morning Mr. Weatherby asked if I could purchase ear plugs for him, and he is in the east wing. Ready to be drawn and quartered? I don't think anyone is. There will be two tables, the ladies at one and the gentleman at the other, a distance apart. Over the years, the ladies grew tired of the exploits of their husbands at McGill. There is only so much they can take about fraternity parties, football games and who did what to whom and who drank more. You will serve the ladies, Mr. Ruskin, the men and I attend the bar. I expect it will be gin and tonic or white wine for the ladies and beer for the men. After six, the men will switch to scotch."

"Not a good choice," I said. "My father taught me a rhyme 'beer then whisky, pretty risky, whisky then beer never fear.' "

"Is that our responsibility to be nursemaids?" Mr. McGregor asked. "We butlers are mortals, not the prominent men of business and politics."

"What about Jeeves," I said. "He helped Bertie Wooster with his tendency to overindulge."

"A character of P. G. Wodehouse in his books to make fun of the aristocracy," Mr. McGregor said. "He had a concoction that improved Mr. Wooster's malaise because of too much alcohol the night before, but he never shared it. Now that you mentioned it, there should be buckets in the basement. Bring them to the kitchen and get wash cloths. The good news is after they party tonight, tomorrow night will be more subdued."

"I am not sure that will apply to the Wests" I said. "They seem to have been practicing."

"Ah yes, your employers," Mr. McGregor said." I will make Mrs. West's drinks weak and the same for Mr. West."

"They will not like that," I said.

"As I mentioned, we all have our problems," he said. At the ladies' table, I placed water glasses on coasters and then stood back with an attentive butler expression.

"Ladies, this is our butler Jenkins," Mrs. Marigold West said. "Isn't he adorable?"

"I don't understand; I thought your last butler was Jenkins?" asked Mrs. Fiona Weatherby."

"He was, but you will have to ask Douglas about that," Mrs. Marigold West said. "I was a little confused."

"And still are," said Mrs. West. "The stupidity of my son- and daughter-in-law never ceases to amaze me." The ladies wore dresses, sunglasses and enormous hats. They chose gin and tonic, except for Mrs. Tallulah Vaughn, who wanted a scotch. When I returned and placed the drinks on coasters, the last one was the scotch.

"Here it is, madam," I said to Mrs. Tallulah Vaughn and placed the drink on her coaster. She looked at me, but her eyes, with her oversized sunglasses, were impossible to read.

"Honey, look at me," she said. "Do I look like I run a whore house? I am Miss Tallulah Conway, and you must never call me madam." I didn't say "a madam" but remained silent. The other ladies looked at each other but never spoke. The only Tallulah Conway I knew was a columnist for the *New Yorker*. I nodded and left, wishing to remain there to listen to what they discussed. If she was unmarried, what was her relationship with Mr. Vaughn? This required an investigation, and I was available. Let's face it I was a magnet for gossip and a few other things.

"My goodness," Mrs. West said. "The fox among the chickens, this will be entertaining." Was Miss Tallulah Conway attempting to irritate the other ladies, or she didn't give a damn? I decided she didn't give a damn, and I was enjoying my job.

"Look serious," Mrs. West said. Just when I found something enjoyable, Mrs. West had to end it. Next was croquet, the ladies against the men, which was sedate until our esteemed cabinet minister remarked about Miss Tallulah Conway's bottom as she bent over. She heard it when she turned around and struck her croquet ball into the minister's nether regions. That ended the game since Miss Tallulah Conway retired to her room after calling the minister "pig." Mr. Conrad Vaughn followed her. In the other corner, the minister was remonstrating with the host about "that God damn New York broad, who did she think she was?" As always, we butlers remained composed, dispensing drinks, and in the case of the cabinet minister, a double and an ice pack.

We rearranged the dinner seating, placing Mr. Conrad Vaughn and Miss Tallulah Conway at one end and the Faulkner's at the other. I served one part of the table and Mr. Ruskin the other. Things seemed under control when Mrs. Victoria Faulkner, the wife of the newly appointed cabinet minister, made a remark about "the rudeness of certain New Yorkers" without singling out Miss Tallulah Conway. Miss Tallulah Conway, alert and perky, whispered to Mr. Conrad Vaughn "how provincial some politicians' wives are." Of course, her whisper reached the ears of Mrs. Victoria Faulkner, who was about to respond when her husband whispered something in her ear. The man was a sneak since he kept what he said out of my hearing, but it had to a bribe. Perhaps a new mink coat or Cadillac if she would stop speaking to the New York bitch. After that, peace descended, like the recent one between the Egyptians and the British, French and Israelis.

After dinner, the men went to the game room to play poker, and the ladies, other than Miss Tallulah Conway, went to the living room to play bridge. Miss Tallulah Conway said she would be in the library to watch a movie on the television. When I served her a drink, the television was off and she was writing, perhaps steps for a successful revenge. She looked up and smiled.

"Mr. Jenkins, why do you do it?" she asked.

"What is that, Miss Conway?" I asked.

"Be a butler," she said.

"This is a disguise," I said. "I am a reporter working undercover to discover a murder."

"Reginald," Mrs. West said.

"I know I asked a silly question and got a silly answer," she said.

"Indeed" Miss Conway," I said. "Is there anything else I may get you?"

"No, Mr. Jenkins, nothing at all," Miss Tallulah Conway said. "Wait, do you have some Ex-Lax pills?"

"I will inquire," I said.

"If you find them, slip them into Mrs. Victoria Faulkner's drink," she said.

"I will need to consult with the butler in residence," I said.

"That was a joke," she said.

"Indeed," I said, and left the library. She should know better that revenge is a dish best served cold. As I was falling asleep, I remembered a story about another Tallulah, the actress Tallulah Bankhead. Miss Bankhead was infamous for not wearing underwear. While filming *Lifeboat*, the film crew complained to the director Alfred Hitchcock. I decided Tallulah ladies were exciting at a distance.

CHAPTER 25

The Ritz-Carlton Hotel and the Annoyance of Mr. Ruskin

Wednesday night festivities ended at midnight, and after we cleaned up, I was in my cot at one in the morning with boxes of support for my feet. My threat of a mongoose kept Daisy away, and, in the morning, Mrs. West let me sleep until my alarm woke me at seven. By seven-thirty, I was upstairs, and Mr. McGregor introduced me to the staff. The butlers ate outside, and once we finished Mr. Ruskin went inside the house. I was about to follow when Mr. McGregor said he wanted to speak to me.

"I didn't sleep last night and walked to one of the outside lounge chairs to sleep, but I still heard Mr. Ruskin," Mr. McGregor said. "He rumbled like a Sherman tank going uphill and I expect they heard him across the river or in Ottawa. We will drive at nine to get more food and liquor. We will park and visit the manager at the Ritz Carlton to make sure the menu and staff are under control for Friday night. He will want to invite us to lunch and under no circumstances are you to be funny. Do you understand?"

"Yes, Mr. McGregor," I said.

"You were funny yesterday, but today serious," he said.

"No more wisecracks," I said.

"Is that what they were?" asked Mr. McGregor.

"They grow on you," I said, "and are an acquired taste."

"Like cod liver oil," Mr. McGregor said.

"More like a single malt whisky," I said, causing Mr. McGregor to snort.

"I thought butlers were not permitted to snort," I said.

"This is a butler-to-butler discussion where all is revealed," Mr. McGregor said.

"Reginald, enough, but I am looking forward to seeing the Ritz Carlton," Mrs. West said. "They built it after I left Montreal." At nine, I learned the schedule, golf for the men and sightseeing and shopping for the ladies with a private guide and two cars. We shopped and were at the Ritz Carlton at eleven thirty and parked down the street in a parking garage.

"You need coveralls and boat shoes. Tomorrow, you take sandwiches, ice, and drinks to the Royal Saint Lawrence Yacht Club."

"Why?" I asked.

"You are the boat butler" Mr. McGregor said. "I decided that you, as the youngest butler deserved it."

"You drew straws without me" I said.

"No, I decided on your behalf" Mr. McGregor said. "I was a sergeant during the war" Mr. McGregor said.

"What has that got to do with me being the boat butler?" I asked.

"You are young and new, and I have a low bullshit tolerance" Mr. McGregor said. We walked to an Army and Navy store for coveralls, then to Ogilvie's, a department store for my boat shoes, sunglasses and a Panama hat. We went to the Ritz-Carlton Hotel for a three-hour lunch where I learned the manager loved opera. Well, that was it. I was Mrs. West's mouthpiece for Italian operas, the best Mozart operas and the most incredible opera singers. Then it was a discussion of the best Paris restaurants and when we finished our coffee with cognac, Mr. McGregor stared at me.

"I thought you were a rube. I had no idea of your

understanding opera or Paris." Mr. Forget insisted that one of his staff drive the station wagon to the residence and take a taxi back to the hotel. Jean even stayed to unload the food and liquor since Mr. Ruskin was in a bad mood which soon worsened. He was annoyed after Mr. McGregor described our meal and the wines. I thought Mr. McGregor was a little unfair until I saw the look he gave to Mr. Ruskin. After two nights without sleep, he had developed a murderous rage against Mr. Ruskin, so I tiptoed around this situation. Mr. McGregor left and a couple of minutes later Mr. Ruskin went to the bar and took out a whisky bottle and disappeared.

Ten minutes later Mr. McGregor asked for my help. Once we finished, I went for a nap. As I was falling off to sleep someone fell down the stairs. I went to help Mr. McGregor, then we set up his cot. After I fluffed his pillow and set the sheets and blanket, he collapsed on the cot.

I changed and went upstairs and found the ladies sitting outside. On a trip to make more drinks, I saw Mr. Ruskin sitting on a chair, holding a whisky bottle and glaring at me. I did not know where Mr. McGregor was, so I took the orders and made the drinks. Once I served the ladies, I explained Mr. McGregor was ill. Before I returned to the bar I went over to Mr. Ruskin

"What's your problem?" I asked. He stared at me and scowled.

"You and that Scot all comfy and what am I?" He asked. "Excluded, that's what I am. Rejected. Mr. George Ruskin will not to be trifled with."

"Getting rather lax," I said.

"What do you mean," Mr. Ruskin asked.

"You ended your sentence with a preposition," I said.

"Who cares, and I don't like lectures on grammar," Mr. Ruskin said.

"Fine, be like that," I said. "We were having lunch together; is that a sin?"

"Without me?" he asked.

"It was a tiny table, and you wouldn't fit," I said.

"Two chairs?" he asked.

"Three," I said.

"I could have sat with you," Mr. Ruskin said.

"Alas, no, the manager of the Ritz Carlton was in the third chair," I said. "He has an amazing knowledge of wine, opera and the best Paris restaurants."

"You are proper...."

"My parents are married," I said. "Must run, try to restrain yourself and work on your grammar; no one likes a party pooper."

"How can I be a party pooper if I was never at the party," Mr. Ruskin said. "You and Mr. McGregor are unpleasant."

"What is this, showing emotion?" I asked. "I thought butlers were serene and imperturbable. You are letting the team down and Jeeves would not approve."

"Whose Jeeves?" Mr. Ruskin asked.

"The most phlegmatic and imperturbable valet, created by none other than the master of humour, P. G. Wodehouse.

"Never heard of him," Mr. Ruskin said.

"More the pity, since once you have tasted the delights of Wodehouse, he will take your woes away," I said. "It appears you have woes a plenty."

"Bugger off," Mr. Ruskin said.

"Nothing worse than a belittling, bitter butler," I said, turned and walked away.

"How long did it take you to think of that one?" asked Mrs. West.

"I am a renowned wisecracking whizz," I said. "Aren't you pleased?"

"No," Mrs. West said. "Not at all. Reginald, that man should be removed from his position."

"You mean fired," I said.

"Yes, fired," Mrs. West said. "He is most unprofessional."

"And drunk," I said. There was no one in sight as I looked around.

"I thought butlers always rose above the fray and were

non-plussed, but Mr. Ruskin requires help," I said. "I wondered if the Butler's Guild will help."

"Oh, fiddlesticks Reginald, there is no Butler's Guild," Mrs. West said.

"There should be," I said. "I keep telling you, no one uses fiddlesticks anymore.

"I do," Mrs. West said. "And I don't care what you say." The ladies retired to their rooms, and I took away their drinks. The men arrived at ten and went upstairs to bed. I cleaned up and was asleep in the basement at eleven with Mr. McGregor in a separate cot. There was a loud crash at around one in the morning, so I walked upstairs to see Mr. Weatherby standing at the front door with an enormous smile.

"Do you know where Mr. McGregor is?" he asked. "He was not in his room."

"Mr. McGregor is in a cot in the basement," I said. "He has not slept for two nights."

"No doubt, and when he awakes, tell him I sent Mr. Ruskin to a hotel," Mr. Weatherby said. "He will be here in the morning but will not sleep in my house again. Good night Mr. Jenkins."

"Good night, sir," I said and returned to my cot in the basement. All was well with the Weatherby mansion, but I was unsure about the hotel where Mr. Ruskin will stay. Perhaps in the morning, I will nip to a bookstore and purchase a P. G. Wodehouse book for our morose butler, Mr. Ruskin. Knowing him he would not read it.

The following day, Mr. McGregor and I had our breakfast on the deck. We were enjoying our second cup of coffee when Mr. Ruskin arrived. He had a black eye and glared at us.

"Rough night," I asked.

"I'd rather not discuss it," Mr. Ruskin said. As proper butlers we said nothing but gave the courtesy nod and looked interested.

"At four in the morning there was a knock on my door. Outside in the corridor I met the man from the next room who objected to my snores" Mr. Ruskin said. "Then he took exception to my telling him there was nothing I could do, so I told him to bugger off." One maid who served him breakfast and was pouring him coffee spilled it and took a napkin to clean the table.

"The black eye was your fault," Mr. McGregor said, which caused Mr. Ruskin to frown.

"I'm told that when a fly lands in a Scotsman's drink, the Scotsman picks up the fly and tells it to regurgitate" Mr. Ruskin said. We didn't laugh.

"That was a joke" Mr. Ruskin said.

"A piss poor one" Mr. McGregor said. "No intelligent person calls someone Scottish a Scotsman, and you forgot about the Irishman and the Englishman. You ruined the punchline since it lands in his whisky. He picks up the fly, pinches it between two fingers while yelling: 'spit it out, you bastard, spit it out.' " This time I laughed which annoyed Mr. Ruskin.

"Have you heard the story of the actions of a gentleman?" Mr. Ruskin asked, but we said we didn't.

"A gentleman is one who knows how to play the bagpipes but doesn't," he said, smiling.

"Are you aware of the definition of a nincompoop?" asked Mr. McGregor.

"Dimwitted?" asked Mr. Ruskin

"A nincompoop is a fellow who tells stories that insults another man's heritage," Mr. McGregor said.

"It was a joke," Mr. Ruskin said.

"I play the bagpipes," Mr. McGregor said, "and you are a nincompoop. This morning Mary, a maid, found an empty bottle of whisky in the room where you sleep."

"Your bedroom as well," Mr. Ruskin said.

"I didn't sleep there last night," Mr. McGregor said.

"Where did you sleep?" Mr. Ruskin asked.

"That is none of your concern," Mr. McGregor said. "I slept in the basement."

"That is where Mr. Jenkins is staying," Mr. Ruskin said. "I bet I know what you were doing?" I stood up, and my six foot two was much bigger than Mr. Ruskin's five foot eight.

"We were sleeping, and any more insinuations, you will have a matched set of black eyes," I said and sat down.

"Goodness, what an awful man," Mrs. West said.

"It is a serious matter to drink Mr. Weatherby's liquor, and I trust you will not do it again. Now I need you to help load some supplies in a taxi."

"I will help Friday night, but I will not help you any other time."

"Fine, leave now," Mr. McGregor said. "I have the authority, and I am sure Mr. Jenkins will assist."

"With pleasure," I said and stood up.

"Good Reginald," Mrs. West said.

"I'll help," Mr. Ruskin said, looking up at me.

"Excellent," Mr. McGregor said. "I always find it pleasurable when three butlers work together harmoniously."

CHAPTER 26

The Souses Excursion

I changed, and we loaded the taxi. I had the keys, instructions for the location of the boat and how to turn on the power, and a note for the club. What could go wrong with a bunch of boozers on a boat, including the man operating the controls? Wrecks, sinkings or explosions but at least I knew how to swim and would remain sober. I thought of a Hardyism, not Thomas Hardy, but Oliver Hardy, "well, here's another nice mess I have gotten myself into." This was what he said to Stan Laurel after the usual mishap.

"The boat is a thirty-five-foot 1956 Chris Craft Constellation, one of the largest boats in the club, and make sure Mr. Weatherby remains sober," Mr. McGregor said.

"How am I going to do that? I asked.

"Less booze and more coffee," he said. That was an impossible task if Mr. Weatherby was anything like my boss. Once in the taxi, I looked out at the city.

"We had a motor launch at the Royal Canadian Yacht Club on Toronto Island. Douglas taught me to steer it and dock it," Mrs. West said. "It will bring back memories." Once we were out of the taxi inside the yacht club, I stood there with boxes and an ice chest. I wore sunglasses, a Panama hat, chinos, topsider boat shoes, a short sleeve blue shirt and a windbreaker. I had my overalls in a bag and looked in the reflections of a window to admire myself.

"Your Panama hat and sunglasses are fine, Reginald, but admiring yourself won't help. You are here to find out who murdered me," Mrs. West said. "Why is it whenever a young man purchases new clothes, they think they are more attractive to young ladies? That is not the case, and you are the same as you were with morning with your horrid pyjamas."

"Those pyjamas were a Christmas present from my mother," I said.

"They are appalling," Mrs. West said. "Pride is a sin, and a humble man looks down."

"Or walks into lampposts," I said.

"Fiddlesticks, Reginald, how am I ever to make you a better man?" Mrs. West asked.

"You have already," I said. "Other than my tendency to make jokes."

"I have, haven't I?" Mrs. West said.

"Yes," I said. "Thank you. Mrs. West said."

"We are on this journey together and I don't know why, but I couldn't have found a better person to share it with," Mrs. West said.

"That was the nicest thing you could have told me," I said, "and it is true."

"I mean it but get on with finding out who brought my life to an end," Mrs. West said.

"Working on it," I said. "I don't understand why someone murdered you. You are a nice spirit and I assume were that as a person."

"Perhaps I am, but I wasn't always," Mrs. West said. "I was unkind, selfish and sometimes acted horribly."

"What happened?" I asked.

"I died," she said, "that's what happened, and I have a new perspective on life which came rather late, since I am dead. Well, not quite dead since we are connected." I ended this discussion since I didn't want to get so attached to Mrs. West that I would lose my detachment and make it personal. I realized I was long past that point.

"I may need you to help me with the boat," I said.

"It is simple" she said. "The controls are forward, neutral and reverse." A man came up, and told me where to find a wagon, and pointed out where they docked the *Griffin*. A strange name for a boat, named after a creature, that was part lion and part eagle. Who knows how many drinks Mr. Weatherby had to pick that name, or was it his secret name for his wife? Being a butler gave me new insights into the rich and famous, and none of it was favourable. I pulled the four-wheeled wagon to the dock, unloaded the supplies and unlocked the cabin door.

"The first thing is to go to the top overlooking the cabin and start the engine," Mrs. West said. "Before you do it put it in neutral. Above the steering wheel are four gauges. Make sure the boat is full of gas and check the oil pressure. There are two Chrysler engines, so you will hear quite the noise." I turned the switch, and the engines started. The fuel gauge showed full, and the oil gauge showed oil. I turned it off, and after placing food and beer in the refrigerator, I made coffee, put on my coveralls and cleaned the boat. Once I was done, I changed out of my coveralls into my butler wear. I went to the clubhouse and got another two bags of ice, which I put in the sink.

"Go to the chart table and study the charts" Mrs. West said. "I expect George will want to head west to the Lake of Two Mountains. I remember boating when I was in Montreal." Ten minutes later, I noticed Mr. Weatherby stepping on board, followed by Mr. Faulkner, Mr. Boulton and my boss.

"Coffee or orange juice, sirs," I said.

"Mr. Jenkins, you have me confused with someone else" Mr. Weatherby said. "Bloody Marys for us."

"Very good, sir," I said. By the time I had them ready, Mr. Weatherby moved the boat, so I waited until we were in the channel before I handed out the drinks. I was the only one with a hat, and it was a sunny day.

"Mr. Jenkins," Mr. Weatherby said. "Take the steering

wheel and watch the compass to head west. Stay well offshore, go around sailboats, slow when you see an approaching boat and stay at fifteen miles an hour. We will go through Senneville to the Lake of Two Mountains and then have lunch at the Senneville Yacht Club. If you have a problem, call me."

"Yes, sir," grabbed the wheel, and sat on the chair holding the wheel, checked the speed and looked at the gauges. There were three sailboats ahead, and I watched them.

"What a joy," Mrs. West said. "Reginald, you should buy a boat." I looked around but the men were down below in the cabin, doing the usual, boozing, talking and playing poker.

"With what money?" I asked.

"A sailboat would be four hundred dollars, and the membership is one hundred dollars to join and another one hundred dollars for fees each year." The sailboats passed us, and we continued west.

"I'll think about it" I said. An hour alter I slowed since the channel was narrowing.

"That is Senneville" Mrs. West said. "Watch for boats coming the other way." Once I was on the Lake of Two Mountains, Mr. Weatherby stepped up on the deck, followed by Mr. West, and sat on the seats.

"I can take politics in small doses, so let them argue," Mr. Weatherby said. "This is the Lake of Two Mountains. Pretty, isn't it?" Mr. West nodded.

"I wrote to you after your mother died, but I am sorry for your loss," Mr. Weatherby said.

"Reginald, pay attention," Mrs. West said.

"It was a loss and a shock," Mr. West said. "I didn't expect it since mother insisted, she was fine. I didn't agree with that, but what could I do? We were not on the best of terms, but she was quite the lady."

"Where were you the morning I died and saying to Marigold 'about time', but you can't confess that to a good friend" Mrs. West said.

"She was," Mr. Weatherby said. "I can remember her

getting after me when I first visited your house."

"My mother always preferred my older brother William, who died in France," Mr. West said. "She expected me to take after him, but I couldn't. She didn't like Marigold."

"Do you know why she died?" asked Mr. Weatherby.

"Old age," Mr. West said.

"Fiddlesticks, no one dies of old age," Mrs. West said.

"No one dies of old age," Mr. Weatherby said.

"I always liked George," Mrs. West said.

"It must have been her heart, but who knows," Mr. West said.

"My heart was fine" Mrs. West said. "The autopsy would have shown the cause, but you refused it." They moved on to other topics.

We were back at the Senneville Yacht Club, where Mr. Weatherby told me to grab the bow and stern lines and jump. I tied the bow line the way Mrs. West told me and then the stern line. The last off the boat was Mr. Weatherby, who looked at the knots and shrugged. Mr. Weatherby's and Mr. West's faces and arms were red. They did not invite me to the yacht club, so I stayed on board.

"Douglas said he didn't expect it, but he told the police sergeant that he did," Mrs. West said.

"Mrs. West, with respect, what your son told Mr. Weatherby differs from what he told the police, but your son did not admit murdering you. He said he didn't agree you were fine, but that doesn't get us very far," I said. "Unless I hear your son confessing to his wife, I have nothing."

"You still need to talk to her when she is drinking," Mrs. West said.

"The drinking part will happen, but a private moment with her worries me," I said.

"Obtain her admission and get out," Mrs. West said.

"You mean run out with Mr. West chasing with a gun" I said

"Fiddlesticks, you will pick a time when he is away" Mrs.

West said,

"That is what worries me" I said. I took out a sandwich and a soft drink from the fridge and ate lunch. At three, they returned, and once the boat was back in the channel, I was back at the wheel. When I had the boat in the open lake, I looked in the cabin to see everyone asleep. Within the hour, I was outside the Royal St. Lawrence Yacht Club, so I put it in neutral and stepped below to wake Mr. Weatherby. After three tries, I stepped to the upper deck and sat there.

"Put down the bumpers on both sides of the boat and place the bow and stern lines together," Mrs. West said. Once I did that, I was back up at the wheel.

"Head in at four miles per hour; note the wind will push the boat once you have stopped," Mrs. West said. I followed her instructions, including reversing the boat and using the wheel, put it in neutral and jumped on the deck to tie the boat. I turned off the engine, took the keys to the boat, found the keys to the car, grabbed the wagon, and loaded up to take to the car. At the car I put everything in the large trunk. Back at the boat I got Mr. Weatherby up.

"Mr. Jenkins, we are not moving," he said.

"Indeed, sir, that is because I docked the boat, and supplies are in the car," I said.

"You did that?" asked Mr. Weatherby.

"Yes, sir," I said.

"Amazing, but let me deal with what is important?" Mr. Weatherby asked.

"What is that sir?" I asked.

"It was on the tip of my tongue but gone," Mr. Weatherby said.

"That happens to all of us, sir," I said.

"Even to a butler?" Mr. Weatherby asked.

"I should have mentioned some of us" I said.

"I knew it butlers are, damn I can't think of the word".

"Indispensable?" I asked.

"Not the word," Mr. Weatherby said.

"Imperturbable?" I asked. I quite liked imperturbable and would try and use it more.

"No," Mr. West said.

"Accomplished?" I asked.

"Annoying," Mr. Weatherby said.

"Why did you name your boat the *Griffin*?" I asked.

"That is a long story but not for now," Mr. Weatherby said. "I must have fallen asleep."

"I tried to wake you on three occasions, but without success."

"How strange," Mr. Weatherby said.

"Indeed, sir, scotch does that," I said. "I have often found that with Mr. West."

"You would, wouldn't you," Mr. Weatherby said.

"Reginald, butlers, never discuss their employer's faults," Mrs. West said.

"It's true," I said.

"What's true Mr. Jenkins?" Mr. Weatherby asked.

"It's true you have a magnificent boat," I said.

"Reginald, stop being obsequious," Mrs. West said.

"I had to explain the sentence," I said. Sometimes she really needs to pay attention.

"What?" asked Mr. West. "I am not following you; what sentence?"

"Twin engines give the boat such power," I said.

"I have difficulty following your thoughts. It's like listening to my wife," Mr. Weatherby said.

"Indeed, sir," I said.

"I'm glad you enjoyed it," Mr. Weatherby said. "Where did you learn to use a boat?"

"My instructor had experience at the Royal Canadian Yacht Club," I said.

"Well, fancy that," Mr. West said. "Good job, Mr. Jenkins. You drive the car, I direct, and I play the music." I brought the other boaters to the car, and we were home by five, listening to the big band music at high volume. It was a quiet dinner;

everyone was in bed by nine, and I was alone in the basement. Well, not quite; I had no idea where the snake was. As I was drifting off to sleep, I realized Mr. Weatherby, escorting his band of heavy imbibers, should rename the boat either *Liver Worst*. That was more fitting than *Griffin*.

CHAPTER 27

Misbehaving

Early Friday morning, I fell out of the cot. Of all the places to land, a cement floor was the worst, and I did not know what caused it. I was alone, so I couldn't blame an amorous lady and decided that if I found a lustful lady, a cot was the last place to do it.

"That must have hurt?" Mrs. West asked, always solicitous about my well-being.

"You try sleeping in one when your feet are four inches too long," I said.

"You didn't fall off the end but from the side," Mrs. West said.

"Picky, but it still hurts, and I did not swear," I said as I stood and felt for sore spots. "Think of all the swear words I could have used."

"Yes Reginald, that is commendable," Mrs. West said.

"I have been on my best behaviour so today I shall misbehave," I said. "Falling out of the cot was a sign."

"Reginald how was falling out of your cot a sign?" asked Mrs. West.

"I restrained from swearing, so I need a reward," I said.

"If you are fired that will not solve who murdered me," Mrs. West said.

"No, but think of the fun I will have," I said.

"When you solve this case, take a trip to Paris and do fun things there like dance the can-can," Mrs. West said.

"Do they still dance the can-can?" I asked.

"I have no idea Reginald, so think of what else will entertain you," Mrs. West said. That set me thinking, and I decided what I wanted would shock Mrs. West, so I remained quiet. I set up the cot, took a shower and changed into butler wear. Breakfast was on the deck with Mr. McGregor, who was reading a paper. I sat down with a cup of coffee.

"Did you ever misbehave?" I asked.

"I'm like the Fats Waller song, 'Ain't Misbehaving,' " Mr. McGregor said.

"Never," I asked.

"Well, hardly ever" and Mr. McGregor laughed.

"What's so funny" I asked.

"In the light opera *H.M.S. Pinafore*, Captain Corcoran was asked if he was ever sick at sea" Mr. McGregor said. "Captain Corcoran was asked 'what never' and he replied, 'well hardly ever.' You need to watch it."

"So, Mr. McGregor, a sergeant in the army never misbehaved?" I asked.

"If I did, I wouldn't share that with you," Mr. McGregor said, still reading the paper. He looked up and smiled.

"There was one occasion on leave in 1944 in France when I was with a young lady," Mr. McGregor said. "I will spare you the details but never use olive oil on your groundsheet since it smells. The problem was in the army your groundsheet is also your poncho, and my platoon kept grumbling about the smell to their sergeant. I had to listen to them griping since I was the sergeant." I had a growing respect for Mr. McGregor.

"My goodness," Mrs. West said. "How disgusting."

"Yes," I said.

"You said yes?" asked Mr. McGregor?"

"Yes, and you have my total admiration," I said.

"Thank you," Mr. McGregor said.

"Reginald, that is dreadful," Mrs. West said.

"What did you do for an encore?" I asked.

"Butlers must never tell," Mr. McGregor said.

"Indeed," I said.

"Quite so," Mr. McGregor said.

"Reginald, stop it," Mrs. West said. I decided I had created enough mischief and took my coffee cup to the kitchen. I told the ladies how beautiful they were in both languages and thanked them for breakfast. You never knew which of them might find it a delight to spend time with an available butler. I hung around the kitchen in my butler wear, smiling and looking approachable. I ensured I wasn't leering or winking, but that ended when the cook told me to leave, so I left. She said it to me in French, but I think it meant to buzz off or jump in a toilet. I was unsure, but since she was using a large knife, I felt it best not to return for a translation. I was learning new skills, like Napoleon and his trip to Moscow, and when to make a decisive retreat. The Czar was a spoilsport, burning Moscow and hiding garlic and baguettes.

As soon as Mr. West was up on Friday morning, I reminded him I had to pack his bags this afternoon. He needed to keep his formal wear, his pyjamas and what he would wear on Saturday. I added I would pack his suitcase at eight the following day and take a taxi to the station since the train would leave at ten on Saturday morning. He looked at me and nodded, but I worried he was oblivious to what I had said and explaining charades would take too long. I felt like mouthing ten tomorrow but decided he was too thick and wouldn't understand.

"Your mistake was not telling Marigold," Mrs. West said as I walked outside.

"Where is she?" I asked.

"Sleeping, then shopping," Mrs. West said. After that, I was busy. I had no idea how much effort went into a large party. At three, Mr. McGregor informed me that the lifeguard had bowed out, and could I swim and give mouth-to-mouth resuscitation?

"Only to good-looking women," I said.

"If you can give that to the attractive ladies, you can do it to everyone, even to Senator McNaughton who is the size of an overstuffed pig," Mr. McGregor said. "Your desire to be humorous trapped you. You will be the one to do the rescue, and no, you will not be serving drinks in a bathing suit. Formal wear only."

"I didn't pack a bathing suit," I said. "How heavy is the senator?"

"Over three hundred pounds," Mr. McGregor said.

"We will need a block and tackle and perhaps drain the swimming pool if he takes a dive," I said.

"I hope not," Mr. McGregor said.

"I must offer up something from the *Goon Show*, 'beware the frenzied fool by the swimming pool' " I said.

"You are referring to the senator," Mr. McGregor said.

"Maybe," I said. "If it is a senator, it would be the honourable frenzied fool."

"Much better; which one said it?" Mr. McGregor asked.

"I believe Neddie Seagoon," I said.

"This calls for another one from the *Goon Show*," Mr. McGregor said, 'you silly, twisted boy, you' "

"Grytpype Thynne," I said.

"Enough with this frivolity. Back to butler duties," Mr. West said.

"Thank goodness," Mrs. West said.

"Must we?" I asked. "I can keep going.

"I know that but duty calls" Mr. McGregor said.

"It is about time," Mrs. West said. "Such nonsense."

"It's an acquired taste," I said.

"It is," Mr. McGregor said. "Have you seen Mr. Ruskin?"

"No," I said. "Maybe he is trapped in a piano."

"No more plots from the *Goon Show*" Mr. McGregor said.

"And there's more where that came from," I said with another classic Goonism usually said by Moriarty.

"Have pity on a downtrodden butler and no more," Mr. McGregor said.

"Or what?" I asked.

"Or else," Mr. McGregor said. He looked haggard, worrying about his duties and butler two. I had Gooned him as far as I could, so butler duties it would be.

"Of course, forgive a Butler's curse" I said. Mr. McGregor eyed me, not sure if that was a joke or I was sincere, and I wasn't sure myself.

"What curse?" Mr. McGregor asked, raising one eyebrow. They taught butlers that in butler school along with polishing silver and sampling scotch.

"The wisecracking curse" I said.

"There is only one solution" Mr. McGregor said.

"What is that?" I asked.

"Keep them bottled up and release them upon your return to Toronto" Mr. McGregor said. "Preferably away from innocent women, children and dogs."

"Children and dogs wouldn't understand my jokes," I said.

"I'm not sure I do myself," Mr. McGregor said.

"I don't wish to know that" I said throwing in another Goonism, but I knew I would be ignored. One wisecrack too many.

"Mr. Ruskin is not happy, his hotel advised him to move out" Mr. McGregor said.

"Due to snoring or drinking?" I asked.

"I have no idea" Mr. McGregor said. "Perhaps both."

"You know what happens to little lambs that go astray" I said.

"I am afraid to ask" Mr. McGregor said.

"They become black sheep," I said.

"Who become a family disgrace," Mr. McGregor said.

"Quite right, but in this case a disgrace to the Butler's Guild," I said.

"There is no Butler's Guild," Mr. McGregor said.

"I told you that," Mrs. West said.

"There should be," I said.

"He is a disgrace as a butler" Mr. McGregor said.

"Indeed," throwing in a butlerism "and what he is doing or

undoing," I said.

"I wish you had not said the last part," Mr. McGregor said.

"Avoiding bad omens, are you?" I asked.

"Over time, I find it best not to attract bad luck," Mr. McGregor said.

"When did he go out?" I asked.

"Eight this morning, and it is now three in the afternoon," Mr. McGregor said.

"Is he lost?" I asked.

"Butler two is eight blocks from the house and has the address and telephone number," Mr. McGregor said.

"Mr. Ruskin is avoiding us," I said. "He was upset that we didn't include him for lunch."

"The table was too small" Mr. McGregor said.

"It was tiny, and I told him that but for some reason he was annoyed" I said. "Butlers must be imperturbable."

"Of all available words, you used that one. Mr. McGregor said. "Why not calm and composed?"

"Two words" I said. "I like the word and by using imperturbable I am describing Jeeves."

"A fictional creation" Mr. McGregor said.

"Yes, but a great one" I said. "Are there taverns in the area?"

"Too many," Mr. McGregor said. "And they open early."

"Not good," I said. "He drained the scotch bottle yesterday?"

"I remember, unfortunately," said Mr. McGregor.

"It is the beginning of a butler's debauchery," I said. "You know the song "What will you do with a Drunken Sailor." Here, it will be "What will you do with a Drunken Butler?"

"I will bar him from the estate," Mr. McGregor said.

"He might sit outside the estate and yell McGregor is a nincompoop" I said.

"I will take the risk" Mr. McGregor said. "If I dodged bullets I can put up with the jabbering of an inebriated buffoon."

"Do you have friendly relationships with the local constabulary?" I asked

"Ah yes, I will call to put them on notice," Mr. McGregor said. "I told them about the party."

"Failing that, we can tie him in the basement," I said.

"I perceived I could rely on you, Mr. Jenkins," Mr. McGregor said. "Mr. Weatherby was impressed by how you docked the boat, but you were supposed to keep him sober."

"I never had the chance," I said. "I was at the steering wheel, and Mr. Weatherby informed me he would serve the drinks."

"How many?" asked Mr. McGregor.

"No idea but he managed to do an adequate job," I said.

"To become drunk" Mr. McGregor said.

"Not the proper description" I said. "Extremely drunk."

"What is the difference, drunk is drunk" Mr. McGregor said.

"Jigger by jigger" I said. "What should I have done, throw the bottles overboard?"

"That would be a waste," Mr. McGregor said. "You remove some of the alcohol from the bottles and replace them with water."

"Where do you put the alcohol?" I asked.

"You are new to this," Mr. McGregor said.

I looked around to see Mr. Ruskin standing about three feet away and grinning. He was in his formal wear, with his bow tie undone. His nose was red, either due to the sun or too much beer, but he was never outside.

"Hello, my band of merry butters, butter two reporting," Mr. Ruskin said, and had difficulty pronouncing his words.

"You mean butler," I said.

"What?" asked Mr. Ruskin.

"You said butter," I said.

"No, I didn't," Mr. Butler said. "Why would I say butter since I am a butter? Oh, beg pardon, I see what you mean, it's that illusive letter."

"Catches us when drinking, like sit and shit," I said. "Or a silent p, in swimming."

"Not helping Mr. Jenkins," Mr. McGregor said.

"Zip my lip, Mr. McGregor?" I asked.

"An excellent idea, Mr. Jenkins," Mr. McGregor said.

"Done, Mr. McGregor," I said.

"Good, Mr. Jenkins," Mr. McGregor said.

"You have been drinking," Mr. McGregor said, looking at Mr. Ruskin.

"Who me?" asked Mr. Ruskin.

"You," Mr. McGregor said.

"Maybe," Mr. Ruskin said.

"You are drunk," Mr. McGregor said.

"Maybe," Mr. Ruskin said.

"You will go to the kitchen and have coffee," Mr. McGregor said.

"Nope, I want a beer," Mr. Ruskin said.

"You will return to your hotel and remain there or drink coffee," Mr. McGregor said.

"Nope, I want a beer," Mr. Ruskin said.

"If you don't drink coffee or go back to your hotel, Mr. Jenkins will take you to the basement and tie you," Mr. McGregor said.

"I'd like to see him try," Mr. Ruskin said.

"A challenge, is it?" Mr. McGregor asked. Mr. Ruskin blew him a raspberry, but Mr. McGregor ignored the rude gesture and walked ten feet away.

"A word, Mr. Jenkins," Mr. McGregor said, so I walked over to join him.

"Were you in the army?" asked Mr. McGregor, looking at me.

"Two years of officer training," I said.

"You learned drill?" Mr. McGregor asked.

"Hours on a parade square with an unforgiving sergeant," I said. "I can drill in my sleep."

"Ruskin starts with R, as does rifle," Mr. McGregor said. "Think of him as a heavy .303 Lee Enfield, so you know what to do. Quick march," shouted Mr. McGregor in a most sergeant-like fashion. I marched over and heard the command, "halt," and stomped my feet by Mr. Ruskin. My heavy oxford shoes made Mr. Ruskin jump since it was quite the noise on the concrete.

"Stop that," Mr. Ruskin said.

"You forgot to say please," I said.

"Piss off," Mr. Ruskin said.

"Such inappropriate behaviour; I will report you to the Butler's Guild," I said.

"What?" Asked Mr. Ruskin. "Never heard of it."

"Membership is by invitation only to the best of the best, so they didn't invite you," I said. "You must be of excellent character, which you are not."

"You are a...."

"An excellent fellow," I said.

"That wasn't it," Mr. Ruskin said, scratching his head, then blew a raspberry.

"Wait for it, wait for it," shouted Mr. McGregor, "shoulder arms." I grabbed Mr. Ruskin and put him over my shoulder. He yelled and tried to hit me when Mr. McGregor shouted, "stop that," which worked.

"Can I order arms and drop him?" I asked.

"You are joking, aren't you?" cried Mr. Ruskin.

"Maybe," I said.

"Not now" Mr. McGregor said. "Perhaps later, so let us head to the basement." The kitchen was full of women. I gave them a smile to let them understand that everything was under control and not to worry. I carried him downstairs to the basement, followed by Mr. McGregor, and put him on the toilet since he might be sick. He started singing, then stopped and blew another raspberry. Mr. McGregor put his arms on my arm and escorted me away from Mr. Ruskin. We watched as Mr. Ruskin stood.

"Sit down, you damn fool, before you fall down," shouted Mr. McGregor, which he did.

"You fellows aren't very nice," Mr. Ruskin said, but we ignored him.

"Find some rope, Mr. Jenkins," Mr. McGregor said and walked back to Mr. Ruskin. While I searched, I heard footsteps and returned to stand next to Mr. McGregor. Mr. Weatherby had reached the bottom and looked at us.

"Why are you three down here?" asked Mr. Weatherby.

"They kidnapped me, sir," said Mr. Ruskin, who hiccupped. He had the sense to retract his tongue but still grinned. This was the occasion to be serious, but that ship had passed. Mr. Ruskin was pie-eyed, and I wondered how he got to the residence. During the plague years, they would take the person suspected of the disease in a cart to the Pest House. The man walking in front would proclaim "unclean, unclean," but in this case, it would be "drunk, drunk" as they pushed Mr. Ruskin here.

"Drunk, is he?" asked Mr. Weatherby.

"Yes sir," Mr. McGregor said.

"Very drunk?" Mr. Weatherby asked.

"I believe so, sir," Mr. McGregor said.

"Do you know they sell quarts bottles of beer here?" Mr. Ruskin said. "I learned an expression 'une grosse Molson,' " snatching away any possibility of mercy.

"What do you plan to do with him?" asked Mr. Weatherby.

"Tie him, since he refuses to return to his hotel or drink coffee," Mr. McGregor said. "He wants beer."

"I see," said Mr. Weatherby, looking at Mr. Ruskin. "I am calling a cab for you to go to your hotel. If you are not on it or return here, I will have you arrested and thrown in jail. Do you understand?"

"Yes, sir," Mr. Ruskin said.

"Call a cab and have Mr. Jenkins do the honours with Mr. Ruskin," Mr. Weatherby said. "Mr. Jenkins seems to know what to do with my boat, so he should be able to handle a drunken butler." I did the honours, and Mr. Weatherby gave me money for the cab. I have no idea what happened with Mr. Ruskin, a nervous breakdown, the influence of too much alcohol, or a broken heart, but it finished him as a butler. It was unfortunate that Mr. Weatherby appeared. Otherwise, we could have tied him and kept the scandal away from our employers. But that did not happen, and once I was back at the residence, lifting and hauling it reminded me of Old Man River, "tote that barge, lift that bail and in Mr. Ruskin's case, get a little drunk and land in jail." Mr. McGregor told me to expect sixteen graduates and their wives, dates or others, totalling thirty-two, not including those staying here.

I wondered what constituted others but left it alone. At four, I knocked on the West's bedroom, but Mr. West shouted he was sleeping. Interesting, he could do that and yell at the same time. At six, we were ready as the pianist began his mellow music with the lady singer and her dulcet tones. Mr. McGregor told me the band would start at nine.

We had been lucky with the weather, and tonight not a cloud in the sky, but it was still hot and wearing formal wear made it unbearable. They gave me soup and a sandwich at five, so I wasn't hungry and sipped water. By seven, I was busier than a cat burying poop on a marble floor. At eighty-thirty, everyone ate dinner, and the waiters delivered wine to the tables by the wagon load. I went to the basement to relieve myself. I found Mrs. Marigold West lying on my cot, and unlike me, she was the right size for the cot.

"Hello Jenkins, I was waiting for you," Mrs. Marigold West said.

"Madam this will be a scandal since the kitchen staff saw you" I said.

"I used the other staircase" Mrs. Marigold West said.

"What other staircase?" I asked.

"Never mind that, I have more important things to do" she said.

"Operating the washing machine?" I asked.

"Jenkins, enough." Mrs. Marigold West said.

"Madam, you must leave," I said.

"Oh, I don't think so," she said. "It is time we got to know each other. You have a big play room but that can be romantic once you get candles. Where is your bed?"

"Only the cot," I said.

"Tight but serviceable," Mrs. Marigold West said.

"Madam, this is wrong," I said.

"Au contraire, I think it's right" Mrs. Marigold West said. "Playing hard to get? I can fix that. The other Jenkins was no fun, but you are my challenge."

"Madam, I assure you I am no fun," I said as she almost fell off the cot.

"I took an oath of celibacy," I said as she grabbed my upper leg.

"Let me touch," she said. "Not much of an oath, you naughty boy," as I jumped away.

"You want me, admit it," Mrs. Marigold West said.

"No, madam, I do not," I said. "It would be most inappropriate."

"Come here Jenkins; you need a real woman," she said.

"That would violate my Boy Scout oath," I said.

"You are a little old to be a Boy Scout and I thought it was to be prepared," Mrs. Marigold West said. "I am prepared."

"I'm not," I said. "Campfires or sharpening stakes, but not this. It would be unfair to my employer, Mr. West, your husband."

"Douglas," she said. "Why his name?"

"That's the one you remember him, the one who loves you with all his heart," I said, hoping to refresh her memory.

"He is not here, but you are," Mrs. Marigold West said.

"Tell her you are aware she spent the housekeeping money on a mink coat," Mrs. West said.

"You used the housekeeping money on a mink coat," I said. "Shall I tell your husband?"

"That is underhanded, Jenkins," Mrs. Marigold West said.

"Indeed, it is, madam, but you left me no choice," I said.

"How do you know that?" Mrs. Marigold West said as she stood.

"Goodbye madam," I said and watched her leave.

"Who told you that?" I asked.

"She was bragging with a friend, but I am surprised she hasn't told Douglas," Mrs. West said. Once Mrs. Marigold West was gone, I thanked Mrs. West and did what I came down to do, washed my hands and returned to the bar. The band played and couples danced. The demand lessened at two and then people left. We cleaned up at three, and I was in bed at five with an alarm set for seven. It was quite the day and night. I learned something about my fellow butlers and avoided something nasty with my employer's wife.

CHAPTER 28

Departure for Toronto

At seven the following morning, I took a shower, dressed in butler wear, and packed my bags. I had breakfast, and at eight, I went to Mr. West's bedroom and knocked to say I was there to pack his bags. After I knocked three times, I heard Mr. West tell me to go away. I returned at eight-thirty where I was told to leave and at nine, on the third knock, I told him I had to get the bags to the station, so I needed to pack them.

"Bugger off, Jenkins, and go away," Mr. West said. That was a redundancy, but I would not tell him, so I returned to the kitchen and advised Mr. McGregor.

"Right then, I will call a taxi, take the tickets, and exchange them for tomorrow," which is what I did. At twelve, a maid told me that Mr. West wanted to see me in his bedroom. I knocked on the door, and he told me to enter.

"We missed the train," Mr. West said.

"Yes, sir," I said. "It left at ten."

"It is now twelve," Mr. West said.

"Five past twelve, sir," I said.

"I don't care what time it is since the train has gone," Mr. West said.

"Indeed, sir, it has," I said.

"And we are not on it," he said. "Did you forget

something?"

"No sir" I said. I decided not to say anything further. He might forget this conversation and my telling him that he was the cause would not help.

"We were to be on that train" Mr. West said.

"Very true, sir" I said.

"This is your fault," he said. He remembered, and I knew what was coming.

"Sir, I advised you yesterday morning that I needed to pack your suitcase at four on Friday, other than your formal wear, your pyjamas and what you were to wear today," I said. "Sir, you told me to go away. This morning I knocked at your door at eight, eight-thirty and nine. They were loud knocks, and on the first and second occasion, you told me to go away. On the third occasion, you told me to bugger off and go away, which I interpreted to mean the same thing. I assume I was correct on that, and I regret not going in your room and pulling you out of bed."

"You are fired," Mr. West said. I decided he was a schnook who didn't deserve a butler, so I would put his name forward to the B.B.B.B., the butler's blacklist of bad bosses. That was one step above the B.B.B., the Better Business Bureau.

"Very good sir," I said. "I will give the tickets for tomorrow's train to Mr. McGregor and find a hotel." I walked to the door and closed it and went down the stairs. I met Mr. McGregor in his office. Once he closed the door, I told him what had happened. He laughed and told me I could stay tonight in the basement, and he would take me out. He added the snake would be lonely and needed company. I was sitting drinking coffee on the deck when Mr. Weatherby sat down.

"A butler who can drive my boat, my car, dock my boat and handle idiots is fine by my books. Douglas is lucky to have you," Mr. Weatherby said. "Has he fired you before?"

"Yes sir," I said.

"Did he rehire you?"

"Yes sir," I said.

"Two things may happen; either he will rehire you or forget he fired you," Mr. Weatherby said. "If you are unemployed by suppertime, I will speak to him."

"Thank you, sir," I said. At four, I knocked on the door, and Mr. West opened it.

"I am here to pack your bags, and tomorrow's tickets are ready," I said.

"I will be downstairs if you need me," Mr. West said. On Saturday night, Mr. McGregor took me to Saint Laurent Boulevard, called the Main, where we drank beer in his favourite taverns and ate hot dogs called steamies, at the Montreal Pool Room.

Sunday morning, Mr. McGregor drove me to the station at nine and shook my hand. I hired a porter who took the bags to the baggage car, gave me a receipt, and I tipped him. I found a bookstore at the train station and loaded up on P. G. Wodehouse. Once I helped my employer and wife to the first-class car, I hopped aboard my steerage carriage. I watched the train leave downtown Montreal and then we were in the suburbs. Once Jane fell asleep, I read out two choice ones from P. G. Wodehouse.

" 'He had the look of one who had drunk the cup of life and found a dead beetle at the bottom.' "

"Really, Reginald," Mrs. Wests said.

"What about this one? 'She looked as if she had been poured into her clothes and forgotten to say when?' "

"That is enough, Reginald. I do not know why you find that writer humorous?" Mrs. West asked.

"He is absurd and light and sometimes that is what I want," I said. "Every time I finish a Russian novel I look around for a poison or a handgun to end it all."

"Then read and enjoy," Mrs. West said.

"You are no fun," I said.

"Why?" Mrs. West asked.

"Half the fun was in annoying you," I said as Jane woke up.

"Who were you talking to" she asked

"I enjoy reading P. G. Wodehouse out loud," I said.

"Read me one," Jane asked.

" 'A melancholy-looking man, he had the appearance of one who has searched for the leak in life's gas pipe with a lighted candle,' " I said.

"That's not funny," Jane said.

"It's an acquired taste," I said and decided that I would divide the world in two, those that liked P. G. Wodehouse and those that didn't. I vowed never to read him out loud, no matter what was the heartfelt plea. Lunch was a choice between a cheese sandwich on stale white bread or a ham and cheese sandwich on stale white bread. I chose the cheese sandwich, washed down with a soft drink. Jane said she would wait, then after watching me eat, she wasn't hungry. At Union Station, I hired a porter, and we took the bags, boxes and garment bags to a taxi, where I waited for Jane to march up to me.

"Never mind what they did or said; hop in front." Once the driver and I were in the front seat, we headed north to the West residence. I paid and, with the driver, carried the bags inside. Once the driver left, I closed the door with three trips, carried the bags upstairs to their bedroom, unpacked, put items in the laundry basket, set things aside for the dry cleaners and took the suitcases to the basement. When they went upstairs to bed, I changed and packed my bags. I wrote that I was entitled to two days off, and my mother needed me so that I would be away Monday and Tuesday.

I called a taxi, and as I waited, my thoughts turned to what I required. The report from the pharmacist, finding the mistress, real estate purchases and my story for the *Toronto Mirror.* I had been away long enough with a murderer to find. It was okay if Mr. West fired me since I didn't think Mr. West murdered his mother. This would depend on observing Miss Walker, the alleged mistress of Mr. West, her size, whether she was right-handed and hearing her.

I thought it ironic that the potential guilt or innocence of Mr. West depended on his little honey. That little honey might be the spitfire, so I must exercise extreme caution. If she was the spitfire, it took me two days before I could comfortably sit after my shoe encounter. How could I make her angry enough for her to say, bastard? I would have to think about that. If Jane was correct, perhaps reading P. G. Wodehouse to her might do it. I could also survey what footwear women wore.

"Miss, could you tell me if you have sharp pointed shoes? If you have, do you use them for walking, kicking a man in his nether regions, or both?" That should do the trick.

CHAPTER 29

The Gumshoe

When I arrived home Sunday night, there were lights on next store. I carried in my bags and made myself a bowl of Wheaties, but Martha must have given up on me. I had been gone a week and never told her I was going. I was better than a cockroach in killing Martha's interest in me.

The following day, Monday, July 8, I put on my casual clothes and, after breakfast, called a locksmith. He had just arrived at his shop, and I promised him an extra five dollars if he could come now and gave him my address. I called Big Fish and asked if he had the pharmacist report, and he said he did. I called my insurance agent, learned what I owed, and wrote out a cheque which I would mail. The locksmith arrived, and once he finished, he gave me my new keys, and I paid him. I called my lawyer's office and obtained an appointment for two.

I locked the door and caught the Queen Streetcar to Fred's garage. Fred explained that they had not finished the roof, but the rest of the car was done.

"A fellow wanted your motorcycle, and I had the papers, so I sold it," Fred said. "You bought it for two hundred dollars, and I sold it for three hundred. My commission is twenty-five dollars, so you have two hundred and seventy-five dollars. It just so happens that I have a 1952 Light Green Pontiac Catalina Coup for sale for two-hundred and seventy-five dollars with new tires. Rain is coming, and you need to stay dry. I have already done the transfer. Call your insurance agent; I have your best interest at heart."

"You also have your best interests at heart," I said.

"Think of me as...," Fred said. "Never mind, but I look out for you."

"Sometimes," I said. "How much did you pay for the Pontiac?"

"I won it in a poker game, but I asked around it is easily worth three hundred, so I am giving you a deal." Fred was always taking care of Fred, but occasionally I benefitted. The car looked in good shape and only had fifty thousand miles, so today was one of those days. I called my insurance agent and asked Fred to send someone to get the licence plates for both cars. I wrote out a new cheque for my insurance and asked Fred to deliver it.

I headed out to see Big Fish and Manny. Big Fish was drinking coffee with Manny when I walked in.

"Take a seat," Big Fish said. My choice was a stool, a small ladder or a wobbly chair, so I sat on the stool. He reached into a drawer, pulled out an envelope, and gave it t

"You owe me twenty-five dollars," he said, which I gave him. The report was dated

July 4, when I was in Montreal. It stated the sample was xylazine or horse tranquillizer and, when ground up, could cause central nervous system depression, blurred vision, disorientation, dizziness, drowsiness, difficulty moving, slurred speech and fatigue. Xylazine could also cause respiratory depression, shallow breathing or no breathing and cardiovascular effects of low blood pressure and lower heart rate. If administered in large doses, xylazine would cause a fatality.

I had the murder weapon, so my next step was to find out more about the woman with the horse tranquillizer at the West residence. She was either the murderer or an accomplice. When I finished with Manny, I learned two things: Miss Eunice Walker had a high rise on St. Clair Avenue, and a man watched her.

Manny gave me his description from observing him in a 1955 Chevy Bel Air Four-door, grey with white trim. The man was in his thirties, wore a grey fedora and was almost the same size as his car. Manny said he was surprised he could get into the car and gave me the licence number. I gave him ten dollars as a bonus since he had to take the streetcar. I called Mr. Wallace and told him I planned to write a story about the woman who took the horse tranquillizer at the West Residence. I added that it was the murder weapon. Could he check with the executor to see if he objected to me mentioning the house or that I was there?

"Mr. Clark, the executor, is an old friend of Mrs. West; if this will help solve her murder, he has no objection," Mr. Wallace said. I called Chuck, who looked up licence numbers for me. I paid him five dollars for each licence number, and I had a credit with him. I do not know how he did this since only the police had access to the motor vehicle branch.

He called me back and gave me a name, Hunston Weir, with an address on Dundas Street. I tried the yellow pages under investigators and found a listing. Hunston Weir, a marital investigator for the deserving spouse and a slogan, "we catch them, you divorce them." An investigator who knew his market, but was gutsy. Any husband who caught Weir eavesdropping or taking pictures of private activities might decide to take a swing or three. I visited Mr. Weir.

It was on the second floor of a Chinese restaurant. The female receptionist was applying nail polish on her fingers when I walked inside.

"I would like an appointment with Mr. Weir," I said.

She didn't look up, and I noticed she was working on a stick of gum as she applied her polish. Looking at her tight dress and fake yellow hair, I wondered where she kept her baseball cards.

"He is busy," she said. "Come back later."

"What time?" I asked.

"He needs to see the men in person below in the restaurant," she said.

"What is your name?" I asked.

"Midge," she said. It sounded like a couch was moving in the office, and a male voice said, "give it to me, baby." I moved, and before the door guardian stopped me, I opened it and witnessed a roll in the hay, but we weren't in a barn, and she was giving it. If I was asked, my only observation was that she was one large woman.

"Midge, help," Weir shouted. Midge got up and slammed the door.

"Too much information," I said. "Shall I give you a description of the woman?"

"Not interested," Midge said. "Damn, now I have to redo my nails. I think you better leave. Mr. Weir will see you at four this afternoon."

"Thank you, Midge," I said." Shall I order take-out for your boss?"

"Don't bother; he doesn't eat there since the chop suey gives him gas," Midge said.

"Then I will pick him up an order; what gives him gas gives me pleasure," I said.

"Whatever," Midge said, studying her nails.

"See you at four," I said.

"You bet, Honey," Midge said, and I skipped down the stairs to the street for my next appointment.

"My goodness," Mrs. West said.

"Such badness," I said. I walked to Queen Street and took the streetcar to Fred's Garage. I walked inside, where he told me he had my Pontiac washed and waxed, the plates were on, and he gave me my registration.

"You will never guess what I saw this morning," I said.

"Reginald," Mrs. West said.

"What?" asked Fred.

"A private investigator in action," I said."

"Was he watching a suspect?" Fred asked.

"Not sure, but he was actively involved," I said.

"Big deal," Fred said.

"She was," I said.

"Reggie, I never understand you," Fred said. We shook hands. I took the keys to my car and headed out to lunch at the Honey Dew, where Mrs. West admonished me, but it was worth it. At two, I waited and signed the papers at my lawyer's office for closing on July 15 and the other on July 31. I called my broker's office and gave instructions for the closing price with the statement of adjustments.

I visited my real estate broker, who was having a late lunch but told me to come in. He told me he had another family of six who would take the second house, and I gave him the closing dates.

"From here on, I charge ten percent for the first month's rent," Mr. Foster said. "You have equity of around sixty-thousand dollars and rental income of five hundred per month. How about buying three more houses and taking out a mortgage on all six properties? The mortgages would be for forty-five thousand dollars, buy three more homes, and your total rental income is eleven hundred a month. Your monthly mortgage payment is less than two hundred dollars. You set aside one hundred and fifty for insurance, taxes and repairs, and you net seven hundred and fifty a month or nine thousand dollars a year. Once a year, pay down ten percent of the mortgage or forty-five hundred, and you still can live on or invest another forty-five hundred dollars. Think about it while I finish my sandwich."

"Do it," Mrs. West said. "Later, you can sell the houses and buy an apartment building."

"Ok, Mr. Foster, find me some magnificent houses and good tenants," and I shook his hand. If he were right, I would own six houses and still have some equity because of Mrs. West and her generosity. Once I was outside, I thanked her.

"Fine, Reginald, call your parents tonight," Mrs. West said. I was five minutes early for Mr. Weir's appointment. When I walked in, Midge was combing her hair. She had reached the point where she was pulling her hair to the back of her neck.

"Seeing you, I have a song in my heart," I said as I closed

the door, sat in a chair and took off my hat.

"We just met this morning," Midge said.

"But who can forget that," I said.

"I did," Midge said, checking her nails. I needed to raise my ante.

"Nice nails Midge," I said.

"Are they too red?" she asked.

"They are perfect," I said. How could I answer her question? As far as I was concerned, red is red. I knew nothing about nail polish but liked buttering up secretaries.

"You are shameless," Mrs. West said.

"I am," I said.

"You are what?" Midge asked.

"I am happy to see you so pretty, Sweetheart," I said.

"Sweetheart, you don't even know me," Midge said.

"Well, I know you are sweet and...."

"I have a heart," Midge said. "Big deal."

"It is, and you are my Sweetheart," I said.

"I bet you say that to every lady," Midge said.

"Guilty as charged," I said, "but you are the one."

"Which one?" Midge asked.

"The prettiest," I said.

"Reginald enough," Mrs. West said. "Does she believe you?"

"Not in the slightest," I said.

"Not in the slightest, what?" asked Midge.

"Not in the slightest chance will you lose the award for the most beautiful Toronto secretary," I said.

"Oh, stop it," Midge said and blushed.

"Ok, if you insist. Is Mr. Weir in?" I asked.

"He is by his little lonesome," Midge said.

"Too bad," I said. "I am surprised Weir can do it with his weight."

"I think his secret is oysters," Midge said.

"Good to know; who was this morning's lady?" I asked.

"I never can keep track, but she was no lady" Midge said. "Mr. Weir is unhappy with you for barging in like that. That was supposed to be private."

"If it was supposed to be private, why do it in an office, and we heard what was going on," I said. "Doesn't that bother you?" I asked.

"Whatever the little gerbil wants to do is fine since he pays me," Midge said. "Sometimes I roll cotton batten and put them in my ears if it gets too bad," Midge said. The office door opened, and Mr. Weir looked at me. He didn't like what he saw, since he tried to snarl. In my experience, you have to be a detective sergeant, any of my former sergeants, Lanny the Louse or an angry husband to do it. Mr. Weir was five foot seven, two hundred pounds in a check suit. He had too much brill cream in his pompadour, and the only thing missing was a fake nose and clown shoes. Whoever had told him that lots of after-shave lotion were the way to go should be kicked out of Toronto.

"I have an appointment," I said.

"I know," he said, giving Midge an evil look, but she shrugged and resumed working on her nails. She was well brought up since she didn't stick out her tongue or blow a raspberry.

"What's your name?" he asked.

"Didn't Midge tell you?" I asked.

"Why would I be asking your name if she had told me?" Weir asked.

"I think you forgot my name with all the action in your office," I said. "Midge calls me Honey, but it is Reggie Clark," I said. "However, I'm taking a liking to Honey."

"Come inside, and Midge, no disturbances," Mr. Weir said as Midge shrugged. He closed the door and told me to take a seat.

"What can I do you for?" Weir asked.

"Such poor grammar, it should be how may I be of help," Mrs. West said.

"A friend tells me you have been observing Miss Eunice Walker at her apartment for the last few days," I said.

"Listen, Bub, what I do is my business, get it," Weir said.

"Bub, did you just call me Bub?" I asked. I was not sure why he didn't respond. Perhaps it was my six-foot-two size, or my sergeants had taught me to snarl.

"I am working on a story for the *Toronto Mirror,* and it may implicate Miss Eunice Walker in the death of Mrs. Alicia West," I said. "I believe her son is involved with Miss Walker."

"A hack," Weir said.

"A gumshoe," I said. "Want to keep this up? How about dick, shamus...."

"Enough," Weir said.

"You're upset since I know more expressions than you," I said.

"Jeez, Clark, you are annoying," Weir said.

"I am, aren't I," I said. "Don't go on; it might go to my head."

"Cut it out," Weir said. "In my work, I like publicity, but I also need to protect my clients. Sorry, Clark, no can do, sort of a solicitor-client thing."

"When were you called to the Law Society of Upper Canada?" I asked.

"I wasn't, but the same sort of thing," Weir said. He tried to look fierce but reminded me of a chipmunk with hemorrhoids. He stood and moved towards the door, but I remained in the chair.

"Listen Clark, I ain't talking, so put an egg in your shoe and beat it," Weir said.

"Whenever I hear that awful expression, I can imagine someone saying hardy har har, but more to the point, who's going to make me?" I asked and resisted making another snarl. That deflated him, and he looked unhappy as I stood.

"We can resolve this the easy way or the hard way," I said. "I can keep confidences, but if this is how you want to do it, fine, but...."

"But what?" he asked.

"I will let your little mind figure that out," I said and closed the door. Outside his office, I looked at Midge, who was working on a new piece of gum.

"Bye, Midge" I said.

"Bye, Honey," she said. "You annoyed my boss."

"Then it was a successful visit," I said. "You can tell him the fun has just begun."

"Whatever," Midge said, and I skipped down the stairs.

"What a disgusting little man," Mrs. West said.

"True, but now he is an annoyed little man," I said. I told Mrs. West that when he tried to look fierce, I imagined him as a chipmunk with hemorrhoids. "I was thinking of sending him a grammar book, but he wouldn't read it. I expect that he dropped out of school in grade eight, so he couldn't understand the big words."

"Really, Reginald," Mrs. West said, then laughed. I stopped to shop and decided to try to fry a chicken breast with boiled potatoes and green beans. I was talking with Mrs. West when Martha rapped on the kitchen door. Martha peered in as I opened the door.

"Were you talking to someone?" she asked.

"Just my resident ghost," I said.

"Reggie, be serious" Martha said, and I was tempted to say I was serious, but I would hear an admonishment or five from Mrs. West.

"How are you?" I asked. She was pretty in a green dress and looked around the kitchen.

"Did you kill the cockroach?" she asked.

"No, they are hard to kill," I said.

"Did you use the D.D.T.?" Martha asked.

"I was worried it would hurt the rats," I said.

"You have rats too?" Martha asked.

"We are not well acquainted yet," I said. "I don't know their names."

"That's a joke," Martha said.

"Yes," I said.

"It wasn't funny," Martha said. "I hate rats more than cockroaches."

"Reginald, you had another reason to keep her away, but you had to be funny," Mrs. West said."

"You changed your locks," Martha said. "I tried to get in."

"My real estate agent told me to," I said.

"Do you do whatever he tells you?" Martha asked. "When are you going to make your own decisions?"

"She has a point," Mrs. West said.

"We shared our keys. Wasn't that special?" she asked. It was time to move on.

"Look Martha, let's be friends," I said.

"That's all we were," she said. "What were you thinking?"

"Nothing," I said. That was now, but before I had erotic thoughts until Mrs. West pointed out what was in store if I succumbed to my desires.

"I should hope so," she said. "Give me back my key," which I found in a drawer and gave to her.

"You disappoint me, Reggie," Martha said.

"I know," I said. "I disappoint many people."

"Why is that?" Martha asked.

"I need to grow up," I said.

"Careful, Reginald, you are giving her a challenge," Mrs. West said.

"Maybe I can help," Martha said, and I noticed her eyes were wide and her lips full.

"We can have dinner tomorrow night," she said.

"I will be back at my other job and away," I said.

"What job?" she asked.

"I am a butler," I said.

"I am trying to get to know you, and all you do is make jokes," Martha said. "Good night, Reggie."

"Good night, Martha," I said.

"She blows hot and cold, and you wait; she hasn't given up on you," Mrs. West said. After dinner, I cleaned up and called my parents. My mother cried, and I promised to call them every week.

CHAPTER 30

The Article

The following day, I drove to Fred's Garage. I told Manny to use my car, and I would pay him ten dollars a day for my revenge. I gave him twenty dollars to go to a printer to have large signs attached to the Pontiac with an arrow. The signs will say, "Hunston Weir, a detective for irate wives at work." I told him to follow Weir and to watch what happened. My 1941 Buick Roadmaster convertible was ready. I took the keys and drove to the Toronto Mirror to write my story, making it a doozy without naming Mr. West. No good would come of that unless I dug up more dirt; so far, it was not forthcoming.

I sat at my desk, put paper n my typewriter and began. A few hellos, but no one asked where I had been. Maybe the scuttlebutt was that the newspaper suspended me or I took leave to dry out.

Who killed Mrs. Alicia West?

A trap was set at 149 Dunvegan Road, the residence of the late Mrs. Alicia West. It was four in the morning on June 2. I believed someone murdered Mrs. West and was returning to retrieve the murder weapon. I waited for this person to return to Mrs. West's bedroom. Once they left the bedroom and arrived at the bottom of the staircase, I leapt forward, tackled them and grabbed a bag. I suffered a scratched face, and the intruder struggled free. When

I grabbed the metal rod, I received a kick that doubled me over. Holding the bag in one hand, I pushed the suspect to the floor and realized it was a woman.

She escaped, but I had the bag and a grappling hook used to retrieve the drugs. I called the police, who arrived and seized the bag with pills and the grappling hook. I kept one pill which I gave to Rexall Pharmacy. The report dated July 4, 1957, stated that it was xylazine or horse tranquillizer. It would kill if administered in a large dose. Someone returned to retrieve the murder weapon. Why would anyone kill a wealthy society lady who headed up many charities? An exhumation is needed to confirm if xylazine or horse tranquillizer killed Mrs. West. Once the police find that the poison killed her, justice and this paper demand a murder investigation. I knocked on Bill Wise's door, and he yelled come in.

"What ya got?" he asked in his deep editor voice, and inside I handed him the story which he read.

"Need's a rewrite. Frank can do it, second page tomorrow," Mr. Wise said. "Good job, but keep after the son or any other person with a grudge."

"Will I get paid?" I asked.

"Go back and keep digging," Wise said, which was a non-answer. I thanked him, left, and wondered if I had this case wrong. Maybe Mrs. West had done something that caused another killer to take her life. How could I investigate this without Mrs. West knowing I was doing it?

I spent an hour in the newsroom catching up on stories, then made extra keys and visited Mr. Wallace at Mrs. Alicia West's Residence. When I pulled up, he walked out and watched me park.

"1941 Buick Roadmaster Convertible and looks in good shape," Mr. Wallace said. "I will be by to pick up my furniture on Saturday." I told him I had made extra keys and gave him one.

"Did you tell Mrs. Murphy since I gave her a key?"

"Yes," I said. Mr. Wallace invited me inside, and I told him what I had been up to, including the trip to Montreal and that my story would be in tomorrow's paper. I gave him a copy of my article.

"There is nothing about Mr. West in your article?" Mr. West asked.

"I didn't have the facts, but this will force an exhumation. The police know you left a message for Mr. Jenkins on behalf of Mr. West that the house would be vacant. As soon as they do the exhumation, who will be the number one suspect?" I asked.

"Mr. West," Mr. Wallace said. "I told the police he had a key; he was away from home and had a motive."

"Correct, and I need to contact Mr. Jenkins," I said.

"He is away until the end of July," Mr. Wallace said.

"Do you know why Mrs. West went to Montreal?" I asked.

"No, why don't you ask her?" Mr. Wallace said.

"That is a topic I will not discuss," Mrs. West said. That was the wrong way to speak to a reporter, but I would let it rest for now. I bought more groceries and drove to a store to buy a charcoal grill, tools, a fire starter and briquettes for hamburgers, beer and wine. When my doorbell rang, I was unpacking. I opened it to see a uniformed sergeant standing there, so I told him to come in and closed the door.

"My beer is warm, so a coffee?" I asked.

"No sir, the sergeant said. "I am Sergeant Philpot, and do you own a 1952 Pontiac licence number, BR 2937?"

"Yes," I said.

"Is your name Reginald Clark?" the sergeant asked.

"Yes," I said, "Is something wrong?"

"We have received a complaint from Mr. Hunston Weir that a fellow driving your car is harassing him," the sergeant said.

"The fellow or the car?" I asked.

"The fellow and the car since on both sides are large signs that say, let me check my notebook, 'Hunston Weir, a detective for irate wives at work.' Do you know anything about this?"

"Yes, I am responsible, and it is the truth," I said.

"Tell me about it; my wife sued me for divorce based on the evidence of Hunston Weir," Sergeant Philpot said.

"You may call him the little Gerbil, his secretary does, and I do," I said. "The little gerbil and I have unresolved issues."

"Normally, one of my constables would handle this. I thought I would drive over to tell you to keep up the good work," the sergeant said and shook my hand. Once I closed the door, I put away the groceries, put the beer in the fridge, set up the charcoal grill, and lit the briquettes. It was hamburgers and beer for dinner, followed by ice cream. I put away the dishes and packed, for tomorrow was Wednesday and a return to my job as a butler, if I still had one. I called Manny, who told me about Weir, who reported him to the police. Manny added that Miss Walker was away. At seven, I drove to Miss Walker's apartment building and spoke to two neighbours who told me she had not returned. I wondered what my reception would be from Mr. West, but I was there at seven on Wednesday morning. Mr. West was not downstairs, and at eleven, I brought him his paper and a coffee to the dining room.

"Thank you, Jenkins," he said. I nodded and closed the door. The next couple of days were the usual, too much alcohol for the Wests, excellent meals, polishing the Bentley and the silver and locking my bedroom door at night.

CHAPTER 31

My Article Reaches Mr. West and Performing his Investigation

By Friday, all Toronto papers had picked up my story of finding the woman in Mrs. West's residence and that the pills were horse tranquillizers, a murder weapon. Mr. West only read the Globe and Mail, but enough of his friends had called, asking if he was aware of the story. I saw a copy of my story, so someone had dropped it off. It was eleven when Mr. West called me into the dining room.

"Jenkins, on Sunday, June 30th, a reporter from the *Toronto Mirror* was in my late mother's house," Mr. West said.

"Really, sir," I said.

"Yes, he almost captured some woman who had hidden horse tranquillizers in my mother's room."

"Indeed, sir," I said.

"Will you stop interrupting until I finish my story?" Mr. West said.

"Yes, sir," I said.

"This reporter gave the pills to the police but kept one and gave it to a pharmacist. The pharmacist's report stated these pills could kill my mother," Mr. West said. "The *Toronto Mirror* is asking that my mother be exhumed to find out if she has traces of horse tranquillizer in her body."

"You are referring to xylazine, called horse tranquillizer," I said.

"Will you stop interrupting?" Mr. West said. "There is no mention of anyone behind this, but you appreciate what happens in these situations?" I remained silent.

"Jenkins, I asked you a question," Mr. West said.

"Indeed, sir, but you admonished me for interrupting," I said.

"Permission to speak," Mr. West said.

"You are concerned that the public will surmise that you had something to do with it since you are disputing the will," I said.

"Who told you I was disputing the will?" Mr. West asked.

"Your mother's former butler, Mr. Wallace," I said.

"Did he do that?" Mr. West asked. "He did not trust me and had the temerity to throw me out of mother's house?"

"Really, sir," I said. "That must have been distressing."

"It was," Mr. West said. "Forget that; here is what I want you to do. Find this reporter for the *Toronto Mirror*. Make friends with him, take him out to dinner, get him drunk and get the goods."

"The goods, sir?" I asked.

"Yes, the goods, the stuff I need to discredit him," Mr. West said.

"If it came out you were behind this, suspicion might grow that you were the one that hired this lady," I said. "You must be careful, sir."

"Jenkins, you are young but wise," Mr. West said. "If this reporter asks you why you are interested, tell him that my mother's former butler was the one who hired you. Do you know what they always say? It's always a butler that does it."

"I am a butler," I said. "We are a much-maligned profession."

"Don't take it personally, and you are in a trade, not a profession," Mr. West said. What a schmuck, insulting me while asking for a favour.

"You can take three evenings off, and I will give fifty dollars for this." One lunch at Morton's Steak House was over sixty dollars. Where did he want me to get the reporter drunk with three dinners and a budget of fifty dollars? The Honey Dew Restaurant, which didn't serve booze but had excellent hotdogs, might be my only choice if I interviewed over three nights.

"Reginald, Douglas is trying to frame Wallace," Mrs. West said. "He is despicable."

"Sir, thank you for your kind offer, but this is a matter of your honour and my duty as your butler. I am off this weekend, so I shall track this reporter down. Reporters drink in taverns, and the food is not expensive, and it will be at my expense."

"I couldn't allow that," Mr. West said, but his cheapness would mean he would not protest much longer."

"I insist, as your butler," I said.

"Well then, thank you, Jenkins," Mr. West said. I couldn't take the money, but I was curious why he wanted to learn more about the reporter. I had given up on Mr. West as the murderer, but I was becoming suspicious again. He was the most stupid man, and it would get worse since the pressure for an exhumation would grow. Since I was the investigator for his mother, I wondered if this put me in conflict. I decided she wouldn't care since I was investigating myself and my job for Mrs. West was to find out who killed her, so I waived the conflict.

I left Friday at five and arrived at the Country Tavern for a beer and to meet my friends since I was here in my report to Mr. West. On Saturday, I checked on Miss Eunice Walker, but she was still away. I painted a room and did some work on my Pontiac. I would have to store my convertible and look around for a garage. I found one two blocks over for twenty dollars a month. Sunday was the church to keep Mrs. West happy, but I became used to it and then made notes for my next meeting with Mr. West.

On Monday at eleven, I met Mr. West in the dining room of his house.

"Sir, I can discuss what I learned about the *Toronto Mirror* reporter who wrote the story," I said.

"Tell all Jenkins," Mr. West said. "Take a seat," which I did.

"The reporter is Reginald Clark, who insisted I call him Reggie," I said. "I met him at his favourite drinking spot, the Country Tavern, where Big Fish and his group play," I said. "Once I plied him with beer and French fries, he opened up. He told me how he had solved many crimes and seemed to know everyone in the tavern. He soon became suspicious, and I told him I was writing a book about Toronto's unsolved crimes. Questions, sir?"

"No, continue," Mr. West said.

"He insisted he bring me to the crime scene, so on Saturday, I was at Mrs. West's residence, and Mr. Clark showed me what happened. What is not in his story is that the intruder kicked him in his private parts when he was wrestling for the pills."

"He got kicked in the nuts; that's funny," Mr. West said.

"He couldn't sit for two days," I said, which caused Mr. West to break out laughing. "I met Mr. Wallace, who had nothing to say. I made a copy of the pharmacist report, which I am giving you." Mr. West's face had paled.

"Once I finished seeing where the struggle took place and reading the report, I was satisfied that a woman was there to retrieve the horse tranquillizers. The one thing not in the article was that Mr. Wallace had called your butler to say that the house would be unoccupied on the weekend. Of course, I dismissed that as nonsense, but Mr. Wallace and Mr. Clark told me this. I expect they have told this to the police, but I am sure the police would disregard this."

"Thank you, Jenkins; you don't think you can discredit this Clark fellow?" Mr. West asked.

"No sir, I found him truthful," I said.

"Ask my wife to come here," Mr. West said. Once I was outside, I closed the door.

"This is it," Mrs. West said.

"It is," I said.

"You must listen even if you get caught and fired," Mrs. West said.

"Yes, Mrs. West," I said. "I will be your snoop."

"What is a snoop?" she asked.

"A furtive investigation," I said.

"You keep me up to date with unfamiliar words," Mrs. West said. I told Mrs. Marigold West to join her husband in the dining room. When I entered the kitchen, Jane, Margaret, and Mrs. Caruthers were at the table.

"I am going to listen outside the library to find out if they are planning to fire me, so don't go there," I said. They all nodded, so I tiptoed outside the library door and stood. Nothing better than the alliance of unhappy staff.

"Marigold, I am scared," Mr. West said. "The press confirmed that a woman returned to retrieve tranquillizer pills from my mother's room, and those pills could kill her. Wallace told the reporter that he called Jenkins to say he would be away, so mother's house was unoccupied, and I knew about it."

"Which Jenkins?" Mrs. Marigold West asked.

"The former Jenkins, and don't interrupt," Mr. West said. "This reporter lay in wait and caught this woman who escaped. He managed to grab the horse tranquillizer from her, which can kill. It makes me the one who sent the woman, but I never did. I had nothing to do with mother's death, which is terrible."

"Not much of a confession, is it?" Mrs. West said.

"Douglas stop that," Mrs. Marigold West said. "Did you make any calls that week to someone who is not a friend or tradesman?"

"No, Marigold, I did not," Mr. West said.

"I bet he called his mistress," Mrs. West said, and I nodded.

"Well, then you have nothing to worry about, even if the police get the records from Bell Telephone," Mrs. Marigold West said. "Douglas, you look like you might be sick?"

"I drank too much, but I think we need to go for a few days on vacation to New York," Mr. West said. "You could do some shopping, and we can visit Conrad Vaughn."

"And Miss Tallulah Conway, his lover," Mrs. West said.

"Yes, Miss Tallulah Conway," Mr. West said. "I am unsure if

they are lovers or just good friends."

"Really, Douglas," Mrs. West said. "If you believe that, you are a fool. Do whatever you want to do but remember they will wait for you with the phone records, and there better not be any strange woman's number on our telephone." I heard nothing else, no confession, no plea for mercy, so I walked back to the kitchen. If Mr. West couldn't convince his wife, how would he do with the police? Once the police discover the phone number for Miss Eunice Walker, he would be busy with divorce and criminal lawyers.

"Douglas should have confessed, but he is weak," Mrs. West said. I nodded and walked to the kitchen, where Mrs. Caruthers poured me a coffee.

"Well?" she asked.

"Not yet; I am still Jenkins the second, in the West residence as a butler," I said.

"That is wonderful," Mrs. Carruthers said and poured me another coffee. I was unsure about that, which depended if Mr. West left. If he did, it did not look good. I still doubted whether Mr. West murdered his mother, but he was taking the wrong steps. The police always believe that anyone who is guilty runs. I expected that Mrs. Eunice Walker would return and we would have a friendly little chat. Maybe Hunston Weir, a gumshoe for unhappy spouses, could join in. Life presents such excellent curve balls.

CHAPTER 32

The Stupidity of Douglas West, My Resignation and Finding Miss Walker

When I returned Sunday night, Mrs. Caruthers told me Mr. and Mrs. West had gone to New York for a few days, and she didn't know when they would return. As I munched on prime rib and sipped my wine, I told Mrs. Caruthers I was leaving and would hand in my resignation letter.

"That's a pity; you are such a laugh," Mrs. Caruthers said. "Mr. West will not provide a letter of resignation for you."

"I know, but I might try something else," I said.

"What, Edward?" asked Mrs. Caruthers.

"Be a reporter," I said.

"Oh, Edward, you are such a card," Mrs. Carruthers said. After dinner, I wrote my resignation letter and gave it to Mrs. Caruthers. I said goodbye to Margaret and Jane and gave Jane one of my P. G. Wodehouse books and told her to try him. I packed my clothes and took a taxi to my home. I was bothered since there might be a chance to learn something, but the possibility of Mr. West learning I was Reginald Clark grew. Besides, I wanted to say I was deserting a sinking ship.

If the detective section learned Mr. West had gone to New York, they might arrest him at home, and I knew most of them. It would be embarrassing to have a detective holding on to Mr. West asking, "undercover as a butler were you, Clark?" I had to get out while I could. If they arrested him, I would not have access to him. Toronto's finest would not invite me to sit in and listen as Mr. West said, "honestly, detective, it wasn't me. Marigold never liked mother, and maybe you should talk to Jenkins, my butler or former butler." The last thing I needed was for Mr. West to discover who I was. I had to find the spitfire who kicked me in my nether region. Manny drove by with the Pontiac, and I drove him back to Fred's garage, then to Miss Walker's apartment, but there were no lights on. I returned home, drove my Pontiac inside the garage, locked it and walked inside to think.

"Well, Reginald, what now?" Mrs. West asked.

"To find out if Miss Walker was the woman at your house, which will mean long hours at St. Clair Avenue," I said.

"What if she is not the woman?" asked Mrs. West.

"Then we are going to have a little chat," I said.

I was up at six in the morning, and after showering, shaving and breakfast, I took the signs off the Pontiac and was at Miss Walker's address by seven. No 1955 Chevy Bel Air was parked near her apartment, so the little gerbil was not there or had changed his car. For him, maybe a large truck or a hearse would fit better. I moved to a new location every two hours and checked for the little gerbil. I did what anyone who consumed water needed to do; I had lunch at a restaurant with a bathroom. I gave up at seven at night and returned home.

On the third day of observation, a taxi pulled up, and a lady got out who matched the description of Miss Walker. I jumped out of my car, ran to hold open the door, and offered to take her bag to the elevator. She had used her left hand to carry the suitcase and handed it to me. I asked where she had been, and she said Ottawa. Once I helped her to her door, I said, have a pleasant day and dropped her suitcase on her foot. I was hoping she would say bastard, but Miss Walker was a proper lady who said, "you idiot." I apologized and retreated down the stairs to the bottom door.

"Is that her?" Mrs. West asked.

"Wrong size, left-handed and not the voice."

"She only said one word," Mrs. West said.

"Which was?" I asked.

"Reginald, I will not repeat it, and how do you know it is not her?" Mrs. West asked.

"The woman at your house had a deep voice," I said. "Miss Walker had a much higher voice like Minnie Mouse."

"Who is Minnie Mouse?" asked Mrs. West.

"Mickey's girlfriend," I said.

"Who is Mickey?" asked Mrs. West.

"They are both in Walt Disney cartoons," I said.

"Reginald, I don't watch cartoons, and neither should you," Mrs. West said.

"I like them," I said. "Miss West is taller, thinner and is not left-handed. I need to go to work, so forget what my boss will say."

When I got to my area, my boss, Mr. Wise, saw me and laughed, and I had never seen Mr. Wise laugh.

"Your story is national, and they have questioned the Minister of Justice about it. It is Toronto's problem, but the minister is from here, and at two, the police chief will announce an exhumation. Circulation is up, and I will pay you. Go to High Park to find the grave, take pictures, and then be at the press conference at two. Oh boy, we are in the money on this one." He shook my hand and danced away.

"My goodness Reginald, you did it," Mrs. West said.

"We did it," I said. I drove to the High Park cemetery, took pictures of Mrs. West's grave, and spoke to the manager, Mr. Jeffries, about how they did exhumations.

"A terrible thing to disturb the remains," Mr. Jeffries said. "It violates the idea of rest in peace, but sometimes justice needs to be done. Poor Mrs. West, and they informed me she was a gracious lady."

"Wonderful, a grave manager's blessing," Mrs. West said. "Are you planning to get an endorsement about my character from the grave diggers?"

"Of course," I said.

"What did you say?" Mr. Jeffries asked. "It is a rather windy day."

"Of course, Mrs. West was a gracious lady," I said.

"We must do it according to the judge's order and not when we are performing a burial, so we do it at six in the morning," Mr. Jeffries said. "You can imagine the feelings of a family burying their loved one and watching a grave being dug and the coffin raised to the surface. I take it you are a reporter?"

"Reginald Clark, *Toronto Mirror* I said.

"That was your story," Mr. Jeffries said.

"Yes, what happens with an exhumation?" I asked.

"I need the court order; then I assemble my team. The police will photograph, and they must wear protective clothing. Once we remove the soil above the coffin, we put screens for privacy. We create side access to take the coffin to the surface; then, they transport the body to the mortuary for examination. Since it is poison, they will test the coffin and the soil around the coffin. I will have a guard at the opened grave to ensure nothing is removed until the body is re-interred, which may take several days. It is rather ghastly, isn't it?" To which I agreed. Walking out to my car, I felt sorry for Mrs. West.

"Reginald, it has to be done," Mrs. West said. "I have to be sure." Once I was in the car, I had to ask.

"Mrs. West, if they find out you died due to ingesting horse tranquillizer, it will become a murder case. If they convict your son, he may hang unless they commute his sentence to life imprisonment."

"Reginald, I was so caught up with finding out who murdered me; I hadn't thought about that."

"Would it be fair to say my next job is to make sure they do not convict your son?" I asked.

"I believe so," Mrs. West said.

"First, you want me to find out if Mr. West murdered you, now to show he didn't," I said. "I wish you would make up your mind."

"Enough of that; you know what to do," Mrs. West said.

"I must tell the police what I know about your son and that Miss Walker was not the woman in the house with the pills," I said.

"Yes," Mrs. West said.

"They will tell me I told the sergeant in Division Fifty-Three that your son did it and make me an unreliable witness."

"Yes, but you can prove it wasn't Miss Walker, which should eliminate my son," Mrs. West said.

"Yes, then I must find out who killed you," I said.

"Yes, Reginald, I suppose you must," Mrs. West said.

"That's why you retained me," I said.

"It was," Mrs. West said.

"There is something you haven't told," I said.

"Perhaps," Mrs. West said, "but not now."

CHAPTER 33

The Police Request my Presence

I was there for the press conference and the exhumation. I wrote like a madman, watching the copy editor increase his whisky consumption. The headline was Widow Killed by Horse Tranquilizer. I thought the story wasn't bad, a smattering of gruesome and what the forensic pathologist would check, written by an intrepid reporter, me. The police crime section read my articles with interest since they arrested Mr. West at the Malton airport on his return from New York. Someone had squealed, but it wasn't me. Mr. Wise kept me busy with follow-ups to the story. Two days later, the police arrested Miss Walker, which was also the wrong thing to do. On Monday morning, July 22, I was at my desk at the Toronto Mirror when my phone rang, and I picked it up.

"Clark," I said, hoping they would confuse me for Superman's alter ego, Clark Kent, who also worked for a newspaper when he wasn't Superman.

"Detective Sergeant Oliver," the growly voice of Detective Sergeant William Oliver. "I need you at my office now."

"I'm busy," I said; it was ten o'clock. "Make an appointment for Morton's Steak House for twelve, and I will tell all."

"Yeah, right," Oliver said. "I can't afford it, and neither can you. Listen, Clark, Lester is standing by and would love to swing by your office and arrest you."

"Say hi to Lester," I said. "For what? I paid my parking tickets and donated to the policeman's picnic," I said.

"There is no policeman's picnic, and the charge is obstruction of justice," Oliver said. "I don't care about your damn parking tickets."

"Tell that to the clerk who grabbed my money when I paid them," I said. "No one has asked me for an interview."

"I did a minute ago, so get your ass over here," Oliver said.

"Send a car to pick me up," I said. "I want to sit in front and push the siren button."

"It's a switch, and no," Oliver said. "Get in your Pontiac and drive here."

"How do you know I have a Pontiac?" I asked.

"You have a 1952 Pontiac," Oliver said.

"No fair checking up on me," I said.

"Did your little mind forget talking to Sergeant Philpot and your licence number BR 2937?" Oliver asked.

"Is that my licence number?" I asked. "No fair talking to other sergeants."

"Tell you what, I will make a new pot of coffee," and he hung up before I asked if he had donuts. There was a coffee shop on the main floor, so I picked up twelve donuts in case I needed to bribe my way out of an arrest. Detective Sergeant William Oliver, called Tank, was six-foot-four and weighed two hundred and fifty pounds. He cut his hair so short you could see the marks on his head. We drank together as long as I paid for the beers and wrote several stories featuring him. He put up with a few press members, including me. I told Jerry I had to meet with the police and did not know when I would be back.

I parked near the police station, and when I went inside, the desk sergeant lifted the counter and told me Sergeant Oliver expected me. He took the donut I offered him. By the time I was at Oliver's office, I was down to two donuts. My motto was a donut a day keeps the police away. The door was open, and I walked in. Sergeant Oliver was talking to Lester Wilson, a detective constable.

"Donuts," I offered. Lester took one, and the sergeant took the bag and looked inside.

"Only one?" he asked. "You mean donut. You got me excited when you said donuts."

"There were twelve when I walked into your building," I said.

"A bunch of pikers," Oliver said. "Lester shut the door," and he left." Once the door was closed, Oliver poured me a coffee and smiled.

"We've been talking about you and what you did to that gumshoe, Weir," he said. "Hunston Weir, a detective for irate wives at work, I like that. He has given evidence against several of us and has had to change his car. Tell me about Mr. West and his babe Eunice Walker. Sergeant Rifkin's notes said you believed Mrs. West's son did it. I want you to tell me what happened when you almost caught the lady with the horse tranquillizers."

"She wasn't a lady," I said.

"Right, she kicked you in the nuts," Oliver said.

"Which hurt," I said. "It was Sunday morning at two, June 30. The entrance to the living room was near the stairs when I heard something. I could see the outline of someone at the bottom of the stairs, and I leapt forward and tackled the intruder to the floor. I thought it was a man, but later discovered it was a woman. She was thin and short, and I grabbed a bag out of her right hand when she hit me on my upper right arm with a metal rod. There was enough light for me to determine she was right-handed. She scratched my face and struggled free. When I grabbed the metal rod, I received a kick to my private parts, which doubled me over. Still holding the bag in one hand, I forced her to the floor and pushed her breasts. She called me a bastard and escaped. I checked what I had and called the police."

"You were there with the permission of the executor?" Oliver asked

"Yes," I said.

"Mr. Wallace had called the West residence and told the

butler that the Alicia West residence was vacant?" Oliver asked.

"That is what Mr. Wallace told me," I said.

"Don't you think that was strange that he made the call?" Oliver asked. "It was an invitation for West to go, which would be stupid. Anyone would know that it was a trap."

"I agree, but what if the woman who showed up were not connected with Mr. West?" I said. "I had turned off the lights earlier in the evening."

"You are a pain in the ass," Oliver said. "I had a good case, a motive. West and his babe were out, and he had a key, and now you throw me this. We have phone records that West called Miss Walker that week. So, mister reporter, how did this mystery woman get in the house?"

"She knew how to jimmy a lock. She was there to murder Mrs. West and returned to retrieve the horse tranquillizer," I said and watched as he scowled and made notes.

"The butler Wallace tells Jenkins, who tells West that the place is vacant and this lady breaks in the same weekend?" Oliver said. "I never believe in coincidences."

"I know it seems inculpatory, but I think it was a coincidence," I said.

"Inculpatory, such big words from the reporter, but it means the same thing, guilt," Oliver said.

"Which you don't have," I said. "One other thing."

"You are going to ruin my day, aren't you?" Oliver asked.

"Yes," I said. "I am. I was watching Miss Eunice Walker's apartment along with the little gerbil."

"Who?" Oliver asked.

"The gumshoe, Hunston Weir," I said. "It was July 12, early, when I saw her getting out of a cab."

"How did you recognize it was her?" Oliver asked.

"I had her picture, and the little gerbil was not around," I said. "I took her suitcase on the elevator, and we talked. She used her left hand to carry the suitcase and handed it to me. Once I helped her to her door, I said, have a pleasant day and dropped the suitcase on her foot. What do you think she said?"

"Is she from Hamilton?" Oliver asked.

"No idea, but she called me an idiot," I said.

"Is that all? She's not from Hamilton," Oliver said. "She had just met you and had you figured out. Pretty astute lady, but this isn't helping. Let me guess; she is the wrong size, has a distinct voice and is left-handed?" Oliver asked.

"Yes," I said.

"You are sure she never called you a bastard?" Oliver asked.

"I am sure," I said. "Before you ask me how I can differentiate, it was a distinctive voice," I said. "The woman who kicked me had a deep voice, and Miss Walker sounds like Minnie Mouse."

"Only a reporter knows what Minnie Mouse sounds like," Oliver said.

"Hanging around you, I am aware of what Goofy sounds like," I said.

"Ok, I deserved that," Oliver said. "West hired Jackson Farnsworth Q.C., a good criminal lawyer who will also represent Miss Walker," Oliver said.

"Isn't that a conflict?" I asked.

"Only if they have different stories and want to lay the blame on the other," Oliver said. "You told Sergeant Rifkin that you thought West killed his mother, and Sergeant Rifkin said that you were wrong?"

"Yes," I said.

"You don't think West bumped off his mother?" Oliver asked.

"That's a double negative," I said. "I don't think Mr. West killed his mother."

"Wonderful," Oliver said. "Are you investigating this other woman?"

"Yes," I said.

"Keep me posted," Oliver said. "I interviewed Mrs. Marigold West. She is on the warpath and is spitting mad about Miss Walker and her husband. As a witness for the crown, I do not know what she will say. She keeps talking about a butler named Jenkins, but I am not sure if it is one butler or two, all named Jenkins. Anything else you want to say?"

"I bet the next Butler will be Jenkins the third," I said. "No, sergeant Oliver, nothing else."

"That wasn't so hard and next time, bring over more than one donut," Oliver said. We stood and shook hands, and I looked at him.

"You will never convict Miss Walker as an accessory to murder, and once the decision to drop her case happens, you will drop the case against Mr. West," I said.

"Come on, Clark, I can't say that even off the record," Oliver said, and I walked out the door. In the car, I laughed.

"What, Reginald?" asked Mr. West.

"If Miss Walker was never in your house, the only link they have for the son to be charged is his relationship to Miss Walker as a co-conspirator to murder," I said. "Once she is let off the hook, they will drop the case against Mr. West. Now we have to talk."

"Yes, Reginald, I suppose we do," Mrs. West said.

CHAPTER 34

A Revelation

"I have been avoiding this, but the time has come. Drive me to my home, and we will talk in the library with Wallace," Mrs. West said, so I drove to the West residence, parked and rang the door. Mr. Wallace answered.

"Mrs. West and I need to talk in the library, and she wants you to sit in," I said. I closed the door to the library, and Mr. Wallace and I sat in chairs. A special meeting, two living beings and a spirit having a heart-to-heart, except there were three of us but only two hearts, and only I could hear Mrs. West.

"In our collegiate, a couple of girls took a year off and returned to school a year behind the rest of the class," I said.

"Reginald, with respect, what I am about to tell you is important," Mrs. West said. "What happened in your school is not.

"It is," I said. "The rumour was they became pregnant. That is why you travelled to Montreal, isn't it?"

"He was the love of my life. When he found out I was pregnant, he had nothing to do with me," Mrs. West said. "It scandalized my mother, who wanted me out of the house, but my father supported me. It took me years to get over it, and Mr. West was a wonderful husband."

"It was a girl," I said, but Mrs. West didn't speak. "Mrs.

West, I figured that out, but I need to know if she contacted you?" I asked.

It was awkward since no one wanted to start. I thought of twenty questions before Mr. Wallace coughed.

"The last Saturday in September last year at ten o'clock in the morning, the doorbell rang. I opened it to see a fifty-year-old woman in a dress with an enormous hat." Mr. Wallace looked at me.

"She looked like Mrs. West. She asked me if this was the Alicia West house, and I said this was the house."

" 'I have something I must tell Mrs. West,' she said. I asked if she had an appointment, but she said she didn't. She was attractive and well-dressed, but she appeared anxious and kept touching her hair. She said this was very important, so I put her in the library, took her hat and purse, and searched for Mrs. West. I found Mrs. West in her bedroom, and at first, she didn't want to meet her, but I suggested she do it. I escorted her to the library and closed the door. I waited in the kitchen to maintain privacy. Twenty minutes later, I heard the front door slam, and Mrs. West returned to her bedroom. Mrs. West had closed her door, and outside her room, I asked her if there was anything I could do, but she said no. I heard her crying, and that is all I can say."

"Is there anything you are holding back?" I asked.

"No sir," Mr. Wallace said.

"Mrs. West," I asked.

"When I walked into the library, the lady stood, and I shook her hand," Mrs. West said. "Mr. Wallace told me you have something to tell me?" I asked. She stood there and examined me but remained silent."

"What happened next?" I asked.

"She was my daughter," Mrs. West said. "What is it? I asked and told her to sit, which she did. She asked if I was Mrs. Alicia West. I said I was, but I did not expect the next question. She asked if my maiden name was Kingsmill, and I said it was. She asked what happened on April 12, but I didn't answer. The lady told me that I was in the hospital, and she was my daughter. I couldn't speak, so I just stared at her. I asked her name, and she said Mary. I asked what she wanted, and she said she wished to spend time with me. I stood and told her that was impossible and for her to leave or I would have Mr. Wallace remove her. She stood and said she left me in an orphanage, opened the library door and then the front door and left. I realize I made a terrible mistake, but I am not the same person I was when we met. I wish I could say now that I was sorry for what I did to her and hug her. I had two dolls with me in Montreal and gave one to my daughter to have something from me. They promised my daughter would be placed with an excellent family, and I still have the twin doll. I want you to find Mary, tell her I am sorry and give her the other doll. I would have kept her if I had known she would be placed in an orphanage, even if my reputation was ruined."

"I think Mary killed you," I said.

"If she did, I provoked her," Mrs. West said. "I know if you discover she murdered me, our connection will end."

"I don't want our connection to end," I said.

"I know, but your job will end," Mrs. West said. I explained what Mrs. West said to Mr. Wallace and said I had to go to Montreal to find Mrs. West's daughter Mary, but where should I start?

"I had the lady's purse in the kitchen," Mr. Wallace said. "I opened it and took down the information shown on her driver's licence," Mr. Wallace said. "It is time for Mrs. West to have her last trip to Montreal. The name and address are Mrs. Mary Chesterton, 2966 Sherbrooke Street."

"You suspected she was Mrs. West's daughter," I asked.

"I had served Mrs. West for almost forty years, and the daughter resembled the mother," Mr. Wallace said.

CHAPTER 35

A Visit to Montreal

The night before I drove to Montreal, I called Mr. McGregor to tell him I would visit the city from Friday to Sunday and did he have a recommendation for a hotel.

"Mr. Jenkins, I will see if you can stay with us in the servants' quarters," Mr. McGregor said. "I will speak to Mr. Weatherby, so please provide me with your telephone number, and I will call you back." I gave him my number and waited. Half an hour later, my telephone rang, and I answered it.

"Mr. Jenkins, or should I say, Mr. Clark, Mr. Weatherby extends his invitation to visit as a guest on one condition," Mr. McGregor said. "He wants the story or as much as you can tell, including what you told the police. He understands that what you said resulted in the murder charge dropped for Mr. West." I said I would be delighted and hung up.

"Your son called Mr. Weatherby, and he has learned of my deception as his butler," I said. "When I return to Toronto, I will meet with Mr. West's divorce lawyer since Mr. Jenkins revealed his problems with Mrs. Marigold West.

"Oh, this will be good," Mrs. West said. "What a tangled web we weave when we practice to deceive."

"That's not fair. I did it under your direction," I said. "My purpose in travelling to Montreal is to interview the lady I think murdered you."

"My daughter," Mrs. West said.

"Yes, and it will be emotional for you," I said.

"And for you," Mrs. Wests said.

"It will, but I must understand why she did it?" Mrs. West asked.

"If she did it, which will depend on finding her and if she will talk," I said.

"Reginald, take the convertible and put the top down if it is not raining," Mrs. West said.

"Won't you be blown away?" I asked.

"Really, Reginald," Mrs. West said. "I am connected with you, even if the wind blows. A hurricane will not separate us." I had my orders, and early Friday morning, I packed, including the doll and after breakfast, headed out at seven in the morning. A few days ago, I had the car checked out and filled with gas. I parked the car in my driveway, loaded my suitcase, and put in a bottle of water, a thermos of coffee, and a mug. I lowered the roof and backed down my driveway.

"What kinds of country and western music would you like? I asked. "I understand you are partial to Hank Snow. I turned onto my road when I heard her.

"I have no idea who or what he is," Mrs. West said. "The CBC will play classical music at two in the afternoon," Mrs. West said. "Until then, do not turn on your radio. I have never heard of Hank Snow and do not wish to listen to him."

"He's got some great hits like "Honeymoon on a Rocketship," I said.

"Not interested," Mrs. West said.

"What happens if I get tired?" I asked.

"With the wind in your face at sixty miles an hour?" Mrs. West asked. "Reginald, sunglasses," which I put on. I stopped at Kingston to refuel and eat and was back on the road. At two, we listened to classical music until we were far from Kingston, and it turned to static, so I turned the radio off.

We reached the suburbs of Montreal at three, and I parked

outside Mrs. Mary Chesterton's two-story duplex. I got out of the car and rang her bell, but no answer, so I waited for an hour, but no one appeared at the building. After one more attempt, I drove to the Weatherby mansion, parked, and took my suitcase inside. This time, I had packed a bathing suit.

Mr. McGregor told me Mrs. Weatherby was visiting her mother, so Mr. Weatherby permitted Mr. McGregor to sit in for dinner with us. It was after the meal that Mr. Weatherby asked me questions.

"How did you suspect that someone would poison Mrs. West?" Mr. Weatherby asked. There was no preliminary discussion; he wanted the story.

"Mrs. West told her butler, Mr. Wallace, about her suspicions," I said. I explained the call Mr. Wallace made to the butler at the West residence to let the butler know no one would be at Mrs. Alicia West's home.

"You suspected Douglas?" asked Mr. Weatherby.

"I did," and I explained what happened the night I almost caught the woman who had left the pills.

"How were you aware that the woman at Douglas' mother's house was not his mistress?" Mr. Weatherby asked.

"When you tackle someone, you sense how they fight. That woman was right-handed and had a deep voice. The mistress I met is left-handed, taller and sounds like Minnie Mouse. I told Detective Sergeant Oliver they would never convict Miss Walker as an accessory to murder. Once the decision to drop her case happened, the same thing happened to Mr. West. Sergeant Oliver convinced the crown attorney to drop the charges." I discussed Hunston Weir, the little gerbil and Mrs. Marigold West trying to seduce me in the basement. I told them about locking my door at night, having been first warned by Jenkins. I added that since I had resigned, I expected that Jenkins the third would replace me. Mr. Weatherby stood, said he had some work to do and left us alone. I looked at Mr. McGregor.

"Do you play the bagpipes?" I asked.

"I can't stand them along with haggis, but that little fellow was annoying," Mr. McGregor said. "You do not know what it is like to not sleep for two nights. I am what you would call a peaceful man, but after two nights, I was ready to kill the little bugger. You can call me Robert."

"You can call me Reggie," I said.

"I prefer Reginald," Robert said.

"So does Mrs. West," I said.

"She tried to have it on with you?" Robert asked, confusing Mrs. West and Mrs. Marigold West, but I couldn't mention my conversations with a ghost.

"Her husband threatened me," I said, "and I had no interest in her."

"If you did, it would be dipping your pen in company ink," Robert said and laughed. I felt queasy thinking about it.

"Reginald, talk about something else," Mrs. West said.

"What happened to Mr. Ruskin?" I asked.

"He fell off the wagon," Robert said. "We were a little rough, but they trained us, butlers, to be tough. Mr. Boulton is putting him in a residential place to dry out."

"He seemed to lose it," I said.

"If you plan to go swimming, forget it," Robert said.

"Why?" I asked.

"The last thing Mr. Ruskin did, as an act of rebellion, was to drop a turd in the swimming pool, and we are having the pool cleaned," Robert said. "It had the consistency of a hockey puck, and I do not know what he was eating."

"No fruits or vegetables in his diet," I said.

"Probably not," Robert said.

"Reginald enough, this is disgusting," Mrs. West said.

"What happened?" I asked.

"If a Butler wanted revenge, there are so many ways to do it, but I thought this one was remarkable. He had to arrange a time when no one saw him."

"Don't forget how drunk he was," I said.

"He did it off the diving board to ensure it was in the deepest part of the pool," Robert said.

"While drunk," I said. "I am surprised he didn't fall in the pool. Let us toast the audacity of a drunken butler," which we did.

"How did you become a butler?" I asked.

"Well, that calls for a drink since it is a long story," Robert said and poured us one.

"I had served in the 51st Highland Division in the war. I ended up in Montreal," Robert said. "Mr. Weatherby manufactures spirits and imports wine. Certain individuals connected with the longshoremen threatened Mr. Weatherby, who hired me as his bodyguard and driver. I lived here, and when his butler retired, I asked to replace him with an increase in salary since I was performing three jobs. They trained Humphries in England, and I watched what he did. Humphries showed no emotion, and he didn't appreciate a joke. He was a stiff old bird who used to fluff up seat cushions. He straightened the pictures each day, and I tilted them each night. He never drank or smoked and insisted on reading to the staff so I would change his reading material." Once he finished his story, we called it a night. I was in bed at eleven, with a bedroom that overlooked the city.

"It is a lovely city," Mrs. West said. "If you find out tomorrow that my daughter brought my life to an end, our connection will end."

"I don't want that, so I will not visit her," I said.

"Reginald, my journey and our connection are for one purpose, to find out who killed me," Mrs. West said. "You have no choice, and you must visit her and find out." It took a long time to get to sleep. After breakfast, I walked to the address with the doll in a package and was there at ten. I rang the buzzer to the downstairs unit.

"Yes?" the voice asked.

"Mrs. Mary Chesterton? I asked.

"Yes, what do you want?" Mrs. Chesterton asked.

"My name is Reginald Clark, and I am here with a gift and

a message from Mrs. West," I said. There was a long pause.

"You are late, and she is dead," Mrs. Chesterton said.

"I am aware of that, but it took a while to get your address," I said.

"You better come in, and I know who you are," Mrs. Chesterton said and pushed the buzzer. This would give her enough time to change for sharp pointed shoes. She stood with the door open. I walked in and stood while she closed the door and told me to sit. Mrs. Chesterton was the size of the woman I grabbed at Mrs. Alicia West's residence, and she had a deep voice. I had seen pictures of Mrs. West, and she looked like her. She was the daughter, but was she the murderer?

"Would you like coffee?" she asked. I said yes and put down the gift. After a few minutes, she put down a cup with a spoon, cream and sugar. She was right-handed.

"I read your articles on the death of Mrs. West, but that is not why you are here?" she asked.

"Nothing we discuss, I will publish or reveal," I said.

"Aren't you a reporter?" Mrs. Chesterton asked.

"I am here as the Godson of Mrs. West and to bring an end to this," I said.

"What end?" asked Mrs. Chesterton, "and what is the gift?"

"The gift must wait," I said.

"Take your time and get it right," Mrs. West said.

"Mrs. West told me to find you and to say she regrets that she didn't allow you to be with her and turned you away," I said. "Since then, she is sorry for what she did, the hurt and your pain." It looked like I had slapped her. Her face went white, and she sat down and cried. I gave her the gift, and she opened it to see the doll. Now she was bawling and rocking herself back and forth.

"Why now? Why not earlier?" Mrs. Chesterton asked. "This was the only thing my mother left me. It was the only thing I had in the orphanage as a connection to my mother, and they took it away," and continued crying.

"Reginald, they told me they would adopt her and not be placed in an orphanage. I would have kept her," Mrs. West said and cried. I waited until Mrs. Chesterton looked at me.

"You know where to kick a man," I said. "It hurt."

"Sorry, but you scared me," Mrs. Chesterton said. "It comes from having an abusive husband," she said. "I figured you would be here. I am the right size, and you recognized my voice. You have no idea how much I hated her, my mother. I had a hard life, and I wasn't at that mansion for money but to spend time with her. That's why I went there."

"Reginald, my heart is breaking for what I have done to her and because I am leaving you," Mrs. West said. "Never turn her in; you are like a son to me. Goodbye."

"Goodbye, Mrs. West," I said. "I will miss you."

"What did you say?" Mrs. Chesterton asked.

"You wouldn't believe it if I told you, but the spirit of Mrs. West was guiding me to find out who killed her and has left me," I said. "She was my constant companion, and I will miss her. She told me she changed after she died and was sorry for what she did to you." Mrs. Chesterton examined me and sighed.

"I believe you," she said. "And I have no explanation why I do."

"The last request she made was that I must never turn you in, and I will respect that," I said.

"Thank you," Mrs. Chesterton said. "I guess your job is done."

"It is, and I hope things will get better for you," I said.

"Knowing my mother was sorry and regretted what she did is incredible, and the doll," she said. "It will. Thank you."

"One final thing, how did you do it?" I asked.

"I spent all of my savings," Mrs. Chesterton said. "I hired a private detective, but you know that. The first few days, he was at the back of the house, then watched with his car at the front. I knew that when they had dinner, opera would be played, and the location was on the second floor of my mother's bedroom and bathroom. She would always turn on the light in the bathroom before turning off the light in her bedroom. I jimmied the lock at dinner time when the record player was on and hid under her bed. Once my mother was in the bathroom, the maid had gone, and I emptied the horse tranquillizer in her tea."

"Why did you leave the rest of the pills?" I asked.

"I wasn't sure if I had left enough to kill her and planned to come the next night. When I put them in the heating vent, they disappeared."

"How did you know that the house would be vacant?" I asked.

"Mr. Ball, my detective, followed Mr. Wallace to a tavern he liked to go to every Thursday night. Mr. Ball paid money to a fellow who talked to Mr. Wallace. I knew when Mr. Wallace was going to Hamilton on that weekend. What I didn't know was that you would be waiting."

"I was expecting her son," I said.

"And you got her daughter," Mrs. Chesterton said.

"Which sent me in a different direction," I said.

"I'm sorry about everything I did," Mrs. Chesterton said. She walked me to the door, where she hugged me. I was subdued at the Weatherby mansion and tried not to let my loss show for the rest of my time there.

I had lost a wonderful, opinionated and cantankerous friend. She loved driving in convertibles, so I named my 1941 red Buick Roadmaster convertible Mrs. West. I couldn't tell anyone since word might get back to Mr. West, who would assume I named it after Mrs. Marigold West, and no good would come of that. Knowing Mr. West, he would spray bullets, and one might accidentally hit me if he didn't shoot himself. A bullet through the head was not how I wanted to end my life.

It was a mystery why Mrs. West connected with me. Perhaps it was my good looks or the fact that I was an excellent reporter. Maybe it was because I needed her guidance, but it made no sense, as were many things in this world. She was from an earlier generation with problems that came from wealth and entitlement. Mrs. West could observe and listen to everyone, but only I heard her when she talked. I never saw her, which meant no visual clues, so I had to concentrate on her voice, which usually sounded annoyed or frustrated. This created problems when I was talking to someone, and she interrupted. There is nothing more aggravating than hearing two voices at the same time.

Occasionally, this made communication difficult, like charging to the bathroom to chat. After a while, certain people thought I had a bladder problem. I didn't hear voices because I had a nervous breakdown; it was only Mrs. West. She was stuck in the afterlife and insisted I do something for her to move on. And the only way she could do that was through me with her moralizing and exhausting voice that drove me to exasperation. However, looking back, my connection with her was the most important thing that had happened to me.

EPILOGUE

I quit my job with the *Toronto Mirror* and, over the next four months, wrote a fictional book; *The Butler Solved It.* A female spirit from the afterlife helps the butler to discover who stole the money from her husband's company, which had caused its bankruptcy. Because of the default, her husband killed himself. There were many characters he met as he solved the case. I had a great time with the little gerbil. By the end of September, I had five rental properties and enough income to set aside half for savings and the other half to live on.

The book became a top seller in the United States and Canada, and Miss Tallulah Conway invited me to New York for an interview along with the American television stations. My book was too racy for the stuffy Canadian Broadcasting Corporation. I invested in three large apartment buildings with the money and hired Manny to manage them. The rest of the money is with my broker, and now I am working on my second book, *The Butler Didn't Do It.* I had enough money to move to Forest Hill, but I liked it where I was. I still do freelance journalism and have written short stories for the *New Yorker*.

One day as I drove along Queen Street, I saw the body of a light-yellow kitten on the side of the road and stopped. I thought it was dead, but it was breathing, and I took it to a veterinarian. A car had knocked it out, but it survived. I named the kitten Alicia, which keeps any cockroaches and rats away and likes to lie on a cushion next to my writing desk. I wonder if Alicia is hungry or bored and wants to be entertained, like Mrs. West, the spirit. Like Mrs. West, Alicia will disturb me in the morning.

Every time I met Detective Sergeant Oliver, he asked me if I found the mystery woman, and I always said my ghost told me to zip my lip. Oliver would shake his head and say, "cut the crap, Clark. You got nothing, but if you do, do not withhold evidence or I will send Lester." Oliver tries to loom over me, but since I am six foot two and he is six foot four, it doesn't make a difference.

Mr. West invited me to his wedding with Miss Eunice Walker, and I was pleased to see Mr. West remain sober. Mr. West said he persuaded his sister to drop the lawsuit against the estate "to piss off Marigold." He told me they were moving to Vancouver Island and had bought a Ford. Mrs. Marigold West kept the house, the Bentley, and the children and hired a butler named Jenkins. I had the 1939 Buick Roadmaster convertible appraised, bought it and gave it to Mr. Wallace. I sent five thousand dollars to Mrs. Mary Chesterton in Montreal, stating it was a gift from her mother. I began flying to Regina to visit my parents and paid for them to visit Florida for a vacation.

I host a barbeque every Friday night and bought more grills, chairs and tables. In the summer or in the winter, everyone crowds into my house. Big Fish, Fred, Manny, George, Sergeant Oliver and Constable Lester Wilson. I always invite reporters who attend. My neighbours and Martha also show up; everyone brings booze, salads and dessert, and I provide the hamburgers and hot dogs. I took up sailing and bought a sailboat and four more Group of Seven paintings.

I produced a country and western record. It is called "Big Fish and His Boys, Tunes to Shake Down the House" under Spirit Records. It became a big hit in Bible Hill and Truro, then Halifax and Canada and we are now working on a second album called "Big Fish and the Boys, More Tunes to Shake Down the House." Even though I like country and western music, I regularly attend operas and play classical music at home.

I learned when not to participate in a conversation, such as when drunk or bored or when an attractive young lady is also bored. Then I gesture to the door, and we leave together. That is how I met Gwyneth, a society reporter for the *Toronto Mirror*, who is now my girlfriend. She likes my sense of humour and the fact that I am down to earth and talk to everyone, but she is not thrilled with Martha. I keep telling her we are just friends, but she must sense something I don't.

I miss Mrs. West. Not a day passes when I don't think of her and her constant presence, and I always listen for the sound of fingers on a blackboard. The inscription in my book was: *To Alicia, a wonderful friend who changed my life.* Friends asked me why I had dedicated my book to my cat, and I would smile at them and say it was a secret. My most important lesson is that spirits and cats can change your life.

www.ingramcontent.com/pod-product-compliance
Lightning Source LLC
LaVergne TN
LVHW010545160826
845677LV00013B/3001

* 9 7 9 8 3 7 2 1 9 2 0 0 3 *